"Liza!"

I turned and nearly lost my balance. Dr. Tim was slipping past a gurney and coming toward me. In a moment he was going to have to defibrillate me.

"Almost forgot." He handed me a prescription. "Can you deal with codeine? You might have a lot of pain the next few days."

I don't know what came over me, whether it was the great New York fairy tale of it all or the sheer exhaustion, but suddenly I was very brave.

"Would you like to have dinner with me?" I blurted out.

"What?" He blinked.

"I...dinner. Sometime. As a thank-you for the...no, that's bullshit. As a date. Would you like to go out with me?"

He looked nervous. I wanted to believe it was excited nervous and not repulsed nervous.

"Doctors can't date patients," he said.

"Oh, I...right. Of course they can't. That was totally... inappropriate." Why does this sort of humiliation happen when I actually can't run?

"So if you needed any follow-up care, I'd have to give you the name of another doctor."

"Sure." I was so embarrassed that I barely registered the way he was looking at me. "Wait, what?"

"And technically you'd need to walk through those doors before we could exchange phone numbers or..."

"Oh!" I got it. "Oh, yeah, of course. Yes."

"So maybe I should walk you out." He smiled this very sexy, warm smile, which I was now able to fully appreciate, knowing I might get to see it again.

"You know any good DVDs, Dr. Tim?"

I got his phone number.

Right
Before
Your Eyes

ELLEN SHANMAN

DELTA TRADE PAPERBACKS

RIGHT BEFORE YOUR EYES
A Delta Trade Paperback / May 2007

Published by
Bantam Dell
A Division of Random House, Inc.
New York, New York

Book design by Robert Bull

Delta is a registered trademark of Random House, Inc., and the colophon is a
trademark of Random House, Inc.

Library of Congress Cataloging in Publication Data

Shanman, Ellen.
Right before your eyes / Ellen Shanman.
p.   cm.
ISBN: 978-0-385-34051-9 (trade pbk.)
I. Women dramatists—Fiction.   I. Title
PS3619.H3548R54 2007
813'.6—dc22
2006034034

Printed in the United States of America
Published simultaneously in Canada

www.bantamdell.com

BVG 10 9 8 7 6 5 4 3 2 1

For my parents
And for Jon

Right
Before
Your Eyes

"When what you really want to do is throw a drink in his face, throw up on his shoes and run, it's worth sticking around to see what happens."
—my great aunt Fran, who sums it all up better than I ever could.

PROLOGUE

HAD I NOT JOINED Parrot for dinner that night, everything would have been different. Everything.

Most evenings out with Parrot are an adventure. I would love it if just once she could manage to get through dinner in a restaurant without recruiting whoever is at the next table to be the evening's entertainment. (Was I the only one who repeatedly got the "stranger danger" lecture?) But as the adventure frequently ends in arrest or vomiting, I should have been grateful that, thus far, our impromptu meeting with a pack of self-important junior tycoons had led only to a crowded bar. A Friday night in New York City can always get so much worse.

River Town Lounge is a somewhat trendy downtown spot where the girls sandwich something clingy and sleeveless between overpriced jeans and hoop earrings, and the men all sport the same Banana Republic shirt. Directly after promising not to desert me, Parrot vanished into the crowd with Kirk, her new acquisition. George, the unfortunately handsome jackass with whom we'd first made contact at dinner, had perceived in me an admirable foe and was attempting to ply me with liquor while we verbally stabbed each other.

"So what do you do, George?" I asked.

"I'm in M'n'A. That's mergers and—"

"Acquisitions, yeah, I know what it is." I was grateful he didn't say "consultant."

"Of course. And you?"

"I'm a writer."

"For whom?" he questioned.

"A playwright."

"Ah. For no one."

"Yeah, I'm having cards made."

"So what kind of plays do you write?"

This is one of those questions I hope people will not ask in a bar, because then I'll have to say something like "Well, right now I'm working on a piece about the perfect suburban widow and the way the neighborhood destroys her when she falls for the wrong man. It's a little bit Ibsen, a little bit Alan Ball." Inevitably, the other person will draw some parallel to *Desperate Housewives* and I'll have to explain why that's completely off base without sounding affected and nasty.

"Gee, George, I'm sure you'd much rather tell me about you. What kind of mergers do you acquire?"

"Point taken. So what do you actually do? For money?"

"I do administrative work." I would not say the word *temp* to this man.

"You temp?"

I hated him.

"What agency? We've always got temps in my office."

So much.

"It must be really hard to have a college degree and be temping."

I was going to kill him.

"I'm assuming you did go to college. You seem like you did."

"What exactly does that mean?" I asked.

"You know what it means. Would you like another?" He indicated my empty glass.

The overtly stylish bartender who was approaching had a "Hello, my name is Richard" sticker on his shirt, clearly an attempt at irony, which prompted George to cry, "Hey, Dick, another Brooklyn Lager for the lady." Dick shot George a crushing glance and said, "It's Richard."

"I suspect that's why it doesn't say Dick on the tag," I offered.

Kirk suddenly surfaced, adding, "Just crack this guy's head against the bar a few times, Richard. That'll shut him up."

"Don't bother, Richard," I said. "His head's so hard it probably wouldn't do any good."

Richard looked George and me up and down and said, "I have a feeling you know."

George smirked. I cringed.

"Hey, I think your friend Parrot and I are going to head to another bar. You guys wanna tag along?" Kirk had discovered the many wonders of a newly available Parrot. I made a mental note to beat her about the head and shoulders for abandoning me on the very night I had come out to cheer her up.

"I'm going home," I said.

"I'm going with her," George said.

I didn't have to say anything. I just looked at him.

Parrot materialized, kissed me goodbye, drunkenly whispered, "I'm going to fuck this Dirk guy—till he bleeds," and staggered out the door.

I headed for the coat check, where George insisted on paying for me, and I rushed toward the door as quickly as possible. He was at my heels.

"Can I get you a cab?" he asked.

"I can get a cab."

He smiled. "I was just suggesting—"

"Not looking for suggestions, thanks." I didn't even look back at him.

"Look, where are you headed? We could split—"

I was outside before he could finish the thought. And as I jumped into the street to hail a taxi, my heel caught on the curb and my ankle turned in the most painful, least natural way an ankle can turn. I made a loud, embarrassing, dying cat sort of noise and began to fall—when George caught me. Why, oh why, did we have to keep having this Nick and Nora, Bogie and Bacall, Turner and Hooch kind of evening? I hated this man! I did not need to have any sort of even fleeting attraction to someone who spent his life hoping that corporations would fold so he could arrange to take them over!

Through the haze of my extraordinary agony, I noticed that George smelled both expensive and very good as he picked me up and put me in the cab, which had shockingly stopped as I went down. And he didn't even make that little "oof" noise that my college boyfriend used to make when he picked me up. Note to men: if you have to make the noise, we'd rather you skipped the picking-up altogether.

Before I could stop him, George slid into the seat beside me.

"Every glorious minute you waste thinking is a minute you could be drinking, loving, fighting or dancing. Think about that. But not for too long."

CHAPTER 1

A S A YOUNG, struggling playwright, you have to feel grateful when anyone wants to do your work. Which was why, when a somewhat intense guy gave me a call and said he went to theatre camp with one of my college friends and he'd read one of my plays and gee, he really felt like he had a handle on it ... I said I'd meet him for coffee. His name was Will Atherton. He was a second-year grad student in a highly regarded MFA program and we had agreed to meet at one of the myriad Starbucks cafes in Union Square.

Getting through the door was a struggle, but I pressed through the thronging caffeine addicts and took a moment to wonder how all these people had so much free time in the middle of the day. I was squeezing this meeting in on my teeny temp's lunch break. I scanned the horde of turtlenecks hunched over iBooks, and realized I had no idea how to pick Will out. I must have looked lost and annoyed, because he spotted me within moments.

"You must be Liza!" a voice barked behind me. I turned to see a shortish, blondish fellow with thinning, unwashed hair and a slightly soft physique.

"Will?" I questioned. Obviously Will. Unfortunately, he had a turtleneck *and* a wallet-chain.

"You got it!" He laughed, though nothing was funny. He pumped my hand like he was trying to bring up oil and I tried not to decide that he'd only matriculated because his family had single-handedly endowed a third of the buildings on his campus.

"It's *so* great to meet you!" Will gushed. He was weirdly energetic and bent over while he was talking. "I actually found a table!" he said, as though this merited congratulations.

"So how goes it?" he asked as we sat.

"Great, and you?" I replied, thinking that I really didn't have time for small talk.

"Good, good," he cooed. "I'm really juiced that you're meeting with me."

"Oh, yeah . . . ," I said. "So how exactly did you happen to read the play?"

"Oh, you know I make it a habit to read everything coming out of Yale."

"Oh," I said, thinking this was sort of odd as I'd left undergrad seven years ago.

"So, your work!!" Will began. "I'm really into it, really feel connected to your vision."

Admittedly, I grew up around one of America's theatrical treasures, my great aunt Fran, so I should be well-used to meaningless showbiz chatter. I went to my first Oscar ceremony when I was eight. But I'm still uncomfortable with the entertainment industry's habitual self-congratulation. I'm not old enough to have "work." According to Will, however, I was someone who "could really make a dent in the landscape of contemporary American theatre."

"So here's the dealy—" Will leaned in closer, and I drew my Frappuccino back a little. "I get to direct one mainstage per semester, use the undergrad actors (great kids!) and I wanna do nothing this winter if I can't do *Georgia Allen's Window.*"

The play in question was my pithy portrait of neighborhood politics in the suburbs, and I must admit I smiled at the thought that it might see the lights of a stage.

"Wow," I said, "I'm really flattered—"

"You prolly wanna know, like, what I'm about: totally valid. Here's my thing—very into the Theatre of Cruelty, Artaud, Grotowski, very physically oriented." Visions of shrieking drama students in unitards writhed in my head.

Immediately I wondered why Will was drawn to my naturalistic drama, but I was trying to be open-minded. Exposure is everything. Unlike acting or dancing or wrapping the Reichstag, writing is one of the few artistic pursuits you don't need permission to do. But if my plays weren't being performed, I might as well stop writing them. I let Will continue and I tried to seem enthusiastic, but a small pebble of fear formed in my stomach as he explained that he wanted to add a character who moved through the audience poking people with a stick and telling them to sit up straight. He seemed to think it would strengthen the feeling of confinement within the play's oppressive neighborhood. I tittered uneasily.

"Thing is, Liza," he explained, tugging on his wallet-chain, "you have to be willing to take risks. You have to make people uncomfortable."

"Hey, go with your strengths." I mustered another laugh so he wouldn't realize I was being a bitch.

"Right, right, exactly," he replied. "So tell me what you think? Where are we? Where do we stand?"

I tried to phrase my answer carefully. "Gee, um ... here's the thing, Will ... I'm really excited that you're interested in the piece. It just sounds to me like you and I have very different ... aesthetics. I'm not sure I see the same things in this play that you do."

"But that's great!" he cried. "That's energy! That's art!

Conflict!" He slammed the rest of his caramel macchiato and pushed a hand through his greasy hair.

I wanted to say, "Sorry, I don't think this is going to work." But the idea of turning down an opportunity, any opportunity, made me want to go home and pore over the stack of law school brochures I keep in my desk drawer. It was just too depressing.

So instead I said, "I'll want to sit in on rehearsals."

"YES!" Will shouted, jumping up and knocking into the table, nearly upsetting my beverage. "That's what I want! I want you in there! Let's make some THEATRE!!"

People were looking. "Okay," I said, very quietly. "Let's."

Will laid out the rehearsal schedule for me, and in a few minutes I was scuttling back to my temp job. Panicking. Afraid that I'd just signed myself up for a horror show, I used the nine-block walk to call Aunt Fran, who can always be relied upon for sound advice.

"You're telling me I've been away three weeks and you haven't scored once?!" Unfortunately, on this particular day she was more concerned with my love life.

"This is not the point!" I told her. "I am having a professional crisis!"

"Sometimes I think you have no priorities!" she erupted.

Fran is decidedly the crazy old bat of our family and my idol. Aged somewhere between sixty-five and three hundred, Aunt Fran is a hard-drinking, trash-talking goddess of the stage and screen. I think she knows secret passageways under the streets of New York, every maitre d' between Manhattan and Malay, and the sexual predilections of every mayoral candidate for the last seventy-five years. There are rumors in our family that she made some explicit films for distribution to the boys overseas during WWII, at the behest of some serious higher-ups in the Treasury Department. She has two Tonys, three very large Dobermans, a stunning prewar apartment on the Upper West Side and, as far as I can tell, the heart of every man she's ever met. Since I was a small child I've wanted to grow up to be Aunt Fran.

I think most of the time she'd say I'm doing a pretty poor job of it. Ever the generous tutor, she consistently works overtime trying to spice up my frankly undramatic life. Our current dispute stemmed from the fact that Aunt Fran had departed for Chicago three weeks earlier, to do a production of *A Delicate Balance* (that was getting raves), admonishing me to use her place as the exotic headquarters for all the trysting I was supposed to do in her absence. I'd done nothing of the kind. Nothing.

"Well, thank God you've rewritten the second act, Liza. It gives me something to live for."

"Right." I tried to get her back on track. "I've rewritten it, for now, but I think the production I just agreed to might really suck. I'm wondering whether I'm making a terrible mistake."

I could hear Aunt Fran's stage manager in the background calling "places" for the matinee, and she told me we could talk more later.

"I have to go and be brilliant now, Niece," she rasped, "but this conversation is not over. You need to take more risks. Go sleep with a stranger; you'll feel better. If I don't see a new notch in your bedpost when I come back, heads will roll."

Little did Aunt Fran understand that I barely had a bedpost, let alone notches. Believe me, I would love to have more sex, but it's not as easy as ordering takeout. I find it nearly impossible to sleep with people I barely know, as they could very well give me a disease, steal my credit cards while I'm dozing or chop me up and leave me strewn in various garbage bags throughout the five boroughs. Acquaintances are even worse, because inevitably they end up interviewing you for a job or married to your good friend and then you have to sit through a lifetime of awkward dinners thinking, "I've seen you naked." Frankly, I don't have time to do the kind of legwork that goes into finding an appropriate partner.

It's not my fault that I'm like this. My mother is a very tense person.

"Your ideal job should involve gin and being fawned over. How about this: when I die, you can be me."

CHAPTER 2

I WAS LATE GETTING BACK to the office. This is one of those little workday indiscretions that is generally forgiven the full-time employee, but hung menacingly over the head of a temp. I had actually gone so far as to mention to my temp agency that my current assignment left a lot to be desired; my supervisor was incredibly severe and actually a little frightening. They gave me no flexibility and inadequate breaks. This felt like a difficult cross to bear during the nine hours a day I spent answering the phone *in a convent*. Did you know they hire temps at convents? Neither did I. But I was right on in thinking the place would be full o' nuns. I had to wear long skirts and read posters on abstinence while answering calls from virtuous and judgmental elderly people. As the daughter of a failed rabbinical student and a former Catholic (my mother is now more Jewish than any of us), my views on nuns mostly came from watching *The Bells of St. Mary's* and *The Sound of Music*. Those nuns were soft and kind and even funny. Ingrid Bergman sorts of nuns. These nuns were bored and tended toward the snippy. They also had a twenty-five-inch phone cord and a filing cabinet seventeen feet away from the switchboard, but felt certain that I should be able to file and greet callers simultaneously.

And try complaining to your temp agency about nuns. Yeah, they don't so much take you seriously.

My head was still spinning from my meeting with Will, but I tried to slip quietly back into my chair without Sister Lorraine noticing. No such luck. If nuns were endowed with superpowers, Sister Lorraine would have X-ray vision. Maybe this is one of her rewards for being sin free. Personally, I'll take sin and a Scotch, neat, but Sister Lorraine had neither a taste for alcohol nor a sense of humor.

"Ms. Weiler?" she drawled from inside her office, as I puzzled over how she had managed to see me through a wall.

"Yes, Sister!" I attempted to manufacture some nun-inspiring good cheer.

"These long lunches won't do."

My face said, "ONE! ONE LONG LUNCH! EASE UP, OLD WOMAN!" But my voice said, "Absolutely, Sister, I apologize." Unfortunately, I think Sister Lorraine heard my face.

"I don't need the attitude, Ms. Weiler."

I cringed. "Of course, Sister. I'll work on it."

"See that you do."

I searched for mirrors or surveillance cameras, but came up empty.

This seemed like a particularly bad time to piss Sister Lorraine off. I made a mental note to be especially impressive for the rest of the afternoon, as I had a major favor to ask of her.

I'm lucky, as a writer, that I can usually stick to a regular nine-to-five routine without too much trouble. Usually, but not always.

Since the actors in Will's production were getting class credit for their work, rehearsals were to be held on university property, Tuesdays through Fridays, from three p.m. to seven. I could not miss out on those rehearsals. Maybe this is true for any playwright, but for a control freak like me who always feels like I'm executing some painful surrender when I give a play to somebody else, the offer to sit in is a gift, a blessing, an opportunity not to be missed. You get to talk with the actors, to discuss ideas with the designers, to whisper in the director's ear. Given my first conversation with Will, there was bound to be a lot of whispering. The way I had it figured, if I could just convince Sister Lorraine to let me come in early and forego lunch for a few weeks, they would only be losing my services for a couple of hours a day. Surely, I thought, they could spare me for those last two and a half hours.

I focused for the rest of the afternoon on being a model employee. In an attempt to earn the nunnery equivalent of Brownie points, I scurried with more vigor than usual when Sister Lorraine called me into her office to take dictation on a memo to the archdiocese. This was after I had lied and said I could take dictation. I don't really think either of us was buying it. It was Friday afternoon, and though I knew I should have waited to ask for a favor, I figured I might have a better shot if the sister had a few days to think it over. I would tell her not to decide right away; she could let me know Monday and I'd still have a few days before rehearsals started. The clock over Sister Lorraine's shoulder read 4:47 p.m. I tried to screw up my courage while we finished the memo.

"That'll be all, Ms. Weiler. You can leave that on my desk before you leave."

"No problem," I said, rising to go, fighting the urge to scream that I was too smart to be a temp, that doing petty clerical work in the face of unchecked condescension screwed massively with my idea of myself. After all, I wasn't spending eight hours a day on *my* career. Applying all the diligence and intellect at my disposal to Sister Lorraine's new

Sunday school curriculum wasn't going to benefit *me* at all. What was going to benefit me was being in those damned rehearsals, and I had every right to be there. I was a temp, for Christ's sake, not an indentured servant!

In any case, now was my chance. I weighed my options carefully before making the absolutely wrong choice. "I'm sorry to trouble you," I began, hoping I looked sweet and perhaps reminded Sister Lorraine of a favorite orphan or choirgirl, "but while I'm here, I have a small, um, scheduling question for you."

"No two-hour lunches," she muttered.

"No! Oh, no, of course not. That would be totally disruptive," I concurred. "No, it's, um . . . I don't know if you know this, Sister: I'm a playwright. I write plays." I heard Faye Dunaway in my head, saying "My name's Bonnie. This is Clyde. We rob banks." Except I sounded stupid and I wasn't getting to the point. I could feel the sister beaming concentrated irritation in my direction. "The point is, one of my plays is being produced and I need to attend rehearsals. And it would mean leaving the office at two-thirty, four days a week for a couple of weeks."

Sister Lorraine didn't even twitch a facial muscle and I thought perhaps she was waiting for divine inspiration.

"So I was wondering if that would be alright with you."

Still nothing.

"Because I'd really like to keep this job. Really. I really would."

I was beginning to question whether maybe Sister Lorraine had died in a very quiet, almost imperceptible way. And then my cell phone began to ring. Repeatedly. Loudly. I froze.

The sister's painful expression led me to believe she might shoot lightning out of her eyes, and she brusquely suggested that I answer the phone, still jingling away in my pocket, which I hastened to do. Parrot took the opportunity to screech "DINNER AT BOCA CHICA AND THEN WE'RE GOING DANCING ABSOLUTELY EVERYWHERE!" into my ear. I took this to mean she was feeling social after weeks of hibernation. As I was both stunned and embarrassed, I hung up on her immediately.

"I am so sorry, Sister." I bowed and scraped. "That was ... awful."

The good sister was not amused. "You'll be leaving that foul instrument at home in future, Ms. Weiler." It was a statement, not a question.

This little gaffe had obviously caused severe trauma to the camel's back. Clearly this was not going to be the right time to pursue my little request. I continued to apologize and started to back out of the office.

"You had a question, I believe, Ms. Weiler."

With a sinking feeling, I straightened up to face her. "I ... um ... right. I guess I did." I gulped. "About my schedule, ah, would that be alright? Sister?"

I waited for the hammer to fall.

"Well, of course." Sister Lorraine softened. "Of course that would be alright."

Stunned, I had to consider whether I had misjudged Sister Lorraine. Maybe she was a frustrated artist herself, torn between her love of all things holy and a creative spirit that yearned to breathe free.

"You've got other affairs and other interests and we wouldn't want to inconvenience you with our silly business of saving souls. No, you go. In fact, why don't you just come in at eleven and leave at twelve? Then you could get a little extra sleep. Would that be more convenient? Because believe me, this entire convent is looking to work around your schedule."

Or maybe she was a bitter old crone who had it in for me.

"Of course not!" the sister shouted. "Why in blue hell would that be alright?" (I didn't know nuns could say *hell*.) "This is not a coffee shop where beatniks while away their days writing poetry and wasting oxygen! This is important work, missy! We have actual jobs here that involve church money and deadlines and FAMILY VALUES FOR GOODNESS' SAKE! NO! NO! NO, THAT WOULD NOT BE ALRIGHT!!!"

A simple "I'm sorry, no" would have been sufficient. I am not a fool. I am not a chimpanzee. I should have kept my mouth shut, but sometimes I can't. And since there was no way I was going to sacrifice my rehearsals for this crummy job, I saw fit to explain myself further. Plus I really can't stand being called "missy."

"Well," I said in a low tone, "I can only hope they don't let you do missionary work. For the record, I'm sure most people are scared to death of you, but with me it's going to take a little more than a black dress and a piece of jewelry. I'm outta here. Have a terrific day, Sister. You be sure and listen for your name when I accept my first Tony." Reeling from the rush of doing something so very naughty, I turned on my heel. I could hear my dead Catholic relatives cursing my mother for marrying a Jew and raising a heathen who bawls out nuns, which I'm pretty certain is a no-no under any creed. In any case, I went straight for my coat and headed toward the exit.

My little play had just turned into a rather expensive endeavor, and that Friday was to be my last at Our Lady of Unforgettable Humiliation. Determined to have the final word, I nicked a package of Post-it pads on my way out. I'm probably going to hell.

"I have few friends in the world for whom I'd drive a getaway car. And thank God, because it's never as easy as it sounds."

CHAPTER 3

M Y MOTHER SEEMS to know, from hundreds of miles away, exactly the wrong time to call me. In this case, she got me halfway between my now-former job and the many drinks I was about to commemorate it with. I have to learn to look at the damned caller ID before I pick up.

"H'llo?"

"Liza?" my mother questioned. She does this. She really questions that it's me picking up the phone. As if there might be another girl with a remarkably similar voice who is now answering my cell phone.

"Hi, Mom." I tried to take a quiet, cleansing breath in preparation for whatever was coming.

"You're not at work."

"Nope. No, I just left."

"They let you leave early from a convent?" She has an uncanny ability to zero in on exactly the wrong thing to say.

"Actually," I assured her, "they were all for it."

"Well, they sound nice. My gosh, the nuns were tough when I was in school."

I am always aware of the moment, early in conversations

with my mother, when I choose: will I appease her and supply polite answers to her innocuous questions, even though I feel like she's boring a hole in the side of my head, or will I revert to hideous bratdom? On this particular Friday, I may actually have skipped the moment.

"No. No," I replied. "They're actually not nice, Mom. They're wretched. I hate them."

"Oh, Liza," she pooh-poohed, with a pinch of disbelief and a dash of disapproval. "The way you talk! You know, I worry that that mouth is going to get you in trouble. I didn't teach you to talk that way."

You see that? Bull's-eye! How does she do it?

"You know, Mom, that's exactly what happened! I mouthed off to a nun and she fired me!"

I was doing it. I was being horrible. And even as I hated myself for being so nasty to my own mother, who really, in fact, didn't know that I had mouthed off and gotten fired, I couldn't seem to stop.

"Oh, honey, it's the sarcasm again. You know I don't find it funny. You sound like a trucker."

I sighed. Even when I was telling her about my actual life, she missed the point.

"I'm sorry, Mom. I'm having a lousy day. Let's start over. How are you?"

"Oh, me? I'm just fine. Just fine." My mother grew up in Florida, where there are many sarcastic people, but settled in Lake Park, Illinois, smack in the heart of the Midwest. In Lake Park, which is petrified beneath the leavings of Chicago's blizzards for half the year, my mother pretends that the sun is always shining and everything is always hunky-dory. Your left hand could freeze and fall off and she'd still tell you it was a "beautiful, crisp, winter's day."

"Daddy's winning a sales award from the Greater Chicagoland Car Dealers' Association. We're very happy about that.

And we've had some nice weather. That Judy Hart is getting married to an accountant she met at graduate school. You should send her a note. Tell her you saw it in the paper."

"Wow, well, I haven't actually seen her in about ten years. Tell Daddy I said congratulations."

"Oh, Liza, you should see this picture of Judy. She's so pretty. She might be prettier now than in high school. You should see."

I had paused to look in the window of an Anthropologie and was now trying to look like I was eyeing a skirt when really I was trying to tame a flyaway. Even my hair was getting on my nerves.

"I bet she is. Anyway, Mom, what's up?"

"Seems like all your little school friends are getting married."

"I was never friends with Judy Hart, Mom." Judy Hart wore lots of pink and always had boyfriends. We didn't exactly run in the same circles.

"Well, I just think there's a limit to these unfocused, running-around years, Liza."

Be calm, I told myself. Breathe. Don't tell her she's about the last person from whom you'd be willing to take romantic advice.

"I'm not running around, Mom." I tried to sound pleasant.

"I just want you to be happy, honey."

"I am happy, Mom."

"You don't sound happy."

"OKAY, FINE! TODAY, AT THIS MOMENT, I AM NOT TERRIBLY HAPPY! I WILL GO OUT IMMEDI-ATELY AND FIND SOMEONE TO MARRY AND THIS WILL SOLVE ALL OF MY PROBLEMS AND GIVE ME FOCUS AND MAKE ME MUCH PRETTIER! OKAY?"

Without a moment of hesitation, she said, "You see, you joke about that, but it might give you focus."

I was barely a factor in this conversation. I considered paying a stranger on the street to hold my phone and agree with her until my mother hung up.

"Okay, Mom." I sighed with resignation. "I'll work on it. Was there anything else?"

"Have you talked to your brother?"

My older brother Jack is in pharmaceutical sales in Los Angeles, but dresses like an indie film director, probably to boost his street cred.

"Not lately. Why?"

"Oh." She sighed. "Well, I called him this morning and I haven't heard back so I wondered if something was wrong. He's bringing his new lady friend to New York for Thanksgiving, you know. I think she's foreign."

"I'm sure he's fine, Mom. It's earlier there. Just give him a few hours."

"Well, alright, Liza. Now, about Thanksgiving . . ."

Foolishly, I had made some noise in late summer about possibly doing Thanksgiving in New York with my friends this year. Within twenty-four hours my mother had engineered a way to get the whole family to the city, so I couldn't escape. It's not that I don't love my family. It's just that my mother spends holidays scurrying around, adjusting sprigs of parsley and checking to make sure everyone's shoes are shined, while my father quizzes my brother and me on our career trajectories. And we watch *It's a Wonderful Life,* which only serves to remind me that it's actually more of a middling life.

"Have you thought about what you're going to bring to Aunt Fran's?" my mother asked.

"She's having the whole thing catered, Mom." Aunt Fran treats her kitchen like one big liquor cabinet. I don't even think there's a saltine in there.

"Well, I think it would be nice for you to show up with a little something. Especially if you're bringing a date. Now, are you bringing anyone special, Liza?"

My mother thinks I date lots of people and just keep it a secret from her. My denials and actual aloneness mean nothing. I had to get off the phone.

"Oh, geez, Mom, I'm late to meet Parrot!" I was sure that would do it.

"Oh, Liza, lateness is such an unattractive quality. You go. Run! I love you!"

"I love you too, Mom. Congratulate Daddy! Bye!" I actually ran a few steps to make it sound authentic. I felt guilty— I always feel guilty when I make an excuse to run away from her—but my mother knows better than anyone how to make me feel disappointing.

One of New York's myriad chatty, idiots-on-the-street took this particularly frustrating moment to tell me to "Smile, gorgeous! I bet you got such a pretty smile." What is wrong with men? I appreciate the compliment, but consider, total stranger, that you have no idea what's going on with my day and maybe I have every reason to look serious. Maybe I have SARS. Maybe a small child just called me fat. Maybe my mother is crushing my soul with her endless attempts to make me into a Talbots catalogue model. You have no idea.

I wanted a drink and to listen to someone else's woes. And after retrieving her six shrieking voice mails, I could only acquiesce and join my best friend at Boca Chica, a relatively hip restaurant on First Street.

Fortunately, as is usually the case, Parrot was there to convince me that I was still safely straddling the middle of the good/bad choice spectrum. Over a FrozFruit bar several months earlier, Parrot had informed me that she'd decided to have an affair with a married man. This, of course, is an only Parrot sort of thing. Deciding. Not a drunk-at-the-Christmas-party-supply-closet affair. But a hotel-room-calculatedly-great-sex affair. I love Parrot dearly, but if her family were not in the mafia, I don't think she'd have any friends.

I explained to Parrot that she had better be careful, as I had no intention of climbing *this* guy's fire escape and jimmying his window open to help her reclaim her favorite bra after it was all over. I'm still amazed we didn't get caught the last time. Parrot, in her inimitable style, explained that:

"It's actually totally cool because I'm not involved at all in their marriage and whatever I do it's totally him who's doing something wrong...I mean I never made any promises to anybody and besides it's not like they have kids so I'm not like wrecking anyone's childhood and really she'll never even know and he's so hot and I really like his car."

It's not that Parrot doesn't think about things. It's just that she has the reasoning powers of a pygmy marmoset when it comes to consequences. Parrot was my first roommate in college. Both her parents, three uncles, two aunts and *seven* cousins came to install her freshman year. My petite suburban mother was nearly apoplectic about the illegal microwave they gave us, but Parrot's dad "spoke" to the RA and assured us there wouldn't be a problem. While we negotiated who got what dresser and tried to decide whether our bedspreads matched, I imagined her borrowing all my stuff without asking and bringing home football players while I was sleeping. I was fairly terrified of her, actually.

Needlessly.

Of course she did do all that stuff. But she also made our room the social center of the floor, listened far into the night every single time my heart was bruised, and always matched me bite for bite when we ordered in cheesy bread. She even threatened my sophomore psych professor when he tried to fail me. I got a B+. Parrot is a loon, but she's my loon.

Naturally, my loon's affair didn't end as she'd hoped. Apparently, and weren't we shocked, this was not a relationship "someone else's husband" felt it prudent to nurture for too long. I was doing my damnedest not to be smug, as Parrot truly is my bestest of friends, although every time she moaned about how much she missed him I was tempted to bury her under a pile of Germaine Greer and Gloria Steinem. This would be pointless. Parrot is a carp on a ten-speed and it will always be thus. Besides, as she'd be quick to point out, half the time I'm riding right alongside her.

In any case, as a result of all this Parrotian despair, I had been on call twenty hours out of every day, prepared at any moment to appear with Chubby Hubby and the occasional bottle of Cabernet. (I'd made it clear that I was not to be called between the hours of three and seven a.m. She mostly stuck to it.) Basically she'd been sitting at home, phoning everyone she knew and bitching.

"It's not like I was gonna marry him or anything," she crowed.

"Not without some significant legal maneuvering," I reminded her.

"It's just that you don't understand this was like so fun and exciting and I had something going on at least I mean you have to be pretty fucking something to make a guy leave his wife—"

"Which you didn't."

"Right, I know but sort of I mean he left her every time he was with me for at least a couple hours right and that's very sexy and hot when someone does that and besides he should so not have been the one to break it off I mean I'm the hot mistress I should so have been the one do you think it was my hair?"

"What?"

"I feel like it's been getting stringy lately and maybe that totally turned him off."

There are times when I genuinely feel like screaming. It requires a great deal of tough love to rein Parrot in, but I am conscientous of the fine line I walk in offering it.

"P, maybe he grew an ethic or two and realized he was a

stinking cheat and had no business taking advantage of a totally fabulous creature like yourself."

Sometimes I'm really impressed with my ability to make
these little lessons Parrot-friendly.

"You're so right you're totally right I am so fabulous."
Then she cried some more.

Despite weeks of my best efforts, Parrot had still been wallowing in alternating states of rage and self-pity. I was thoroughly pleased, therefore, to find that on this particular
evening she had clearly managed to get her engines revved
once again. Since I've known her, Parrot has never allowed
incidental details, like being in a public place, to prevent her
from yapping interminably about wholly inappropriate subjects:

"The thing is it's not like he was really rejecting me it's
just that he's really actually a fucking mess and he can't handle a mature relationship which is very interesting because
I was obviously not asking for any sort of serious commitment of any kind and really we could just have had a good
time and I think it would have been really nice to get regular sex with no obligations attached but if he couldn't handle that fine because I am an extremely attractive woman
in my absolute prime and it's completely his loss and his
wife is a complete failure as a woman as far as I can tell and
there is nothing there for him so he's just going to drown in
his life and he will probably change his mind and come
crawling back and I will be more than happy to let him watch
me with any one of the string of boyfriends I am about to
ruin."

"Sure, sure," I said. What else was there, really?

I was trying hard to focus on Parrot's impressive, if off-
putting, revelations, but I couldn't help noticing all the attention she was drawing from our fellow diners. I was raised in
an almost obsessively polite family; nothing is so painful to

my mother as ordering at a drive-thru window, so unaccustomed is she to raising her voice. Whereas Parrot's generally extraordinary decibel levels are always compelling strangers into conversation, and she just attributes it to being irresistible.

It therefore came as little surprise that at this point, I noticed a self-important snickering coming from the next table. Mind you, Parrot, on her best day, is not one to snicker at. There's no telling what she might do. This was not, by any stretch, her best day.

Attempting to avert an incident that might catapult Parrot back into hiding, I said, "Gee, P, it sounds like you're being really healthy about this."

No dice.

I might as well have been in another room. Parrot had sensed her quarry and was already tracking the scent.

The snickerer, whose back was turned, was one of the pretentious, suit-jacketed, capitalists who've come to frequent the East Village in the past few years, turning every formerly hidden gem into an after-work skank-fest/raw bar. It used to be that east of the Bowery you could actually order a beer without holding an Ivy League degree. Not so anymore. Sometime during the mid-'90s the word went out among the white-collared masses that the dirty '80s were over and great, safe fun was to be had slumming it with the artists and the indigents downtown. Now they come in droves to collect a Russian waitress here, a pierced sculptor there. You know, it spices up the sexual catalogue. You ask them what they do and they say, "I'm a consultant." Very informative. What does that mean? Remember when people had jobs like "bricklayer," "secretary," "prostitute"? I miss that.

"Excuse me," snapped Parrot. "Do I amuse you? Am I a clown to you?" she asked, with absolutely no irony.

So now, from his table of similarly clad cool-boys, the snickerer turned.

I have only one requirement for these soulless assholes—that they not be cute. When they are, it ruins everything. Everything.

"I'm sorry. You said 'regular sex.' I couldn't help overhearing." He was bold. I hated him already.

Parrot, however, who was only just reawakening to her considerable sex drive, clearly saw her table of potential tormentors as a buffet.

"I'm sure you couldn't," she replied, and tossed her dark curls. "I think it's sad that regular sex is such a joke to you."

This was going nowhere good.

"Well, I like to shoot for something more along the lines of extraordinary." He was a pro. And his friends were enjoying this. Parrot would soon be in over her head. I prayed that she would be distracted by something shiny or just give up and refuse to take the bait.

"Well," she quipped, "keep listening. You might learn something."

There it was. She was open. Big mistake.

"That's alright," he fired back. "I've seen the *Ricki Lake Show*. I doubt you've got anything new for me." And he said it with a grin stolen from my own bag of tricks that's meant to soften the blow. I simply had to speak up.

"Parrot, you're obviously speaking with someone who's seen it all before." I shot him a look of disdain so he knew who he was dealing with.

"Oh, dear, does it show?" He acknowledged me. "I've been working so hard to stay fresh."

"You should try coming out during daylight," I parried. "The sunshine does so much." Thinking that the proverbial bud had been nipped, I turned back to Parrot and my monkfish.

But he wasn't done. "I should introduce my friends. This is Kirk and Steve. And that's Kyle. I'm George. And you are?"

Great. "I'm Parrot, and this is Liza." *Great. Great.*

Now Kirk, by far the least impressive-looking of the group, chimed in, "You know we're just finishing up and we thought we'd head out to River Town Lounge after this. Would you ladies like to join us?"

And of course he would pick a bar that was only worth frequenting Sunday through Tuesday when no one is there. I was thinking ... absolutely fucking not. And Parrot said, "Sure." Why? Why?!

Despite the raging telepathic death threats I was sending her, Parrot asked for our check and refused to make eye contact with me. She's not oblivious, she's selectively attentive.

George began to make a noise about paying for us and I was forced to explain my feelings about being obligated to total strangers. He suggested, as he threw down a gold card on his own check, that I talked like I was doing a scene from *Key Largo.* Certainly he could not have fathomed my obsession with early Lauren Bacall movies and instantly I felt as though he'd somehow managed to begin undressing me. This was infuriating, as were his noteworthy brown eyes and wavy hair. Against my better judgment, I followed Parrot's lead and we departed.

She was already working her giggly magic on Kirk as our newly formed party made its way across Houston Street. I could feel George jockeying for the spot next to me but I stepped ahead and firmly pincered Parrot by the elbow.

"What?" she tweeted, clearly annoyed at being interrupted.

"You are *not* going to abandon me to this guy, Parrot. I am tired and grumpy and jobless and really, really not in the mood."

"Of course I'm not I would never do that," she protested.

"Again. You would never do that *again,* you mean."

"Liza, I really like this guy."

"You've been talking for seven and a half minutes!" I argued.

"I—"

"No, P! Not tonight, please, I'm begging you!"

She considered my puppy-dog eyes carefully before swearing on her vintage Pucci dress that she wouldn't leave me.

Naturally she broke said promise within minutes of stepping through the door to the bar, which George held with a smirk. She disappeared as soon as we were inside and didn't surface again until drunkenly declaring her intention to leave a few marks on poor, dim Kirk.

Which was why I felt it wholly appropriate to blame her for my wretched ankle injury and a good deal of what followed.

Well ... part of it.

*"A man who notices your shoes either
wants to see them on his floor in the morning or
wants to wear them."*

CHAPTER 4

ONE MOMENT I HAD BEEN on my way
home, and the next I was being ferried toward medical
care in the company of an irritating corporate raider with ter-
rifically gorgeous brown eyes and a truly extraordinary ego.
My night, like my ankle, had suddenly taken a turn.

"St. Vincent's, please," he told the driver.

"Wha...I...who said I'm going to the hospital?!" I
protested.

"In fifteen minutes your ankle's going to be the size of
New Jersey. I heard the pop."

"Well, we're closer to Beth Israel!"

"It's a Friday night. We're gonna be there for a while.
Fewer crackheads at St. Vincent's. How bad does it feel?"

Like seven angry pit bulls gnawing slowly through my bones.

"It's not that bad," I insisted.

"You don't have to be brave for my benefit."

Which was good because I really wanted to cry a little.

"I don't even know you! I have no idea why you're in this
cab and I'm certainly not thinking about your benefit!"

"Okay, fine. Why don't you let me take a look?" He reached

for my throbbing, pulsating ankle, which at the moment even I didn't want to touch. Already it was more than a third its usual size.

"Ow! No! Don't touch it! You're gonna make it . . ."

George had pulled my whole leg into his lap and I was very, very glad that I had shaved.

". . . worse."

"You should have it elevated. Is that worse?"

Umm . . . nope. But I hate you. So start making it worse.

I said nothing.

"Do you think you could sit there and keep quiet while I take your shoe off?" he asked, smirking again. Just in case I had missed it.

"Why do you need to do that?"

"Because it'll hurt less if I do it now. Didn't we just talk about being quiet?"

"Are you trying to make me feel better?" I snapped. "Because you really have absolutely no bedside manner to speak of."

"That's hardly fair. We're not even in bed."

Afraid to open my mouth again, I tried hard to call upon my rapier wit while George gingerly worked my boot off. I'm fairly certain that this hurt like the dickens, but looking at him was somehow numbing the pain.

"Nice kitten heel," he remarked.

"You realize if we'd gone to Beth Israel we'd have been there by now," I poked.

George chuckled as the sound of the meter receipt printing punctuated my statement. We were there.

"Good point," he said.

Then he refused to let me pay.

I insisted on getting out of the cab myself, so George held my boot and kept an arm out, clearly ready for me to take another dive. He then denied me access to said boot, assuring me that he'd relinquish it when I was comfortably seated. I

explained that this would certainly interfere with his immediate departure. He countered that he wasn't going anywhere
and asked why I was being so difficult. Outraged, I hopped
my way to triage, and George stood by while my insurance
was noted and my admitting forms filled out.

Finally I was told to sit and await my doom. Emergency
rooms make me nervous. George settled me on a green plastic bench in between a moaning old woman and a large
Spanish-speaking family. He was right. Friday was a busy
night.

"Okay, look," I said, snatching my boot from his hand,
"you've gone well beyond the call of duty and when I tell
this story I'll be sure to say how chivalrous you've been, but
really, go now. It's still early and I'm sure the lonely women
of New York are wondering where you are."

He looked down at me, so cocky I wanted to sock him,
and said, "Okay."

What? What do you mean okay?

I mean, good. That's what I was hoping you'd say.

"Good luck," he said. And he shook my hand.

This was infuriating! You don't ride across town with
someone's thigh under your arm and then shake their hand
goodbye! Which only proved he had no soul.

"Thanks," I said. And I watched him walk through the
sliding glass door and into the street.

"Forget make-up sex. You need to try argument sex. Trust me."

CHAPTER 5

I WAS A LITTLE DRUNK and a little nauseous and my ankle felt like a flaming beach ball. I looked around at the sea of distressed and bedraggled ER patrons and realized I'd never been in a hospital by myself before. I felt seven years old. My ankle throbbed some more and I wondered how I would even get up from my seat when they finally called my name. However many hours from now that might be. Even as I sat there I was sure that Parrot was uptown in some grimy, fratty apartment, banging the shit out of Dirk or Kirk or whatever his name was. And here I was, spending my Friday night alone and in pain and that freaking guy had flirted with me and then just LEFT me sitting ALONE in a SCARY EMERGENCY ROOM to fend for myself with a HORRIBLE PAINFUL INJURY! Which was exactly what I would have expected from a guy like that.

Another second and I would have been in tears.

"McGurdy! Rose!" called an admitting nurse.

Old Moany to my left hobbled up and sneezed on the nurse, who tried to be very Julianna Margulies about it and not wipe her hand on her smock too conspicuously.

In only seconds I felt the newly vacant seat next to me being refilled.

"Take all four," said a voice as a familiar hand extended two foil packets of Advil.

I looked to my left, stunned, but fairly certain I was right in thinking I would see . . .

George. Who was back. With a huge bottle of water and two bags of frozen peas.

I thought I might throw up.

I took his Advil and he opened the water for me.

"I got you a Volvic, which is something I like to do for any girl on a first date."

I nearly choked on my pills. "I hope you've been tested. And we're not on a date."

"You're right. Advil, injuries. Definitely feels more like the morning after a date."

"This is why I would never date you."

"I don't remember asking."

I resisted the temptation to kick him with my good leg.

"Got a little snack?" I glanced at the peas.

"Yeah, that's it. I was hungry." He bent down and lifted my foot up, wrapped the plastic bag from the deli around my ankle, laid one bag of peas under my heel and draped the other over it.

It was becoming increasingly difficult to maintain my complete disdain for this man. And I was really working at it.

"I guess I should thank you," I managed.

"It would be polite."

"Okay. Thank you. I thought you were off."

"Thanks for thinking so little of me. I just went around the corner."

I didn't know what to say. So I tried, "So why so much expertise with the ankle?"

"I played rugby in college."

At this point I really had to question whether perhaps he'd

been manufactured in the basement of some women's magazine to be awarded to a lucky sweepstakes winner, and that we were only sitting here now because a lone editorial flack had taken pity and released him into the wild to charm at random. Rugby. Please.

"Really? Where was that?"

"London School of Economics. You?"

"Yale. The London School has a rugby team?"

"Local team. Yale. That must make temping hurt."

Just when I was beginning to find him palatable.

"Oh, right, in your world there are 'professionals' and then there's everybody else. No MBA?"

"Finished last year at Kellogg. So are you saying that you enjoy temping?"

"No, but you know they don't exactly offer lots of terrific entry-level playwriting jobs."

"Ever think about grad school?" he asked.

"Occasionally. Ever think about charm school?"

"Not once. Although your friend Parrot is clearly a graduate."

"Careful." I get to make fun of her but no one else does.

"What, you get to make fun of her but no one else does?"

"I know she's a little crazy, alright? But a little crazy is not always a bad thing."

"She balances you, you mean."

It was like being in some kind of romantic horror movie. Every time I turned a corner, there he was, three steps ahead of me.

"So, let me guess. You went into finance because you didn't have the personality for insurance sales?" I asked.

"I'm exceptionally good at what I do and it's the fastest way to become a millionaire before thirty-five."

"Wow, you said that with no shame whatsoever."

"Neither would you. You just don't happen to be in a field

that affords the opportunity. Which you probably resent if you have any sense."

"Excuse me?"

"It's not an insult, it's just true. You could be the most successful playwright in history and you probably still couldn't afford to buy a decent apartment in this city."

"Okay, a) that's not true, and b) forgive me for thinking there's more to life!"

"I didn't say there wasn't. But who wouldn't rather get paid shitloads of money to do their job? I just chose a job that actually rewards merit in a fairly reliable way. There's nothing wrong with wanting to live well."

"Well, why even bother working? Why not just snatch yourself a rich wife?"

"I'd love to. You know any rich women who are looking?"

"Please, I'm in theatre. No one I know has any money."

"Last time I checked, the only people who could afford careers in theatre are the ones who have money. You have any student loans?"

"That is so incredibly none of your business!"

"Oh, I get it. You have to play starving artist or nothing you do is meaningful. If the bank balance is too high nobody will take you seriously."

"You see? This is what I hate about people who spend all their time thinking about nothing but money," I snapped. "You just decide that you know what makes the world go round and really you don't know a thing about the lives most people lead."

"Oh yeah, and you're Maxim Gorky. See, this is exactly what I hate about artists. You all think you're the moral center and you look down on anybody who works nine to five but you'd be perfectly happy if my tax dollars were subsidizing you!"

"That is ridiculous!! Only a person—"

"Excuse me!" broke in a Latin-accented voice.

George and I arrested and gazed at the soft-spoken man to our right, cradling a dozing three-year-old boy. "My son"—he indicated—"has a fever and he's finally sleeping. Could you just have this little lovers' quarrel at home?"

"We're not lovers!" I insisted, as George rushed to say, "We're so sorry."

We didn't look at each other.

"We really are sorry," I said.

"No problem, man," the gentleman whispered. "Just keep it down."

My cheeks were flushed. My face was hot. I had sort of forgotten what I was doing there. It felt like we'd been sitting on that bench arguing for a hundred years.

I looked at my watch. More like an hour and a half.

We sat in silence. There was a little puddle by my foot where the pea-ice had melted and dripped from the bags.

"How's your ankle?" he finally ventured.

"I didn't mean to be obnoxious," I replied. "It's better. The ice helped."

"That's okay. You can't help it." The smirk was back. "I didn't mean to imply that you'd die poor and disenfranchised." He grinned.

"And I didn't mean to suggest that you were completely devoid of human qualities and that no one would visit your grave."

"I didn't take it that way." He almost laughed.

We managed to sit in strangely comfortable silence for almost ten minutes. Until I made a comment about the benefits of socialized health care. It was another hour and forty-five minutes before my name was called, during which time we managed to argue passionately over several subjects we actually agreed on (the war, gay marriage, U.S. dependence on foreign oil) and a few we didn't (Hollywood moviemaking, the most exciting city in Europe and Simon

Cowell vs. Ryan Seacrest. We were twice more told to keep it down. Being around him was like being slightly more awake than usual, as if my synapses were firing faster.

Not that he stopped pissing me off or making fun of me for being exceptionally uncoordinated. When my name was finally called I told him to go. He seemed genuinely surprised, which I presumed meant he thought maybe he was going to get laid after all. I told him that if he wasn't gone by the time I got out, I'd have Parrot's family leave a horse head in his bed.

"You know, most girls would be grateful for what I've done tonight," he said, annoyed.

"Well, why don't you go and maim another one and I'm sure she will be."

"Fine." He grabbed his jacket from the bench.

"Thank you. Goodbye." I barely worked to keep the sarcasm out of my voice. I began limping toward the curtained bed to which I'd been directed.

"Good luck," I heard him mutter. I spun around (with difficulty) to deliver the parting blow . . .

George was gone.

I stared after him, certain he'd reappear momentarily with a bag of Peanut M&M's or a handful of wildflowers.

"Elizabeth Weiler!" a nurse called disapprovingly. I had no choice but to hobble after her.

For a second I wondered if I'd done the wrong thing. Except I knew guys like this; they thought you were fun when they were looking for a brainteaser, but eventually they'd hear the siren song of vapid arm-candy and you'd be left wondering what the hell happened. I was not about to be taken in. Besides, only for the most pigheaded cretin should it take more than three hours to figure out that go means go.

"I can't resist a man in uniform. On a slow day,
I'll take a waiter with a nametag."

CHAPTER 6

A T SOME PAINS, I hoisted my sorry self onto a bed and waited to be dissected. And this was where my evening suddenly changed for the better. Out of a sea of screaming winos who didn't want to take their meds and surly teenagers who had beaten each other up, there emerged a doctor, my doctor, the very doctor I had always dreamed I might someday turn my ankle and be treated by.

I would love to say that I'm immune to such clichés, but … wow, such a cute doctor.

Picture the child of Cary Elwes and Albert Schweitzer. Sandy hair, glasses, hands you'd like to sit in. He threw back the curtain, looking at his notes and not at me, and said, "So … you are … Elizabeth." And then he looked up. And he froze for a second, as if to say, "Good God, it's not every day a woman as astonishing as you limps into my ER." I explained directly to his stunning green eyes the nature of my injuries.

"Another senseless plastic bag accident. I'm seeing them all the time," he said. I looked down and realized I was still wearing the makeshift sheath George had wrapped me in. I hastened to tear it off, but he stopped me.

"This is very technical, Elizabeth." He used my name gingerly and I explained that everyone calls me Liza. I smiled to suggest that he could scream it in the heat of passion if he liked.

"Why don't you let me do that?" he asked, reaching for my ankle. I did let him, and he wadded up the bag and threw it in a red trash can marked "biohazard," which I thought was a wildly appropriate way to describe George. "Looks like you did a real number on yourself, huh, Liza?"

"Oh, I really did, Dr. . . ."

"Tim. My name's Tim."

Tim. Oh, yeah. That's gonna work just fine.

"Does it hurt when I do this?" He gently twisted my ankle to the left.

"Yes! Yes it does!" I sort of squeaked without meaning to.

"Okay, Liza."

There was a kindness that radiated from him, this gentle sweetness that felt like a warm blanket after three hours of snarking back and forth with George.

"I think some X-rays are in order. I'm going to have an orderly take you down and I'll meet you back here in, let's say, forty-five minutes?"

"It's a date!" *Stupid! Stupid! Stupid! Stop speaking!*

Dr. Tim grinned and excused himself. After a few minutes, a rather portly man named Tito wheeled me into an elevator, deposited me in radiology, and returned to chauffeur me back to a different bed in the ER. I was reminded of those children away from home on Christmas who worry that Santa won't be able to find them.

My knight in shining lab coat had no such trouble. He returned, touched me a great deal, which I knew was his job, but I liked to think he maybe did it a little more than he had to, and he definitely seemed to enjoy looking at my X-rays and describing my sprain. "So no dancing for you this weekend, Liza. Too bad. I imagine you've got a fella who'll be willing to set you up with a stack of DVDs and some Chinese food, though."

I giggled in spite of myself. "Oh, no! No guy at all! No DVDs. Not a wonton, Dr. Tim."

I watched with pleasure as he took this in.

"Liza, let me tell you what my major concern is with the ankle. It's going to be extremely important that you stay off it, and this whole DVD deficit could really get in the way."

"Really, Dr. Tim, you think so?"

I thought the giggling might not end until I was forty-five and had had six of Dr. Tim's children.

"I tell you what, Liza—"

Suddenly the surgical curtain was pulled back by an evil nurse who requested Dr. Tim's help with a silly car accident victim, as if that were more important!

"I've gotta go do this, but you stay off that ankle!" he said, turning quickly to go.

"Oh! I ... okay! I will! Thanks. . . ."

And he disappeared. I sat there for a moment, clutching my new crutches and watching my perfect future evaporate into mist. After an adequate amount of self-pity had washed over me, and a nurse explained that they needed the bed, I hung my head and began hobbling toward the waiting room.

I scanned the room for George, but thank God, he was gone. In the course of one evening, I had traded good ankle for bad, gained and lost one frog and one prince with equal aplomb. So basically I was just a lonely cripple with no prospects. Not so different from the way I'd begun the night, just less mobile.

"Liza!"

I turned and nearly lost my balance. Dr. Tim was slipping past a gurney and coming toward me. In a moment he was going to have to defibrillate me.

"Almost forgot." He handed me a prescription. "Can you

deal with codeine? You might have a lot of pain the next few days."

I don't know what came over me, whether it was the great New York fairy tale of it all or the sheer exhaustion, but suddenly I was very brave.

"Would you like to have dinner with me?" I blurted.

"What?" He blinked.

"I ... dinner. Sometime. As a thank-you for the ... no, that's bullshit. As a date. Would you like to go out with me?"

He looked nervous. I wanted to believe it was excited nervous and not repulsed nervous.

"Doctors can't date patients," he said.

"Oh, I ... Right. Of course they can't. That was totally ... inappropriate." Why does this sort of humiliation happen when I actually can't run?

"So if you needed any follow-up care, I'd have to give you the name of another doctor."

"Sure." I was so embarrassed that I barely registered the way he was looking at me. "Wait, what?"

"And technically you'd need to walk through those doors before we could exchange phone numbers or ..."

"Oh!" I got it. "Oh, yeah, of course. Yes."

"So maybe I should walk you out." He smiled this very sexy, warm smile, which I was now able to fully appreciate, knowing I might get to see it again.

"You know any good DVDs, Dr. Tim?"

I got his phone number.

Honestly, not the worst evening ever. The shameless, girly part of me had gotten out for some exercise, which was good, because she spends a lot of time in her stall. And being off my feet would leave me plenty of time to call Parrot and tell her how much my ankle hurt.

Over. And over. And over.

"If you wake up and you know where you are,
you're doing pretty well."

CHAPTER 7

I AWOKE THE NEXT MORNING wondering if I'd dreamed the previous twenty-four hours. Luckily, I had a throbbing ankle and itchy Aircast to reinforce reality. I popped a couple of Advil on my way to the living room, where my roommate Jeremy was lounging and slurping at a bowl of Cocoa Puffs.

"Whoa, L-Train! What the hell happened to you?" sweet Jeremy asked with concern. I explained.

"You're a disaster master!" he said, awed.

I reminded him of the way that two completely different men had fawned over me and of the fact that I now had an excuse to lounge around eating ice cream and watching Lifetime Television for Women. Jeremy immediately abandoned his cartoon so I could watch *The Golden Girls*. I don't know what I would do without him.

A much younger Jeremy and I were freshman hallmates. I liked him immediately, as he was one of the only boys in our dorm who could acknowledge Parrot's eccentricities and like her anyway without having sex with her. When Parrot was "entertaining," I sought refuge in Jeremy's room, where we bonded over Cowboy Junkies albums and *Hill Street Blues* reruns, nostalgic even as teenagers. While he was proofreading a term paper for my E. M. Forster class during sophomore year, Jeremy and I got shamefully drunk on Boone's Farm strawberry wine and spent a sweet but awkward evening making sweet but awkward love. We immediately stopped speaking to each other for several months, but found ourselves at a frat party during second semester and both apologized profusely. He's my most favorite male, and for the past several years a harried academic, working through a doctoral dissertation on *Clarissa*. Last year, though he's normally a pacifist, Jeremy delivered a black eye to an ex-boyfriend of mine who tried to convince an entire bar full of people that I'd refused to sleep with him because he was too generously endowed. In reality, I had refused to sleep with him because he had too quickly revealed his overwhelming ego and underwhelming vocabulary. I like a man who has more to say in the morning than "You make coffee?" Jeremy is my lifeline.

But when we decided to get a place together after college (neither of us could have lived with Parrot in a setting that involved paying bills and keeping more than one room clean), we were both caught unprepared for the brutality of the New York real estate market. Creative types attempting to find housing with some measure of dignity or even cleanliness are almost universally rejected and demeaned by the real estate powers that be. It doesn't matter what you promise them. You just don't fit the formula. Come on, they're called brokers because they want to break you.

Finding an apartment in New York is such an arduous, Byzantine process that someone could make a video game out of it. Of course, no one would play, because frankly anyone who's been through it and managed to stay out of an asylum would rather eat a car piece by piece than ever even think about it again. We spent weeks, maybe months, comb-ing the internet as though the formula for a cancer cure was hidden somewhere on Craigslist. We soared into the air every time a landlord said jump, producing credit histories, refer-ences, testimonials. And when we finally found a place that didn't evoke steerage on the *Titanic,* we got shot down. This happened three times. Jeremy and I looked at every vermin-infested shoebox in Manhattan, until one rainy afternoon a broker snapped at us for being too picky and I had a break-down.

"You listen to me, Nancy or whatever your damned name is! I don't know where you people came up with this unspo-ken rule that anyone who doesn't work in an office should expect to be comfortable living in squalor, but it's crap! I'm sorry that my annual income is not equal to forty times the rent, but I don't want to wake up with bugs on me! I don't want to shower in the freaking kitchen! I don't want to let the staff from the restaurant downstairs use our oven to make tortillas and I don't care if it was okay with the last tenant! And I really don't think that a man and a woman not roman-tically involved should have to share a room! What if one of us gets laid, Nancy? Hmm? I realize it's unlikely, but where is the other one supposed to go? Can we come to your house, Nancy? WELL, CAN WE?!"

From what I remember, Jeremy dragged me out into the street at this point, where I began to cry. He used my phone to call Aunt Fran, who called someone who called someone. Two days later, because this is the sort of thing Aunt Fran can make happen, Jeremy and I came face-to-face with a New York myth: a rent-controlled three-bedroom in Gramercy. It was spacious and sunny and there were no dodgy, window-less rooms with odd smells. We would have done anything to get this apartment, to secure our belongings within its sturdy, roach-free walls and to abide there forever and ever. There were only two catches: one, if anyone asked, we lived with an old woman named Mildred, a long-ago Hollywood costume designer who had probably been dead for decades when we moved in, and two, the third bedroom was occupied.

Tabitha was Mildred's granddaughter or great-granddaughter or demon spawn. Rather than pay the fairly modest rent in order to have an enormous apartment to herself, Tabitha had devised a system that would allow her to live absolutely rent free: we paid the whole thing. I have to admire her ingenuity—Tabitha always gets what she wants.

Our entrance interview felt like the inquisition. I think Tabitha has so many of my financial records that she could seamlessly assume my identity, not that she would want to. I would later come to realize that she probably selected us because she could tell that neither of us had much of a social life and she didn't want strangers having too much sex in her nice apartment. But she seemed alright at first. She was an assistant curator at some boutique, women's art museum. Zero sense of humor, but we were looking to share an apartment, not a desert island.

People to whom I described Tabitha frequently had difficulty grasping the extent to which she absolutely sucks, and whenever possible, I showed them her room. She'd painted it a horrible salmony-peach nursing home shade, which would have made even dead Mildred wince. She had Ethan Hawke novels on her bookshelf, both of them, and a vast collection of ceramic ponies. And she kept her prom pictures framed on her dresser. Her prom pictures. At twenty-eight. There's no reason for that.

Some people work to surround themselves with friends and colleagues who will challenge them; Tabitha had to be sure she never stood next to anyone who might outshine her. Yes, Jeremy and I could have run intellectual circles around her, but Tabitha knew that her future ATM, I mean husband, wouldn't care about smarts. He'd care about her twinset sweaters and her overarticulation of the letter T and the immaculate condition of the space behind her toilet.

By her bedside, Tabitha kept a pair of earplugs in a dish shaped like a cat, which she used whenever Jeremy or I so much as spoke in the apartment after nine p.m. And anytime we watched *South Park,* which she found morbidly offensive. She left Post-its on our pillows to remind us that utilities were due and offered constant critiques of our "bohemian" lifestyles and general "sloth." It was like living with Pol Pot with French tips.

Jeremy and I were enjoying our Saturday morning on the couch, he making fun of me for being a klutz, me repeatedly trumpeting my own dating bravura, when the gorgon puffed in from her morning run with a carb-free muffin and a self-satisfied "Good morning, lazybones!"

Jeremy and I grunted and attempted to camouflage ourselves into the couch. After a few moments, Tabitha's whine began to drown out Estelle Getty's Sicily story.

"Um, roomies?"

I hate it when people request your attention before they start talking. Just talk. With minimal effort we turned our heads.

"We need to have a chitchat."

We braced ourselves for a scolding. I rapidly scrolled through the possible offenses in my head: Had I forgotten to pay her for the electric? Used the last tampon? Failed to refill the Brita? Panicked, I realized I wouldn't be able to flee on my ankle.

Tabitha's overlong pause alerted me that I should mute the TV.

"I have some news."

Mm-hmm.

"I don't know how to say this. I hate to break up the team. We have so much fun here ..."

Wha . . . ? Wait a minute, RED FLAG! TOO FRIENDLY! OH, GOD, SHE WAS FINALLY KICKING US OUT!!

"Tod and I are getting married. I'm moving in with him in two weeks and then we're buying a place with the money from his trust as soon as we find something on a block where we really feel at home. Of course you'll both be invited to the wedding and I'm going to register at Neiman's, just so you know."

Since we'd met her, Tabitha had never spent a moment without a hapless man floundering somewhere on her plate. She'd patrolled the streets of Manhattan with the urgency of a starving jungle cat, meeting men on the subway, in unisex bathrooms, in the dentist's waiting room. She gave internet dating a bad name. Tabitha is the reason why relatively healthy, normal people who meet their mates online fear a stigma and lie to their friends. Mere months ago she could be overheard on the home phone, shrieking at the WebLove administrators, trying to have a user named CaptainHootie36 expelled from the system for using explicit language to describe his intentions. I tried to explain that "shove it up your ass" is not necessarily a romantic advance, but Tabitha ignored me.

There was, therefore, no justice in the fact that Tabitha had been getting it good for seven weeks. Tod, one D, was a recently laid-off associate from an investment house he felt it "inappropriate to name." They had dated from ages seventeen to twenty-two and many would suggest it was this tragic breakup that prompted Tabitha's casual dating frenzy. After years apart, they ran into each other at Whiskey Blue and rekindled their love over some overpriced, specialty martinis. Tabitha had had the grating grin of an undeserving lay ever since.

Jeremy and I just looked at each other and screamed the silent scream we'd learned to share with only our eyes. It was so unfair, so fucking unfair! Tabitha was going to move on up and we were going to be homeless, and she'd only been dating this guy for seven weeks! We were poor and struggling and we never did anything to anybody but we were getting screwed, and she was getting fucking flatware!

"And, because we've had so much fun here, and so many happy, happy memories, I'm going to let you two keep the apartment!"

The heavens opened, the angels wept.

"You're letting us stay?" Jeremy found the courage to speak.

"Well, of course there's going to be an eentsy-weentsy rent increase. You will have a whole extra bedroom now."

I might actually have hugged her, even with the rent increase, but the phone rang. Tod-with-one-D wanted to know whether we'd taken the news okay. Apparently, it was "going to be hard on Liza and Jeremy."

I didn't know how to feel. On the one hand, I barely needed to express my ecstasy at the prospect of the pall that was Tabitha being lifted. On the other . . . this made me so pathetic. Tabitha, by all accounts, the worst girl I know, had found someone who wanted to legally ensure she'd always be around. And this was just the beginning, I knew, just the eerie foreshadowing of that thing that happens where everyone you know suddenly starts making the decision to become an adult. And one day you turn around and you're thirty-nine and you realize that all the people you know have been replaced with these scary suburban versions of your old friends. They drive sensible cars into their city jobs and they park in garages where they rent monthly. And they invite you to their barbecues so you can meet their successful neighbor, the lawyer. And he has premature ear-hair, but you're supposed to be okay with that because you seem to be "unfocused" and your friends are just trying to give you a kind shove in the "right direction." Oh, fuck.

I wish someone had warned me that there would come a time in my life when I was supposed to look like I knew what I was doing. I would have tried to prepare. Instead of finding myself out of college, mysteriously in my late twenties and still flailing. Did everyone else take some sort of class in how to do this?

I think I was out that day.

As soon as Tabitha left the room to take her betrothed's call, Jeremy and I called a housing conference.

"How soon do you think she's leaving?" he asked.

"How fast can you pack her stuff?" I replied.

"We're dreaming. No one is this lucky," he assured me.

"I don't want to wake up," I said.

"Yeah, well, I think you're gonna have to, when she tells us how much she's hiking the rent. It's gonna be tight, but I'm doing okay with the TA gig."

I was awake.

Jeremy and I had always dreamed of having the place to ourselves, but in six years we'd never had a realistic opportunity. It sounded like perfection. Like the best idea ever. Like . . . something I couldn't afford.

Shit. "Big J," I began, crestfallen, "I lost my job yesterday."

"No."

"Yeah. Big-time. Bad business with the head nun."

"Damn," he said. "I'm sorry. But they'll get you a new assignment, right? You're always working somewhere."

I imagined the angry call Sister Lorraine had undoubtedly made to my temp agency.

"I screwed up," I said. "I have a solid feeling I'm about to be in temp purgatory."

"Man," he said, "I don't know what to tell you." We sighed in unison and I felt terrible for darkening this happy occasion.

"You know it's just like her to have her wildest dreams

come true and still be trying to bilk us for extra cash. She knows we don't have any money. I may need to have a word with her about this little increase—"

"Liza," Jeremy interrupted me, "you're gonna have to come up with something. For me. We can't lose this apartment."

One look in Jeremy's sincerely terrified eyes told me he was right. I had to do something that did not involve arguing with Tabitha. I had to find a new job, pronto.

"I promise," I told him. This was my problem and I was going to handle it. After all, humility couldn't really be as bad as it sounded.

"Asking a man on a date is not a risk.
Stealing a lawn chair from Zsa Zsa Gabor ...
now, that's a risk."

CHAPTER 8

FIRST THING MONDAY MORNING, I called my temp agency. I was contrite, repentant, ashamed. I basically apologized all over myself. My supervisor, Carmella, was having none of it. She suggested that I take some time to think about whether I really wanted to be temping. This, I explained to her, was a foolish suggestion, as naturally I didn't *want* to be temping. I *wanted* to be reading in a porch swing on Nantucket with a pitcher of martinis at my side. But I *needed* to make a living and therefore I *needed* to temp. Except I said it in a very sweet and groveling way. Carmella was unimpressed and explained that even though she'd be happy to try to find me a new assignment, it was going to be tough. This was her way of telling me the temping gods were peeved and I'd have to do my penance before I got another gig. I wheedled and cajoled, but Carmella was immovable. Clearly, I was going to have to look elsewhere.

That evening, I met Aunt Fran for drinks at Temple Bar. Her Chicago run had ended only the night before, but thankfully she makes me a priority and she met me only hours after landing at LaGuardia. After suffering months of her absence, I was so glad to see Aunt Fran that I nearly forgot how much energy one is required to muster in her presence. I was barely settled in the cushy banquette when she gave me a sharp look and cried, "You met someone, you little minx!"

How does she do it? I must emit some strange I-met-a-man pheromone that only Aunt Fran can detect.

"I'm glad to see you too and thanks for not mentioning the crutches."

"Cut the small talk, Niece, who is he?"

I hesitated for a moment at the odd realization that I wasn't sure which name I was going to cough up.

"Tim," I said, and I listened for the way it sounded coming out of my mouth. "His name is Tim."

"No names," Aunt Fran rasped, "I want details."

"He's a doctor. An ER doctor, actually. The one who fixed my ankle."

"Doesn't look fixed to me, but carry on."

"He's very sweet, smart, I think. We haven't gone out yet."

Aunt Fran looked long and hard at me. "Very sweet, smart, you think, and you haven't gone out yet. And that's where you're getting the look from? I don't think so."

"What look?" I protested.

"The glowing, hot-pants look," she insisted. "I know that look. Sean Connery gave me that look once. Sweet and smart, you think, does not give you that look. Somebody else?"

I felt my ears reddening. "No, definitely nobody else, unless you count the asshole who should actually be taking responsibility for nearly breaking my ankle in the first place."

"Now you're talking."

"No, absolutely not, this guy was a jerk. One of these incredibly egotistical financial types who probably gets laid all the time and thinks that life is just one long happy hour."

"I'm waiting for the bad part," she insisted.

"Oh, trust me, the hours I had to spend listening to him in the hospital waiting room more than counted as a bad part. Why are you looking at me like that?"

"Who, me?" she asked. "I'm just enjoying your story."

"Well, it's over. There was no story. That was it."

She kept looking at me.

"So how are you? How was your flight?" I was going to force a new subject.

"Hmph," Aunt Fran grunted. "To be continued, Niece. I killed in Chicago. Did you read the reviews?"

"Every one," I promised. I never miss a single one of her reviews.

"So what else has transpired in my absence?"

I explained that I'd tussled with a servant of God and lost.

"Nuns," Aunt Fran muttered. "Nuns don't know what they're missing, Liza. If they did, they wouldn't be nuns."

It was probably this irreverent attitude toward religion that made Aunt Fran so willing to help my parents elope when they were still in college. My very Catholic mother, Margaret "Peg" Flaherty, had fallen for my very Jewish father, Jason, when the two were only sixteen. By junior year of college my mother had converted and a year later Aunt Fran had flown the pair to Vegas for an impromptu wedding that infuriated my two sets of grandparents equally. I'm not sure if it was the *Romeo and Juliet* factor or just the opportunity to piss off four old farts that had motivated Aunt Fran, but she and I share a powerful awareness that I would likely not exist without her intervention.

I gave her the lowdown on Tabitha's departure and my current unemployment bind.

"Mm-hmm" was all she said. I waited for more, but Aunt Fran returned her attentions to her cocktail. There was an awkward pause, at least for me.

"Well, gee, I hadn't thought of it from that perspective. Now I know exactly what to do! Thanks for the advice," I said, with perhaps a touch more attitude than is appropriate when speaking with one's great aunt.

She looked hard into my face and I could feel myself backing down.

"Exactly what sort of advice were you looking for?" she drawled.

"I don't know," I replied, "job advice? John Guare needs his plants watered, Edward Albee is looking for a cleaning lady, something like that."

"You're aspiring to be some rich old man's domestic?"

Aunt Fran has always been my protector, my confidante and my oracle, but she's never come through in the one area where she could help me the most. For all her Tonys, all her connections, all her celebrity, she's never offered me help as a playwright. Yes, she's read my material, she's shown up for every performance, she's encouraged and nudged and even disciplined me to write more, to write better. But she's never offered to pick up the phone and send my scripts to a literary manager or an agent. Never pulled a string to get me into a writing program or leaned on any of her myriad adoring colleagues to just give me a leg up. And we both know connections are everything.

"I'm aspiring to make enough money to stay in my apartment, Aunt Fran," I said, "preferably without losing my mind."

"You'll figure it out, Liza. You're a competent, resourceful young woman and I sincerely doubt you will be foolish enough to end up roaming the streets and eating out of Dumpsters."

"And if I did, just imagine what the tabloids would say about *you,*" I joked, because I couldn't take the tension.

"Wouldn't be the first time." She grinned. "But we have more important business to attend to. You need to bring this Dr. Whoever to Thanksgiving so your mother will leave me the hell alone."

I almost choked on a cocktail onion.

"I haven't even gone out with him yet!"

"Well, get on the stick!" she crowed. "Another drink for my niece!"

It was still early when I got home, and the combination of Aunt Fran's prodding, two strong drinks and the crisp fall air had given me the courage to do something important.

I called Dr. Tim. I mean, of course I called him! If he hadn't given me his number I might have taken up skydiving, skateboarding, sumo wrestling, anything that would up the probability of another visit to the ER.

The first call is always hard. Jeremy insists you have to wait two to four days after meeting to prove you're not desperate. Two minimum, four maximum. (Although most men seem to insist that the max should be a week. I don't know why. If you like someone, don't you want to call them?) Parrot always coaches me beforehand, to silence the little voice inside screaming that he won't remember me, to be prepared for either voice mail or live action and to rehearse the intro. There's nothing worse than having your intended pick up the phone and realizing you've forgotten your own name. I've done it. Or forgotten to clear your throat. Or forgotten *his* name because all you can remember is the silhouette of his significant and perfect torso. Done and done.

In Dr. Tim's case I was prepared. I was ready with the first three sentences, but I never got to utter them. I'd barely spoken his name when he said, "Liza, I was hoping you'd call."

Dr. Tim, I was hoping you'd take me away from all this.

"I have to tell you, it took a lot of guts to make the first move the other night. I was so glad you did."

For once, it seemed I'd found a guy who didn't regress three stages of human development when he was on the phone. Men, where do you all learn this skill? Is there some sort of mandatory seminar in your late teens during which you're instructed to buck even minimum etiquette during the simplest phone call? You grunt, you conspicuously engage in another activity, you generally send the message that you'd rather be doing anything other than chatting with us. And you don't realize the paroxysms of despair into which we are hurtled after every conversation. We have to go and call all our friends and dissect every single monosyllable until we are firmly convinced of your affection or lack thereof. A five-minute phone conversation with a man leads a woman to six or seven forty-five minute sessions with her closest friends. You guys don't even realize. Or maybe you do. Maybe you work for the phone company.

In any case, Dr. Tim must have been raised by Emily Post. He was articulate and thoughtful throughout our conversation.

"How's the ankle?" he wanted to know.

"A little painful," I admitted.

"Keep icing," he said. "Sprains are no fun."

"Well, I could make a good case for this one." I smiled into the phone and hoped he would hear it.

"How so?"

Apparently he didn't.

"Oh, well, meeting you—"

"Oh, gosh, I—I'm an idiot. Long shift."

"Don't be silly!"

"Too late," he quipped. His slight nervousness and self-deprecation were unspeakably sweet, as was the fact that he quickly asked me out.

I explained that I was still somewhat immobilized, and suggested, horror of horrors, that he come over for dinner. This was a calculated risk as I figured I was less likely to make a fool of myself limping around my own house and knew that I could get away with being more casual. Crutches and a skirt look awkward.

"I am such a heel," he said. "Of course I'll come to you. And don't do a thing; just leave it all to me."

We made a plan for Wednesday evening. Breathless, I hung up the phone and screamed. Jeremy came bounding into the living room as if maybe I were being murdered.

"What? What's wrong?"

"We have to clean."

*"The only difference between me and an artist is that
I like to sit at home and count my money."*

CHAPTER 9

A MERE FORTY-EIGHT HOURS stood be-
tween me and my date with the doc. But there was the
not-so-small matter of the first rehearsal of my play to attend.
After a morning spent poring over want ads, I hobbled my
way to the university's theatre building early Wednesday afternoon. Will, resplendent in various takes on black polyester,
was standing outside when I arrived, looking nervy and
smoking a clove.

"Liza!" He dropped his cigarette and stamped it out as
though I were a teacher catching him behind the gym. "Oh,
you're here! It's so great! I am so pumped!"

"Yeah." I hobbled toward him. "I'm ... pumped too."

"Oh, man," he moaned, observing my ankle, "you look
like you jacked yourself up pretty good." There's nothing I
love more than an Exeter grad who uses the word "jacked."

"Yeah, well, skateboarding accident."

"Ha, right. Totally." He giggled.

"So, let's get to it, huh?" I encouraged him to show me inside, as he was currently blocking the double doors.

"Right! Yeah, let's. Listen ..." He seemed twitchier than

when I'd last seen him. "I just, um...okay, this is weird," Will stuttered, shifting his weight back and forth from one foot to the other repeatedly. "I'm, like, actually...I'm gonna be on TV."

This clarified nothing for me and I indicated as much.

"I'm actually...I'm like doing this...okay, it's a documentary show?" He'd switched to upspeak, which I assumed meant he was especially nervous.

"A documentary show?" I echoed. "You mean a reality show?"

Will blushed. "Yeah, okay, I don't like to call it that. It makes it sound like I'm doing *The Bachelorette* or whatever. But it's like this show, *High Hopes!,* that follows young artists trying to make it and every episode they follow a different person. And they're doing one on me. It's on the Applause Channel."

I readjusted my crutches to disguise the convulsive laugh that wanted to escape my mouth. Will Atherton, arguably in the Top Ten of Pretentious Twithood, was going to be the subject of a weekly reality show about struggling artists? On the Applause Channel, no less, a network that was irritatingly, if shrewdly, attempting to make entertainment out of the business of entertainment, and for the most part, conning the American public into watching.

"Wow" was all I could manage initially. But Will still looked petrified and I knew I should find a way to be supportive. "Well, that's great! Right? I mean, good for you! Exposure. Exposure is always good." I really wasn't up on the etiquette for this sort of situation.

"Yeah, no, yeah! It's great! It's totally great! It's actually kind of a big coup because, like, they only profile you if they're really into your work, you know, and think you have some kind of future, so...I'm psyched. Definitely." He rocked on the balls of his feet and looked at the pavement and I knew there was still something coming.

"So, I was kind of wondering . . ." He paused and I couldn't take it anymore.

In an attempt at a friendly joke, I said, "Come on, Will, don't keep a cripple standing around!"

"Right, okay. So this is the project. They want to shadow me doing your play."

Obviously. Why had I not caught on to this when he brought it up? Clearly the reason he was standing outside foaming at the mouth and waiting for me was that—

"The camera crew's inside, aren't they, Will?"

He sucked air through his teeth. "Yeah," he admitted. "Yeah, they kind of are. Which means, um, you sort of need to agree to this. Name and likeness, whole nine yards."

"It's not a likeness if it's actually me," I muttered.

Will made a finger-snapping, clapping gesture and said, "Right."

I couldn't believe this. Here I was, maimed and certainly not camera-ready, and this little pipsqueak asks me to be part of his weird, creepy foray into reality television at the very last minute? Immediately, I was torn.

Reality television presents a sticky wicket for me. On the one hand, I have been known to watch it. But the mudslide of real-life crap with which the viewing public has been deluged has made me ill. Just to be clear, reality television is not the proper setting for selecting a marriage partner or reuniting unsuspecting adoptees with their biological parents. I don't want to be present at anyone's plastic surgery, and I certainly have no desire to watch anyone eat maggots, on- or offscreen. Apparently, absolutely nothing is sacred anymore and there is no length to which the American public will not go to see itself on national television. The reality epidemic is reaching critical mass. We've covered it, people. There's nowhere else to go. And what happened to truly great, memorable television? Who doesn't remember where they were when J.R. was shot? We cared about who killed Laura

Palmer, we wanted to "be careful out there." Personally, I was ready to jump down on Jump Street. What are kids today going to remember, the skating costumes from *Project Runway*? The ethical pitfalls of being *America's Top Model*? Or perhaps the heartrending disciplinary dilemmas of *Nanny 911*. Please, Hollywood, I beg of you, shell out the extra cash and go back to telling stories. Jack Bauer and Meredith Grey cannot shoulder the burden alone. We need to bring fiction back to television before the only things on are *Jailbait & Switch* and *The Bi-Sexual Style Manual*.

I knew right off the bat that I wanted no part of this *High Hopes!* business. Clearly it was going to be some sort of pathetic and humiliating look at young people devoting themselves to a dream that was futile and exhausting, and I don't need television to experience that.

"Not cool, Will," I told him. "You have a lot of nerve springing this on me at the last minute. I have no desire to be a part of this."

"Okay," he said, "okay, right. I get that. Let's dialogue about it."

"There's no 'dialogue,' Will! I'm not into it! And I think it sucks that you would foist it on me at the last minute because you thought I'd feel obligated. No, I'm not doing it. You can find another play to do on television, or you can get rid of the cameras and we'll start the rehearsal."

Will Atherton is a perfect example of why children should not be given everything that they want. Even as I took the hard line I could see that it wasn't penetrating; he was just repositioning for another tack.

"Okay, look," he said, and he began to lean forward and talk with his hands, "you're right, and if I was you I'd be pretty furious too, but I'd like to think that maybe, if I was you, if I was a smart businesswoman, I would see how maybe this could be a boost for me, you know? Like maybe I would think about all the millions of people who would actually see *my* play on their TV, and maybe some of them are producers, right? And if I'm you, this shrewd chick, maybe I'm seeing how suddenly my play is out there, you know, like it's a commodity now, *I'm* a commodity. You see where I'm going?"

"You think I'm going to be the next Naomi Wallace because my play is on this stupid TV show?"

"I think the last playwright they profiled got three commissions within a year."

I'd like to say I was unmoved by his argument, but the word "commission" stopped me dead. Will must have sensed that he was getting somewhere.

"Yeah," he went on, "within a year. All you need is for people to see your work, Liza. And then it's no more temping, no more scrambling. What would you rather tell people when they ask what you're doing right now? You wanna say you're working on something, blah, blah, blah, or you wanna say, 'No, motherfucker! My fucking play is on fucking TV'?"

Motherfuckers notwithstanding, the part of me that wanted to walk away was being brought to its knees by the part of me that wanted to believe maybe I was finally getting a break. Maybe this was my shot, my right-place-right-time. I couldn't help thinking how good it would feel to tell people, to tell Aunt Fran, that I was finally making something happen.

"You're asking for blind faith here, Will. I mean, I haven't even met the cast! What if they suck? What if the play sucks? Then it won't be about commissions, it'll be about finding another line of work!"

"This play, Liza"—he put his hands on my shoulders and looked into my eyes—"this play is brilliant. It's brilliant. And these actors are attending one of the best theatre schools in the country. You will be astonished at what they can do."

"I don't know ..."

"What it really comes down to, is do you believe in your work? Because if you do, those words are going to shine through anything and everything those actors and I bring to the table. Do you believe in your play, Liza? That's the only question you need to answer."

Needless to say, I could think of a few other questions. But I did believe in my writing. I do believe in it. I looked at Will, and I forced the last part of me that wanted simply to deny him to lay down and die.

"Fine." I sighed. "Fine, I'll do it."

Will jumped in the air and made a triumphant air-guitar gesture to express his pleasure. "You will not regret this, Liza! Awesome!"

I insisted that he show me to a ladies' room on our way into rehearsal. (If I was going to be filmed and given no time to prepare, I could, at the very least, apply some lip gloss.) Satisfied that I'd done the best I could under the circumstances, I followed Will through the winding halls of the theatre building and was delivered to a vast but stuffy rehearsal studio lined with mirrors and dance bars. It all brought back terrible memories of after-school ballet classes.

Will began to introduce me to the actors and I couldn't help thinking they all looked far too young to inspire anyone to suspend disbelief.

"This is Gina," Will cooed, "great dancer." Gina blushed and I wondered if she knew there was no dance in my play. "And Suzi, who is such a terrific emoter." I was sure he was joking. Suzi looked painfully vacuous and kept nodding at me and letting out a single clap every few seconds. "This is Graham Parsons, and this is Graham Fineman."

"Two Grahams," I commented, because what the hell else was there to say?

"Liza, we have got the best two Grahams in the theatre department. Be excited. Be very excited." Will clapped me on the back and I almost fell over. It took a great deal of restraint to avoid popping him with my crutch.

And there were the TV crew, two thirtyish men, one of

them scruffy and holding a camera, and a woman who introduced herself as the producer and told me to forget they were there and that I shouldn't be nervous about being on TV. I attempted to seem like an old hand at TV appearances, though secretly I was praying that I wouldn't look fat. I signed release forms, and forced my doubts to pipe down while the actors stretched and engaged in absurd vocal warm-ups, even though we were just going to read the play.

Will, the cast and I all positioned ourselves around a circular table and made ready for the first read. I attempted to sit as far from Will as possible in the hopes that I wouldn't be caught on film as often (the point was to show the play, not me), but I noticed that Suzi nearly tripped one of the Grahams in her attempt to sit directly next to Will. She probably figured five minutes of screen-time would do for her what an ice-cream soda and a tight sweater had done for Lana Turner.

Hearing my own writing is always a surreal experience. I tend to turn bright red as all the blood rushes to my face and my mouth twists into a goofy grin that I have no intention of producing. The realization that my audience had just gotten exponentially larger did nothing to calm my usual nerves. The play is a story about the perfect housewife; having lost her husband in an accident, she has an affair with a much younger man, who uses her and throws her away. But her neighbors feel that she's behaved indecently and they drive her out of town. It's dark and my mother should never read it, as she'll certainly decide that it's some reflection on her.

But during the first read, I was fixed on a more immediate problem: *the cast*.

They were dreadful. Horrendous. Excruciating to watch. Suzi read the whole piece like she was auditioning for a movie-of-the-week. As an actor, Gina was a terrific dancer. And if we had the two best Grahams in the theatre department I'd have shuddered to see the two worst. The entire thing was like listening to the kids from *The O.C.* reading

C-SPAN transcripts. About as compelling and nearly as believable. By the time we got through the first act I was utterly panicked. Will wouldn't look at me and I knew he must know what I was thinking. I was careful to keep my eyes on the page every time I caught the camera circling in front of me, for fear they'd capture my horror on tape.

When Will dismissed the cast for a five-minute break between acts, they all trotted off to water themselves and I seized the opportunity to ream him.

"Can I see you for a minute?" I asked, as Will jotted down whatever brilliant idea he'd gleaned from the trainwreck we'd just watched.

"Sure. Shoot," he said, rising.

The camera was still rolling. "In private, maybe?" I pushed.

Will looked at the crew and understood. "Oh, yeah, okay." He led me into the hallway. I didn't notice that he'd left the door to the studio ajar.

"What's up?" he asked, sunny and pleased.

"Well," I ventured, "what did you think of that?"

"Not bad, not bad," he crooned in his pretentious artsy voice. "It's gonna be an interesting journey."

I was conscious of the need to contain myself. "Are you maybe a little concerned about them?"

"Concerned how?" he asked, seemingly oblivious.

"They're a little . . . unprepared for this kind of play, aren't they? I mean . . . they sound like teenagers playing house."

"Look, it's the first read, Liza. You've gotta give actors the chance to grow into a piece."

Yes, this was true, it was too early to ask for perfection, but I wasn't comforted.

"How can they grow into it when half of them can barely get the words out, Will? I mean, that was . . . that was rough! To say the least! You do understand the stakes are much higher for me now, right? I'm not trying to be a pain in the ass here, but are we sure this is the right cast?"

Will's cheeks turned red and I thought he might snap at me, but instead he took my hand and squeezed it as though we were close girlfriends. He looked into my eyes and asked, "Do you trust me, Liza?"

Considering our rocky start this afternoon, I couldn't quite believe he was asking.

"It's really important that you trust me. I am the captain of this ship. I will steer. But you have to trust me."

I was so angry, mostly at myself for signing those releases before I saw a reading, that I was afraid to open my mouth for fear I'd explode.

Clearly ready to take advantage of my silence, Will pulled me into a warm embrace. He patted me firmly on the back and said, "You wait and see, Miss Playwright. You just wait and see. We're going to do something terrific."

He released me and strode confidently back into the rehearsal room. The camera had been on us the whole time.

"I can buy my own damned dinner.
What else have you got?"

CHAPTER 10

I WAS THOROUGHLY SHAKEN by the whole afternoon, but I spent the train ride home trying to come up
with reasons why it might be okay. The last thing I wanted to
do was get ready for a romantic evening, but the memory of
Dr. Tim's shy grin was a happier prospect than anything else
I could think of at the moment. I only wished we'd already
gotten past that hideous first date.

It would be fair to say I don't go on a lot of dates. To me,
they're like interviews for jobs you're not really sure you
want, but you spend most of your time trying to make sure
you'll get an offer anyway. Jeremy, who thinks he has me all
figured out, refers to me as a "great befriender," meaning I
get to know a guy in a non-date setting, then develop a mas-
sive crush, which usually results in total social paralysis. So if
anything ever actually comes of it it's because the guy makes
a move, and by the time this happens we always seem to
know each other too well to go on actual dates. But I say
there's a beauty to this system. For one thing, you already
know you like the person before you get involved, and for
another, you haven't had to sit through an awkward three

hours in a restaurant, where small talk has to be generated and really all either of you can think about is that you're up on the auction block and will there be any bidders? I'm not good at this.

"You date all the wrong guys," Jeremy would say.

"What is wrong with the guys I date?"

"They're just not . . . impressive."

"J," I would remind him, "you have worn the same sweater every day for two weeks, and I eat peas out of a can. We, ourselves, are not totally impressive."

"That's not what I'm talking about," he'd argue. "I'm not saying they're convicts or anything, they're just kind of a rung below you. You need somebody as smart as you, somebody with his shit together and like, a vague idea of what he's doing with his life. You need a challenge."

I don't know, a challenging date just sounded so punishing.

But somewhere in my youth or childhood, as the song says, I must have done something good. Because Dr. Tim looked to be my grand reprieve. He arrived at my door, precisely on time, bearing three DVDs, Chinese food and two bottles of wine.

"I wasn't sure whether you liked red or white." He smiled.

"I'm equal opportunity," I said. "Come on in."

I took the DVDs from him and set the food on the kitchen counter. "*Annie Hall, Unforgiven,* and *The Conversation.* Nicely done. You have excellent taste in movies, sir."

"Yeah, I asked the clerk at Blockbuster for some recommendations. I have to confess, I'm not a movie guy."

"Well, let's see what we can do to change that." I tried to sound coy. I had a handsome doctor in my apartment and for some reason my nerves weren't even making an appearance.

Over dinner, we began the obligatory exchange of CVs. Dr. Tim was a middle child from northern California, and a proud member of the hospital softball team. I nearly choked on a snow pea as he described his volunteer work with underprivileged teens. The man's whole life deserved a public service award and still he managed to make me feel like *I* was the special one. I practically told him my whole life story and still he asked for more.

"More?" I asked. "I feel like all I've done is talk about myself."

"Well, I like hearing it," he said, leaning back on one elbow. "Tell me about writing plays."

He seemed so genuinely interested that I decided to share the tale of my traumatic afternoon.

"Wait a sec." He laughed. "So you're telling me that not only is your play being done, you're actually going to be on a reality show?"

"Oh, God, it sounds so desperate and cheap, doesn't it?" For some reason, I didn't feel embarrassed talking to him.

"Are you kidding? I think it's amazing! Look, you're an artist, you can't hide your art in a dark room and never share it with anyone, right?"

"Sometimes I think I'd be better off," I admitted. "I'm really thinking about trying to pull out of this deal."

"No!" he insisted. "You're taking a risk, you're putting it out there! I really admire that. You're venturing off the beaten path. You have to be willing to stand up for your work and have faith that it'll see you through or you might as well just have a nine to five. I mean, I'd be doing something pretty different with my life if I hadn't caved and gone into medicine."

"But you save lives!" I sputtered.

"There are plenty of doctors, Liza, but very few real artists." He looked at me fixedly. "So what else," he continued, "tell me more."

Talking about writing with most people, I feel like they're wondering when I'm going to clean up my act and get a real job. Dr. Tim made me feel legitimate, like maybe I wasn't a total idiot for agreeing to be on some stupid television show. Like maybe I really was good enough to shine through all the crap.

"I don't know, there's this summer reading series at the New Manhattan Playhouse that I'd like to submit to. It's really prestigious and the playwrights get lots of feedback and development support. It would be a big step. I'm sure they'd never take me."

"Hey," he said, leaning over to brush my cheek with his thumb, "don't talk like that. I believe in you." It seemed like a strange thing to say to someone you barely know, but I decided to roll with it. He was so easy to be with, like he'd decided the minute he looked at me that I was wonderful and I didn't have to prove a damned thing.

Normally I don't like to rush into a relationship. I avoid sex on the first date as a general rule, because first-date sex seems to be the surest formula for ensuring that a desirable man will never call again and that an awful one will choose you as a mate for life. With Dr. Tim, it wasn't even on the table.

Halfway through the third movie, I caught him staring at me while I was looking at the screen.

"What?" I asked.

"Liza, can I kiss you?"

"God, I thought you were waiting for an engraved invitation." I leaned in. Kissing him was very soft and sweet and only lasted for a few minutes before he pulled away and said it was time to leave.

"You don't have to go," I told him.

"No, I really do. Or you'll never get rid of me." He grinned. "I'd like to see you again."

"I think I'm available." I smiled back. Without question, my best first date ever.

Further, he called the next day (before I'd even had a chance to decide that I'd never hear from him again), just to say that he'd had a really terrific time and was thinking about me as he fell asleep. He asked to see me again over the weekend, and not just for a "wanna hang out?" kind of date; he already had a plan that involved a picnic and the planetarium. It was like he'd read a book on what women want. I hung up the phone and smiled to myself and wondered why everything suddenly seemed so easy.

"Just smile pretty and keep a flask in your purse."

CHAPTER 11

WHILE I WAS ENJOYING an ER fantasy come to life, Parrot was shockingly still shagging Kirk from the terrible ankle night. They'd seen each other nearly every day since, and she filled me in daily with rapid-fire phone summaries or poignant text messages like "he can go for hours" or "we did it on the stoop of his building." Parrot and I were swapping details on the phone one night after my third date with Dr. Tim when she suddenly interrupted herself to say, "Ohmigod you know who asked about you that George guy from the ankle night he's like best friends with Kirk and we went to a hockey game tonight and he was like where's your friend and I was like she's out with somebody else and he was like that's too bad so I totally think you should come out with us and maybe hook up with him."

"P, I just spent twenty minutes telling you about the fabulous man I'm seeing. George was a jerk. I think you're missing the point here."

Though I said nothing to Parrot, who would've latched on like a dog to a bone, the mention of George's name did pluck some chord inside me, and the vibration made me uncomfortable. I tried not to dwell on it.

I also tried not to dwell on my continuing failure to find a new job, though I was starting to lose sleep. Repeated calls to my temp agency had yielded nothing; they were still pissed off. My sprain pretty much ruled out bartending and cocktail waitressing, and though I wasn't dying to work in a bar, there were few other opportunities for good money and a flexible schedule. Rehearsals were no fun, but the more time I spent watching Will attempt to make my play completely unrecognizable, the more I knew I needed to be there. Every choice he made provoked a tiny battle, and I knew I was fighting for my televised chance at a career.

As Tabitha's move-out date drew closer, she seemed to swing between increasingly unpredictable moods. One day she was bequeathing to me her old lingerie bags, and the next she was having a meltdown because I'd eaten the last can of tuna. (Her only consolation, she said, was that mercury poisoning would come for me first.) While Tabitha was packing boxes one evening, Jeremy put a glass of milk down on one of her bride magazines, and in a huffy rage she announced that our rent increase would be five hundred dollars. Poor Jeremy and I could barely speak. We tried to argue, tried to wheedle and cajole, but once she'd spoken the number, Tabitha wouldn't take it back for fear she'd look hasty and unstable. We couldn't exactly play hardball or we might have lost the place altogether. But how was I supposed to come up with an extra two hundred and fifty dollars a month?! It was more than either of us had predicted. No, we still wouldn't be paying near what the apartment was worth, but I wasn't bringing in a single cent! My bank account was dwindling with each passing day, and with every dollar I spent I thought of the promise I'd made to Jeremy. I was going to have to take the next job that came along, no matter what it was, or I was going to be out on my ass.

Had it not been for Dr. Tim, I would no doubt have sunk in my own quagmire. He never seemed to tire of telling me it would all be alright, of reinforcing that I was special and that everything happened for a reason. There were days I almost wished he'd just let me wallow for a bit, but his support and adoration meant more than I wanted to admit. For our fifth date, he had promised a foreign film and delicious tapas from a place he swore by in the East Village. His arrival to pick me up was unfortunately to coincide with Tabitha's return from whatever packing supply depot she'd begun to haunt. Crating her sensible shoes and high school memories had made Tabitha weepy, and her nerves seemed to be stretched so tight I was almost afraid to make a peep in her presence. I heard her twitter in the hallway and groaned at the thought that I was going to have to introduce her to Dr. Tim. The only thing Tabitha liked better than evaluating her own dates was trashing mine.

Her key turned in the lock and I was surprised to find her yammering, as she entered, not into her cell phone, but at my suitor.

"Liza! I have just been talking with your charming new friend here! Isn't he just sweet!" she chirped.

"Hey there, lady!" he greeted me.

"Well, I guess you two require no introduction," I said.

"Oh, Tabitha was just coming up the stairs and—"

"—and he offered to help me with my boxes!" she interrupted.

"I offered to help," he added, pulling another sheaf of cardboard through the front door.

"What a sweetheart!" she raved.

"Yeah," I agreed, "he's pretty damned sweet." Dr. Tim blushed.

"So much better than usual for you!" Tabitha whispered to me as she dragged a giant roll of bubble wrap toward her room.

"So sorry about that." I turned back to Dr. Tim. He hugged me and gave me a kiss on the cheek.

"No problem! So good to finally meet Tabitha."

In a totally uncharacteristic move, I had actually held off on trashing Tabitha to Dr. Tim. He had such an admirable ability to see the good in every situation; I suppose I was a little afraid to let him see all my vitriolic potential too soon. Tabitha flew back into the room and I recognized the desperation of another mood swing.

"Okay, Liza, have you seen the packing tape? It's not in my room. I'm doing ponies tonight and I need the packing tape! Now, where is it?" I could tell that she was on the verge of a tantrum.

"Oh, is this it?" Dr. Tim piped up. "On the coffee table?" He grabbed the roll and extended it to Tabitha.

"OH! Thank you. Thank you, thank you, thank you," she crooned at him, one hand on her chest for effect. "I'm getting married and we're moving and redoing an apartment. Lots going on! I'm doing ponies tonight—no time to lose." She turned to go.

"Ponies?" he asked me.

"Ceramic ponies," I explained.

"PORCELAIN!" Tabitha called from the other room.

"I stand corrected." I winced. "She has about a million of them." I adjusted my necklace in the hopes that he'd notice the very cute dress I'd hauled out in celebration of my newly crutch-free gait.

"Gosh, she seems pretty stressed out, huh? Moving is so tough," he said instead.

So is living with her, I wanted to say. But Dr. Tim didn't seem to be registering Tabitha's awfulness. I reminded myself that he couldn't be blamed for not having a judgment reflex as finely honed as mine.

"It sure is," I concurred. "So shall we go?" I twirled slightly to pick up my keys in a second attempt at exhibiting the dress. Surely this would be enough to make him throw decency to the wind and take me to bed. It had been five dates, after all.

Something small and equine shattered in the next room.

"NOOOOOOOO!" Tabitha screamed. My first instinct was to usher Dr. Tim out the door before he was subjected to a tantrum. But I knew I'd look insensitive and brutish. "Are you alright?" I called gingerly.

"I broke Sterling!" Tabitha cried, with just the hint of a quaver in her voice. "I've had him since I was eleven! I can't believe I did that!"

We both heard the echo of her fragile frame throwing itself onto the bed in agony.

"Oh, Lord," I muttered.

"I have an idea." He smiled at me. "What do you say we skip the movie, I'll go pick up takeout for the three of us, and we can help your roommate pack?"

WHAT?! EXCUSE ME?! HOW ABOUT WE GO DOWN TO THE EAST RIVER AND YOU CAN HOLD MY HEAD UNDERWATER AND HUM WHAM SONGS UNTIL I BLACK OUT?!

"Oh, Tim, that is so not necessary. She's really organized. I'm sure she has a plan and everything...."

"Yeah, but come on, it would be a really nice thing to do. Besides, I want your friends to know I'm an okay guy."

"Technically we're more roommates than friends...."

I had played the whole thing completely wrong. Here he was thinking that Tabitha was my friend and now all he saw was a person under stress and in need of help. It was so like him. If I tried to explain Tabitha now I would only come off as petty and unsympathetic.

"Although I have to say it's a shame to waste that dress, especially now that I can see your whole leg...." He kissed me and I was convinced. For one night, I could play the role of a really nice person.

Two hours later, over the remains of some fabulous Greek takeout (the man had takeout down to a science), the three of us were hunched over the coffee table giving special wrapping care to individual hooves and tails. Dr. Tim and I had made solid progress on a bottle of Sauvignon Blanc, but Tabitha had refused a glass as "someone should stay sober around the breakables."

It turned out that Tabitha and Dr. Tim had both attended Stanford undergrad and were both Cancers. Dr. Tim seemed charmed by Tabitha's babble and she by his willingness to listen. I mostly munched on my spanakopita and tried to enjoy dating someone that Tabitha couldn't poke a hole in for once. If she really had been my friend I would have been delighted with the evening.

"So do you have a date set yet?" he was asking.

"We do. For next September. I told Tod I needed a full year and I was absolutely not going to be rushed putting this wedding together. I mean, we're only doing it once, right?" she yipped.

"One only hopes," I muttered, winding way too much tape around a tiny palomino.

"Well, Miss Liza, I haven't seen too much of you lately." Tabitha turned to me. "How have you been keeping busy? Has good luck been visited upon your career or did you waste it all on this terrific man?" She flashed Dr. Tim an enormous smile and I seethed quietly.

"Oh, she's doing great!" Dr. Tim stood up for me. "She's got this play that's going to be on a television program—it's gonna be phenomenal. I can't wait." He beamed at me.

"It's a little reality thing." I tried to brush it off. "On a cable channel."

"Television! Well, isn't that terrific? Finally getting paid for your writing, Liza, that's a big step!"

I was not about to correct her. "Yeah," I agreed, "good stuff."

"Now if we could just get this little job thing sorted." Dr. Tim elbowed me gently and kissed me on the temple. I cringed. I'd been super-careful to keep my unemployment from Tabitha. The last thing I needed was her assessment of my unfortunate situation.

"What's this?" Tabitha asked, and I could see her little gnome ears perking up.

"Oh, it's nothing," I said. "I'm switching jobs."

"That's exactly it," Tim supported me. "It's just a switch with a little vacation in the middle." He was definitely not helping, and Tabitha put it together pretty quickly.

"Liza! Did you lose your job?!" she gasped. "That's so horrible! What happened?! I can't believe you didn't tell me!"

"Yeah, well, I didn't exactly feel like advertising." I tried to smile.

"How did it happen? When did it happen? What did you do?"

I hated the fact that she immediately assumed I'd *done* something to get fired, and the fact that I actually had didn't make me feel any better.

"It sounds like just a great, big misunderstanding to me," Dr. Tim defended me. "Now we've just got to find her something else!"

I was starting to feel like he might suggest a telethon in my honor at any moment. The "Save Liza" campaign was becoming a bit much.

"OH, MY GOODNESS!" Tabitha shrieked. "Oh, this is too amazing! Liza! I was just saying to Tod last night that with working full-time and moving and redoing the new apartment I'm gonna be just swamped. So he was saying that maybe I should hire somebody to help me with wedding stuff!" She paused, her mouth gaping happily in a giant grin.

"You mean like a wedding planner?" I asked.

"No, no, no, no. Wedding planners are for disorganized people who don't know what they're doing, Liza." She shook her head disapprovingly. "No, I'm talking about more like a wedding assistant! You know, somebody to help with the list-making and the errand-running and all the phone calls and little details that would just drive me crazy if I had to do it all myself. You'd be perfect!"

I felt spanakopita rising in my throat.

"Oh, Tabitha," I began, "that is really so nice, but—"

"Oh, it would be so great. You could work on your own time and as long as you met all my deadlines I could be really flexible. And you have all those years of temp experience so I'm sure you're qualified! Oh, come on, say yes!" she whee-dled.

"That's incredible," Dr. Tim interjected. "You see that? You just ask and the universe gives you what you need! Just like that night that you showed up in the ER." I looked at him, so proud of himself, blissfully unaware and absent-mindedly stroking the nose of a three-inch thoroughbred.

I took a deep breath, thought of a Tabitha-free apartment and asked her how much the job paid. My only hope was that she wouldn't be able to cough up enough to make it worth my while.

Damn Tod-with-one-D and his stinking trust fund.

"I've yet to see a person suffer in adequate silence;
otherwise I'd be all for it.
In the meantime, ask for what you want."

CHAPTER 12

IT WAS ONLY A WEEK and a half before Thanksgiving, and luckily Tabitha wasn't planning to kick the wedding planning into high gear until after the holiday. If I tightened my financial belt I could definitely make it that long, which gave me time to focus on my family's impending ground assault and Will's ever-worsening rehearsals.

Every day he had a new change to suggest. Like maybe Georgia Allen should do her direct address to the audience completely naked, or maybe the busybody next door should break stuff for no reason.

"We need to physicalize some of the torture these characters are experiencing, Liza, or nobody's gonna get it," he whined.

"Nobody's gonna get it, because you're trying to do an entirely different play from the one I wrote!"

"You're very closed, for an artist," he said.

"It's naturalism, not a music video," I retorted.

Clearly, our conversations were less than productive. Rehearsals were starting to feel like a battle for my very soul, and I found myself doing defensive rewrites almost daily, trying to shore up the action against Will's bad taste. And always, there was the camera, in my face or over my shoulder or circling for a better angle.

I probably should have been more careful, and I might have been, if I hadn't been so distracted by my family's subtle pressure to bring a date for Turkey Day. My father left a message on my cell reminding me that I could "bring whoever you like, Lizaloo. Anybody at all. Boys or girls. Just so you know. We love you!"

While my mother could spend three days wandering in the desert and not even mention she was hot, my father is explicit about everything. They're quite a pair. I knew he was just as excited as she was about having us all together for the holiday. I just wished they would both leave me alone about bringing a date.

The fact that my brother was bringing his girlfriend only placed added pressure on me to show up with somebody. I called him to complain.

"Jack Weiler. Speak."

"That's how you answer the phone?" I spat.

"Occasionally. What's up?"

"Are you totally set on this Thanksgiving thing or could I possibly convince you to derail it?"

My brother and I fight like cats and dogs, but in a good way. Actually, I spent the first seven years of my life convinced that Jack was the product of an experiment in which a puppy was turned into a human boy. He told me I should never mention it to our parents because they were slightly ashamed and might make him start sleeping outside and that if this happened his dog behaviors might return and he might chew up my toys or pee on me. When I finally confessed this to my father he actually cried from laughing so hard.

In recent years, Jack and I have reached a sort of understanding. I harass him about dating bimbos and selling drugs for an evil pharmaceutical empire, and he gives me crap about being completely secretive about my unimpressive string of quasi-boyfriends and my floundering career. Underneath it all we're actually quite respectful and supportive. Usually.

"Hell, no," he returned. "Mom and Dad are paying for me and Melania to fly out there. Free weekend in New York, yo."

"Utter torture and mortifying interrogation for me, yo!"

"I thought it was your idea," he said. "Mom said you didn't want to deal with holiday travel and we had to come rescue you."

Manipulation! Treachery! Deceit! I had said I wanted to spend Thanksgiving with my friends!

"She just hears what she wants to hear," I said.

"Man, did you have other plans?" he asked.

"Does it matter?"

"Probably not. Melania's pretty psyched though."

"Excellent. You should probably get her Hooked on Phonics before you come. Or can this one read?"

"Honestly, I never asked. But she's in modeling school so there's probably some kind of reading involved. I assume you'll be bringing your—oh, wait! You're not seeing anyone, are you?"

Logic would suggest that this was where I told Jack all about my fabulous new doctor boyfriend. But I didn't. I opened my mouth and all of a sudden I didn't want to say it.

"I hate you. I'll see you at Thanksgiving," I said instead, wincing slightly at my own omission.

"Looking forward to it." Then he woofed into the phone like a wild dingo and hung up.

Why hadn't I said anything about Dr. Tim? He was the ultimate parent-pleaser. Boyfriend-in-a-box, no grooming required. No, I could not imagine allowing my family to put him on a slide and examine him for husband DNA, but there was something else there too. I guess I wasn't . . . sure. Yes, we were having a wonderful time, but maybe the relationship wasn't exactly going where I'd hoped it would . . .

After our fourth date, as he'd dropped me off at my doorstep, I began to realize that Dr. Tim was relatively satisfied with the five to ten minutes of making out we did on my stoop. I tried inviting him in, that night and on three subsequent occasions, but as we neared date eight, I started to get really antsy. I simply hadn't been trained to deal with a man who wanted to take me on great dates without . . . anything else.

Jeremy, who had noticed me coming home alone after a series of supposedly successful evenings, advised that maybe all Dr. Tim needed was a firm go-ahead from me. I resolved to give him just that.

After a lovely evening that included dinner, a movie and a stroll around Bryant Park, Dr. Tim began to make the usual rumblings about putting me in a cab.

"Why don't we share a cab?" I ventured.

"Don't be silly, Liza. I live all the way uptown. We're going in opposite directions."

"Right," I said, "but maybe tonight we could go in the same direction." I fingered the top button of his coat and tried to look suggestive.

"Oh, um . . . I hadn't thought of that." He did not seem to be overwhelmed with joy, but I was unwilling to give up until I knew I'd made myself clear.

"I mean, we've seen a whole lot of each other these past few weeks . . . and I'm starting to want to see . . . more of you . . . if you know what I mean . . ." I knew how awkward this sounded, but I was hoping his libido would edit my lameness into something sexy. I tried to reach up and kiss him, but he pulled back and took my hands off his coat. Suddenly November felt a lot chillier.

"Liza," he stalled, "I don't think we should."

Immediately, I began to prepare for the dump speech. Clearly he didn't find me attractive, thought my thighs were immense, that I talked too much and had no career. Obviously he was done with me.

"Oh," I said. "Okay." I moved toward the street and raised my arm. "Taxi!" I called. Of course there wasn't an available cab in sight.

"Liza, no, listen to me." He reached for my hand. I tried to force my face into neutral and looked him in the eye. "I want to."

"You don't have to say that," I told him.

"I'm not just saying it! My God, I think you're beautiful! I think about you all the time. I think about *it* . . . a lot."

"So . . . I don't understand . . ."

"It's just so fast, Liza. It's only been a month."

And suddenly I felt like the slut that ate Manhattan.

"Oh," I said, unable to come up with anything else.

"I don't know how you work," he went on, "but sex is really special for me."

Oh, really? Well, I'll sleep with anything that moves apparently, three minutes after I see it.

"I just want us to be sure before we take that step."

"Wow," I said. "That's . . . rare."

"Just give it some time. Try it my way," he continued. "I think you'll really find that sex means more when you wait."

It was as if my mother had telepathically programmed him to obstruct my unladylike behavior. Needless to say, I went home alone that night. Again.

I was determined to stop myself from torpedoing this romance, just because I was a little upset, just because I'd been caught off guard by Dr. Tim's *Crucible*-esque, prudish quality. Okay, maybe more than a little.

I mean, what was the big deal? So he wanted to wait! So we'd be old-fashioned about it—there was something really lovely about that. Wasn't I always saying I was tired of the guys who *only* wanted to sleep with me? Why did it seem like such an issue that he wasn't ready at exactly the same moment I was? And who says the guy always has to want sex? Dr. Tim was kind and compassionate and supportive and adorable and a perfect gentleman. And he was the only thing keeping my ego out of the toilet of late.

But Parrot's frequent tirades about her terrific sex life had started to feel more like lectures, and instead of brushing her off again, I decided to be honest when she asked me about Dr. Tim.

"So ohmigod is the sex just amazing?" She perked up.

"Um, I don't know if that's the right word," I attempted.

"No but seriously is it like totally amazing because I need to know I mean I'm having like the most amazing sex right now like lose your mind forget your name sex and it's so fun and if you're having it too then like everything is perfect and we can double-date and nobody will get offended if somebody has to run off and have sex sometimes in the middle of dinner."

Forgetting for a moment that I couldn't really picture Dr. Tim and Parrot sitting at the same table, I tried to figure out how to make her see that he and I would certainly make it through the meal without deviating from the menu. I didn't say anything.

"So?" she nudged.

I didn't know how to explain.

"Liza did you hang up on me I hate when people do that without warning me first—"

"I'm here, P," I assured her. "It's just that the sex ... isn't."

So I 'fessed up to my best friend, and I'm always grateful that when it really counts, she says the right thing. Parrot chalked it all up to his superior quality as a boyfriend. "Most guys are like in your pants the second they get close enough Liza you should be totally grateful to be with someone who respects you for who you are and takes you out and buys you

dinner and like always pays for your cabs I mean I have dated
so many guys who slept with me and never bought me anything."

"P," I explained, "I know he's great. It just makes me
wonder . . ."

"He's totally into you you're just being an idiot."

"Okay, fine," I conceded, "let's just say he is really into me.
I'm beginning to feel like some kind of weird nympho! I'm
not Amish, for fuck's sake. Would you be satisfied under
these circumstances?"

"Oh hell no I'd have dumped him after the first week," she
admitted. Oh, well. She tries.

Dr. Tim was great in so many ways, and clearly he was
feeling full-speed-ahead in all areas but one. Maybe I'd
found the last truly chivalrous, old-fashioned man in New
York.

Lucky, celibate me.

"I'll be out back pretending it's just another Thursday."

CHAPTER 13

I HAD AWAKENED THANKSGIVING morning fully prepared to enjoy my dinner and my kin. But a sickening veil of guilt and fear dropped over me before I even set foot on the floor. Because he'd received no better offer, Dr. Tim was working Thanksgiving, bandaging children hit by footballs and patching up overconfident bird-carvers. He'd just assumed I was going home and I chose not to correct him. He would be treating heart attacks brought on by creamy mashed yams, and dreaming of me, slicing canned cranberry sauce somewhere in the Midwest. Except I wasn't going to be in the Midwest because I was a great big stinking liar.

Perfecto, the doorman in Aunt Fran's building, is a remarkably intuitive man. He had obviously noticed the cavalcade of Weilers who had preceded me in entering Aunt Fran's luxurious penthouse.

"You look like your mother." He chuckled.

"Did they seem happy or were they anxious?" I asked him.

"I don't know. I don't know them."

"Right. Sorry."

Perfecto sensed my dread. "They were smiling," he added. They're always smiling. I didn't have the heart to tell him.

Aunt Fran has one of those amazing apartments that takes up an entire floor, so the elevator just opens into the foyer. Pronounced FWA-YAY. I took a deep breath as the little light on the elevator panel crept toward "PH."

The doors slid open too soon for my taste, and there stood my father, wearing one of those handmade, too-colorful, Bill Cosby-type sweaters, arms outstretched. What do you want? The man owns car dealerships.

"Lizaloo! Look at you! Who's the prettiest girl in New York?" he barked, crushing me in a good old-fashioned Dad-hug.

Over his shoulder, however, leaning insouciantly against a doorway cradling a Diet Coke as if it were champagne, was the answer to my father's question. I could only assume that this was Melania, my brother's Slovenian flavor du jour, and certainly, unquestionably, the prettiest girl in New York.

"Hi, Dad!" I croaked, my father's enthusiasm nearly crushing my rib cage.

"Lemme look at you. My God, you're just prettier every time I see you, Lizaloo. Are you taller? You sure there's no special fella in your life?"

Melania looked bored in the background. And then she jumped as though somebody had pinched her ass, which, in fact, somebody had. My brother emerged from behind Melania, looking practiced-hip in a rust-colored corduroy blazer and obviously expensive jeans. Jack looks like the "average" guys who advertise high-speed internet connections on TV. Slightly tanned, possibly athletic, but with really snazzy glasses.

"E-Lizard-Breath is here! Whoo-hoo!" he shouted, advancing to give me a back-slapping hug. He's also incredibly immature whenever I'm around.

"Excuse me, Wes Anderson, I was looking for my brother. Could you put those D&G frames to use and see if he's around?" I returned. (Okay, fine, maybe I act like a twelve-year-old too.)

"You know, maybe it's just my glasses, but you look like you're filling out there, little sister. Could you be putting on a little holiday weight?"

"Possibly. You seem kind of droopy. Could you be suffering from erectile dysfunction?"

My father guffawed. He enjoys nothing more than watching his children spar. Melania made a tiny mewling sound that I suppose could have been laughter. "Damnit, I'm being rude." My brother noticed her. "Melania, this is my bitter, lonely sister. Lizard, this is my awesome girlfriend."

I think I almost crushed the woman's hand. A better candidate for osteoporosis I have never seen. A bird would describe her as birdlike. But she said hello like a normal person and told me she liked my coat, which I was still wearing.

"Liza! You're here!" My mother surfaced in an apron and I wondered if she'd brought it with her or if Aunt Fran actually owned an apron.

"Hi, Mom!" I hugged her. "You smell good!"

"Thank you, sweetheart! It's Chanel. Your father bought it for me. Just because." She beamed at him and my father blushed.

Hmm, interesting. My parents are not usually ... romantic. I made a mental note to ponder the strangeness of this in private with Jack.

My mother looked me up and down. I braced for a thinly veiled expression of dismay.

"You look wonderful, Liza."

I waited. And waited. Nothing. And my hair was definitely in my face. On purpose.

"Thanks ..., Mom," I ventured.

"You really do."

Something was amiss. My parents were being weirdly lovey-dovey, my mother seemed pleased with me. Normally, I would say my mother and father were distant from one another, if not downright tense, which always seemed sad to me considering their romantic beginnings. Of course, in our family this wasn't discussed. Even my father just acknowledged it tacitly, almost Waspily; why actually talk about anything when you can let a deep-seated problem fester to a breaking point? Mine were the parents who would never divorce. They might while away forty years talking about nothing but the weather, but they'd stay the course. Anything less would be uncivilized.

I don't know what I expected, but this sudden warmth between them was highly disconcerting. I needed to find Aunt Fran. I heard the elevator rumbling behind me and three excitedly barking dogs. The doors opened and Aunt Fran's enormous Dobermans, Adam, Eve and Snake, bounded into the foyer. Aunt Fran followed at a more reasonable pace, a joint dangling lazily from her mouth. (Aunt Fran always smokes grass for the holidays. She calls it her "special occasion cigarette.")

"Niece, nice of you to drop by. We're practically ready to eat. You've missed the cocktail hour, but I saved some in a thermos for you to take home." Clearly Aunt Fran was not going to fill me in on all the strange familial doings at this particular moment. My mother patted my head as I greeted the dogs.

"We're so glad to see you, Liza. Are you hungry? What do you think of my apron?" she asked.

"I think it looks pretty foxy, myself," my father offered.

I had a sudden urge to search both of my parents for signs of body snatchers, but I was kind of enjoying this weird pod family. They made me glad to see them. I decided not to push it.

"I thought there were caterers" was all I could produce in response to my mother's question.

"There are," Aunt Fran rasped, "but your mother insisted on helping them. Frankly I think she just wanted to be close to all the pretty boys."

"Oh, they are very handsome, Liza, you should see," my mother added.

"Feel free to take one home, Niece. Dumb as dirt, every one of them, but I'll wrap him up for you if you find one you like."

Thankfully, as I was somewhat dumbfounded, one of the admittedly handsome, "dumb as dirt" cater waiters summoned us to dine. I hung my coat in the closet and filed in to my place at the table.

The astonishing thing about Aunt Fran's world is that she always manages to make everything look somewhat celluloid. In a good way. Our catered Thanksgiving spread looked like it was straight out of a French's Fried Onions commercial, and my father got a big kick out of the way one of the cater waiters ceremoniously offered him the carving knife. (I felt very strange being served by five obviously out-of-work aspiring actors, when I myself had been saved from catering only by Tabitha's enormous wedding to-do list. But I comforted myself with the thought that they were probably models and not actors and therefore deserving of very little sympathy.)

We all chattered comfortably as we commenced to stuff ourselves. Aunt Fran was drinking in exceptionally impressive volume and I had a feeling she was remembering that she didn't particularly enjoy playing hostess. My family is especially gifted at the sort of small talk that makes strangers feel welcome; my parents started right in on Melania.

"So what do you do when you're not busy keeping Jack out of trouble?" my father asked her. This, I told myself, was why I hadn't brought Dr. Tim.

"Melania's a model." Jack beamed, gratuitously answering for her. I noticed the cater waiters perking up in the background.

"And she's hired you to talk for her?" I asked.

Melania released a tiny warble.

"And do you do runway or print work or . . ." Oh, sure, my mother could be interested in Melania's modeling, but my career wasn't worth discussing.

"Mostly print," she answered. We all waited for something more, but Melania seemed to have finished. Apparently she didn't share the family's gift for yapping. Fortunately, we had Peg Weiler, who has never once allowed a dinner party to succumb to the inevitable seven-minute lull.

"So, Liza," my mother chirped as she passed the asparagus, "how's the writing?"

This was perhaps the first time in my memory that my mother had asked this question. Did I suddenly warrant the same consideration as a catalogue model? What had this woman been taking?

"It's, um . . . it's actually, going pretty well. I told you I have this little play going on downtown." I had chosen to keep the national broadcast under wraps until closer to airtime. No need for them to tell all the neighbors right away.

"And when does it become a big play going on uptown?" my father wanted to know.

"Well, Daddy, I'd need a place to do it, and a producer, you know. There are a lot of steps between here and there. Right, Aunt Fran?" I wondered if my parents could possibly understand that all of this was well within Aunt Fran's power, if only she would deign to help me.

"She'd need to stop rewriting it, for one thing," Aunt Fran muttered, and I knew I was being checked.

"Anyone special in your life?" my mother questioned.

I shot a quick glance at Aunt Fran to see if she'd blabbed about Dr. Tim, but her face was a blank.

"Not really," I said, and my stomach turned a little. I thought of just telling them, right then and there. Yes, there was somebody, but I was scared, and frankly I wasn't really sure about him even though he was absolutely perfect on paper and that was why I hadn't said anything. But instead I nibbled at a forkful of cranberry sauce.

Aunt Fran coughed very softly, to let me know she didn't approve of my behavior. Or maybe it was just years of drinking and smoking catching up with her.

"So how are you guys?" I attempted to deflect all the attention.

As though on cue, my parents looked at each other and just glowed. "Well, we've actually got some news," my mother sang. And my father giggled. Like a schoolgirl.

"You tell them, Jason," she said.

"Well, kids, you may not realize this, but your mother and I haven't always had the perfect relationship."

My brother caught my eye.

"But in the last few years, we've done a lot of work on ourselves, lotta soul-searching. And, well—no, you do it, you tell 'em, Peg."

"Okay, thanks, because I really wanted to do it!"

"I know you did," he mooned at her.

"Somebody do it before I die of old age," Aunt Fran snapped.

"Alright ... Jason and I ran away to Mexico two weeks ago and renewed our vows on the beach in Oaxaca!"

"We sure did!" my father added.

No one said anything. Jack looked like he was trying hard to think of an appropriate toast to make. Aunt Fran smiled her "I-love-you-but-you're-getting-on-my-nerves" smile. Melania looked blank, which I assumed meant she was thinking.

"Wow, that's ... that's really ... amazing, you guys ...," I attempted, while thinking I was definitely dining with someone else's family. "That's ... wow ... congratulations."

"Yeah, man, here's to Mom and Dad." Jack joined me and

raised his glass. "You guys are ... an inspiration." Jack tends toward the sappy.

"Thanks, guys. Your mother and I are so glad to be here, sharing the holidays with you. All together." My mother nodded vehemently. "We're so happy together and we're so happy being with you."

And they really did look happy. Actually, I had to admit, they looked happier than I'd ever seen them. Whatever time my parents had spent away from their children had obviously led them from empty nest back to love nest.

My father raised his glass. "And making love to your mother on the beach in Mexico has really given me a new outlook on the world."

Aunt Fran, the least shy among us, promptly spit Scotch all over her plate and all over the cater waiter who was attempting to serve her more turkey. Said cater waiter dropped the serving platter and the dogs, sensing a feast, came tearing in from the living room. Jack leapt from his chair, partly out of horror, I'm sure, but partly to help wrest the turkey carcass from Eve, the opportunistic Doberman, who was ready to run down the hall with it, and as he did so, knocked Melania's chair rather fiercely, propelling the piece of roasted squash she was gumming directly into her windpipe. (One might venture the theory that Melania was simply so unused to consuming solid food that she choked from mere inexperience, but one would quickly be told that wasn't funny and to stop being so catty.) My mother gasped, my father bolted out of his own chair to assist Melania and I had to catch the bit of tablecloth that he'd accidentally tucked into his belt before he pulled everything off the table.

In this moment, time slowed to a remarkable and excruciating crawl. My thoughts, in this order, were:

1) My mother isn't being critical because she's having great sex.

2) Wow, my parents are having more fun with their flawed, thirty-plus-year-old marriage than I am with my brand-new relationship.
3) I'm really screwing the pooch on this Dr. Tim thing.
4) I hope Melania isn't about to die. Dr. Tim would know what to do—I wish he were here.
5) Oh, shit. Melania's going to need medical attention. We're going to have to take her to the emergency room, where Dr. Tim is currently on shift. And not only will I have to introduce him to my entire family, I'll have to explain why I lied to keep him away from them. Then he'll hate me and never speak to me again and I will spend the rest of my life wondering why I let this kind, noble man get away.

I had a little moment where there was warmth and fuzziness in the pit of my stomach and I realized I really did wish that I'd been brave and just brought him along. You can spend your whole life being afraid, or you can take a risk and maybe end up having great sex with your spouse on a beach in Mexico when you're in your mid-fifties. (Then I got grossed out again.)

This was when my father's expert administration of the Heimlich maneuver to Melania's negligible rib cage resulted in the largish chunk of squash catapulting across the table and smacking me squarely in the left nostril. It stuck for a second, and actually kind of hurt. It really was a big chunk of squash.

Not surprisingly, we didn't get to the pie. Which was sort of fine because I got to take the pecan home untouched. Melania recovered nicely, though her conversational skills went from unimpressive to nonexistent. Jack was mortified and probably still reeling from the revelation that our parents had had sex more than twice, as was I. My incredibly in-love parents, though I don't think they realized they were to some degree the cause of the ruckus, were concerned and decided to see Melania and Jack back to their hotel. As they were retrieving coats and hats, my mother pulled me aside.

"There's something I think we both know needs to be discussed," she said quietly, as she wound her scarf around her neck. I braced myself and wondered how she knew.

"Look, Mom, it's not like I'm keeping anything from you—"

We'd had such a nice, if uncharacteristically relaxed, evening. I didn't want to have this discussion now.

"I don't want to overstep, sweetie, which is why I didn't bring this up in front of everybody else—"

Clearly I was busted and there was no getting out now.

"—but I would button one more button if you're going out in public."

"You . . . what?"

"Those waiters must have gotten an eyeful. You do have a bosom, Liza."

That was it. My bosom. Just when I thought she'd had a complete personality transplant . . .

Relieved, I didn't even think of arguing. "Okay, Mom. I'll keep it in mind."

We all hugged and kissed goodnight, and while the cater waiters tidied up the kitchen, Aunt Fran and I sat by the fire stroking the dogs and trying to recover.

She seemed in remarkably better spirits, probably because Aunt Fran likes nothing better than witnessing the birth of a story that will be told for years. After a half hour or so I summoned up the courage to ask her what was on her mind.

"You're not pleased with me this evening, are you?" I asked.

She paused and took a goodly sip of her drink. "Why do you say that?"

"Oh, now we're being coy. You're definitely pissed at me."

"I hate that expression. I am never anything as nondescript

as 'pissed,' Liza. I am frequently hocked off, occasionally furious and often seething. Pissed is for sissies."

"Understood," I relented. Maybe my increasingly barbed shots at Aunt Fran's failure to boost my career had made an impact.

"Currently," she went on after a moment, "I am ... disappointed."

Like an arrow in the heart, that word. Where do one's elders learn this trick? Smack me, ground me, stop speaking to me, but tell me you're disappointed and I wilt.

"Ouch. Okay. Why?"

"Because I think you're being cowardly and I don't understand it."

"How, please?" As much as I'm frequently tempted to run the other way when Aunt Fran makes frank observations about my life, I know it's medicine I'll have to swallow sooner or later. Because she's usually right.

"Why didn't you bring your young man tonight?"

I answered slowly. "Because I wasn't sure I wanted to." I was trying desperately not to get defensive.

"It's dinner, Liza. One dinner. If you'd decided in the middle of the meal that you never wanted to see him again you could have been rid of him by dessert. What the hell are you running from?"

"I'm not running! I'm being thoughtful. Too many people rush into relationships. I'm just waiting until I'm sure." I sounded just like Dr. Tim, the part of Dr. Tim that I found less than exciting.

"And how exactly will you know when you're sure, hmm?"

"I don't know." I knew I was being cornered. "I just will."

"You're acting like a preteen, Liza. Even your perfect mother is finally taking a bite out of life, and you're still cleansing your palate and pretending the main course hasn't come yet. You're so afraid of being wrong, of anything being messy, that you won't even give this fellow a chance. Won't even let him in. And if you don't let him in you're never really going to know whether to throw him out."

I didn't know what to say. I hate having myself explained to myself. So accurately. I nodded mutely.

"Get a little messy, Niece. It's fun, I promise. Don't you see all the other kids doing it?"

I felt the tears forming behind my eyes. I didn't even like finger painting as a child. How was I supposed to risk mess with other human beings?

"Break a heart. Have your own broken. It's good for you. It's life. Participate in your own."

She handed me a Kleenex and poured me another drink. "Remember," she crowed, "it's like Lucky Luciano used to say to me: if you want to make an omelet, you've got to break a few legs."

I wished Parrot were there to share in that last moment. She would really have appreciated that.

*"There's a hell of a lot to be said for guts and
a decent suit."*

CHAPTER 14

FRIDAY NIGHT, twenty-four hours after our
Thanksgiving went bust, I managed to drag my brother
out for a drink. Melania had met up with a few of her modeling friends and I gathered Jack was just as happy to leave
them all feasting on a single lettuce leaf somewhere farther
uptown. He was relatively unfamiliar with NYC, but my
brother has always had a respectable appreciation for a great
dive bar. I took him to the Cherry Tavern on E. Sixth Street,
where you can get a Tecate and a shot of tequila for five bucks
if you hit it on the right night.

We managed to grab a couple of seats near the pool table
and I tried to get the scoop on what the hell was going on
with our parents.

"I thought they were gonna start pawing each other at the
table," Jack said.

"Since when do Mary Ann and the Professor actually do
it?" I asked.

"Since they realized marriage didn't have to feel like a gu-
lag, apparently. Honestly, Lizard, I could still throw up from
last night. Do we really have to talk about this?"

"No, of course not. Why don't you tell me how you managed to find Albert Einstein trapped in the body of a PennySaver model?" I can say these things to Jack and he doesn't take them personally. There's a limit, of course, but we've spent nearly thirty years pushing it.

"She's not dumb, Liza."

"Uh-huh." I wasn't buying it.

"Okay, she's not *that* dumb." He knocked back most of the beer he was holding.

"Seriously, what is it with you and these extremely hot, vapid girls? None of your female friends are idiots. You grew up around smart women. What is the deal?"

"Whoa, why am I getting the third degree here?" he shot back.

"I'm just curious about your boring and no doubt expensive bimbo habit," I replied.

"Okay, fine. But you're not gonna like the answer."

"Which is?" I couldn't wait for this one.

"Which is that smart girls are frequently a pain in the ass. You go on three dates and they start using words like 'serious' and 'commitment,' and you fall for it because you like the girl and you don't wanna be a dickhead, and the next thing you know you're fucking trapped and married for thirty years like Mom and Dad."

I was tempted to attack Jack's position, but the moment we each took to ponder our parents' newfound romance took the heat off of what might have become a sibling tiff. Besides, he had a point, and for a second I had to wonder about my own dating habits. Most people in a brand-new relationship wouldn't be thinking so much, right? They'd be "seeing what happens." Whereas I was spending all my time trying to figure out what was missing and how much I would actually miss it if I kept on going down this road. Like I was going to turn around one day and realize I'd made a terrible mistake and it was too late to get out. What if I was just manufacturing doubts about Dr. Tim to keep myself safe?

"And by the way," Jack continued, "at least I date women. At least I'm actually getting laid. Can you say the same?"

Hmm, tough to answer that one. Though I'd briefly floated the topic to a select panel, I was still lacking answers. I needed to talk to somebody. I needed to know if I was the one being too uptight.

"Okay," I ventured cautiously, "cone of silence?"

"Oh, my God, you're turning tricks for extra cash."

I punched him in the arm and he laughed.

"Okay, okay, cone of silence!" he promised, and made his two hands join in a point over his head.

"I am seeing someone," I confessed.

"I knew it! You know Mom and Dad are totally onto this. She kept trying to manipulate me into asking you at dinner last night."

"WHY? That makes me so insane. Why can't she just come out and ask me? Why does everything have to be so indirect?"

"Because she's Mom," he answered. "If anyone really knew how she was feeling they'd probably be terrified. Back to the dude. Who is he? Can I beat him up?"

"He's this ER doctor I met when I sprained my ankle. Which is much better, thanks so much for asking, jackass."

"How's your ankle?" he retorted.

"Shut up. He's awesome. He's this terrific guy. He's smart and funny and sweet and he's really great to me and we have a lot of fun and . . . I don't know. He's great." How to explain to my brother that I couldn't seem to kindle my initial spark with Dr. Tim into raging flames of passion?

"See, I don't get why you don't get this," Jack marveled. "Do you know how much easier it would have been if you had just brought this guy to dinner? Why do you think I always, always bring a date to Thanksgiving? It completely deflects Mom's judgment reflex and Dad spends the whole time trying to figure out the new person's teasing angle. I can't believe you haven't caught on!"

It was true, I reflected. My brother had dragged a different woman to our family Thanksgiving every year since he was a freshman in college.

"I just assumed you were exceptionally horny and couldn't go without for four days."

"Well, I am," he replied. "But that's a secondary concern. You think I think a lot about whether I'm gonna stay with this woman or, oh, it's such a big deal, she's meeting my family. No! She serves a purpose, she makes it fun for me, maybe we'll stick, maybe not."

"Yeah, but I'm sure you don't say that to them. You probably say something really faux-sweet, like, 'Melania, you're really special to me, and it would mean a lot if you'd come and meet my family.' And then three days later you're done with them and they have no idea what they did wrong or how your feelings could have changed so dramatically. I can't believe my brother is one of those guys." Those guys that you have to see coming a mile away, or they will leave you in pieces on the floor, wondering how you could ever have been stupid enough to give them so much power. I know those guys. I know the girls who fall for them, and they always end up looking like fools, because everybody else could have called it in the air. No relationship is worth that much of my dignity.

"Okay, fine, I'm evil incarnate." Jack was unconcerned with my impression of his behavior. "So what's the deal with this guy? You like him, he's 'awesome.' Are the Weilers that embarrassing?"

"Yes," I chided him, "you alone are the great shame of my life. I don't know. It seemed too soon."

"Whoa, whoa, wait," he stopped me. "Something's up. Criminal record? He's ugly? What?"

"No! I told you, he's terrific."

"I got it!" He jumped. "The sex sucks! Dump him, Lizard! Dump him fast, dump him now! Incredibly not worth it."

"The sex does not suck!" I protested.

"Dude, I know how it is. It's like, you like somebody, you're having fun, but between the sheets it's like you'd rather wash your car. I know the drill. Trust me, show him the door."

I could feel my cheeks flushing as he went on.

"Jack, would you listen to me?"

"Nothing to listen to, little sis, if the bangin's rough, the deal is off!"

"JACK!" I practically shouted. "THE SEX CAN'T SUCK BECAUSE HE WON'T HAVE IT WITH ME!"

In a play, this is the moment in which the entire bar would fall silent, the leading lady would realize she'd been too loud and after a few seconds everyone would return to their respective beverages and conversations. In my life, however, this was the moment when George and I realized we were in the same bar.

Seriously. My mouth should come with a warning label.

My brother was practically hysterical. "That was the fucking funniest thing I have ever seen!" He guffawed. "You just made an ass out of yourself in front of an entire bar! Christ, Lizard, I hope no one knows you here!"

I would have strangled my brother, but I couldn't move. My ears were hot and I could feel myself turning scarlet from forehead to waist. Someone did know me there. Someone I hadn't seen for a month. Someone who looked better than I would have wished.

Someone who was coming over.

"Are you always getting into trouble," he asked over Jack's shoulder, "or just when I'm around?"

I could have screamed. How dare he talk to me as though we'd known each other for years when really this was only our second meeting.

"Apparently you do know people," Jack muttered under his breath with amusement.

"George," I managed. "How...interesting...to see you."

"Sorry to hear about your...difficulties," he smirked, clearly in reference to my humiliating outburst. "But it's nice to see you upright."

Jack was thrilled to bits at watching someone else torment me for a change. Nobody ever threw me off my game like this, to the point where I couldn't come up with a damned thing to say.

"I don't think we've met." My brother turned to George. "Jack Weiler. Liza's older and better-looking brother."

"George Doren," George replied. "Liza's ambulance service."

"George took me to the hospital when I hurt my ankle," I explained. Jack shot me a look that I knew meant he registered how busy I'd been that night.

"Lizard, we have got to buy this man a beer!" Jack demanded. "You owe him. As a representative of the Weiler clan, allow me to repay you in liquor. What are you drinking?"

"Totally unnecessary," George responded, but followed with, "Maker's and Coke."

"Coming up," Jack said, hopping up to head to the bar. "Join us," he added, snagging a chair for George before I could register my objection. Then he disappeared into the throng by the bar.

"We have to stop meeting like this," George joked as he sat down.

"My sentiments exactly." I attempted to seem flip.

"You look terrific," he said, sending me flying off guard again. "I mean, you don't look like you're having any trouble walking."

"I'm sitting," I said.

"Okay, I take it back. You look like a hideous gimp."

"What are you doing here, George?" I demanded.

"I'm drinking. Crazy, I know."

"I mean, what are you doing *here*?" *In my bar,* I wanted to add.

"I'm so glad I am here," he rolled right past my inane question, "since it sounds like you're having kind of a tough time."

Oh, Lord, I thought. *Here it comes.*

"I mean," he continued, "I—along with everyone else— couldn't help overhearing your...complaint, shall we call it?"

I hadn't the first clue what to say.

"Who's the guy?" he asked.

"That is so none of your business," I spat.

"Is it serious?" He was so delighted with my misery.

"I don't know," I said. "I think maybe. It might be."

"Wow, sounds great. Maybe, might be serious and no sex. That's a keeper."

I had to regain my footing or he was going to keep winning.

"So," I attempted, "is there a wet T-shirt contest starting soon or are you just here to scam drinks off of people's unsuspecting brothers?"

"Ooh." He acted as though I'd punched him in the chest. "That was harsh! You know, you're not very nice to me."

"That's because I don't like you," I told him.

Even though you look exceptionally sexy in that blue button-down with the cuffs rolled up. With your hair and your eyes and—

"I don't think that's it," he said, staring directly into my eyes so I couldn't look away.

The sound of a commotion at the bar saved me. I heard my brother say, "Hey, man, it was an accident. It's a little crowded, you know?" Some drunk asshole was in his face and I gathered that Jack had spilled a drink on him.

"It wasn't a fuckin' accident," the cretin slurred, "you wanted to get me fuckin' wet!" He stood up from his barstool and I noted that the guy was a good deal bigger than Jack. My brother and I share the same poor editing skills when it comes to a witty retort, and I got a bad feeling in the pit of my stomach. People at the bar started to move away.

"Yes," Jack retorted, "that's exactly it. I wanted to see you wet. It's a dream. I'm thrilled. Thank you for this moment."

I saw the huge guy make a move toward Jack. Before I could say a word, George was out of his chair and stepping between them. "Hey, buddy," George said, in a voice more humble than I thought him capable of, "my friend is really sorry. He didn't mean to do it."

The huge guy took George in and I watched him trying to calculate how tough it would be to fight George and Jack at once. George is tall enough and a formidable guy, but this fellow was one of those enormous, sketchy East Village dudes who make a career out of prowling around looking threatening. If George was scared, he didn't show it, unlike my brother, who was finally taking in the fact that he was about to get his ass handed to him.

"Get out of my way," the huge guy growled at George, who put a hand against the guy's shoulder and refused to move.

"He's sorry, man. He doesn't wanna fight you."

Jack really didn't. I knew he wanted to run. But the Neanderthal seemed to be more interested in George.

"You wanna fight me then, tough guy?" he mumbled, clearly not too drunk to do some real damage.

"Me?" George smiled. "Nah, I was just gonna buy you a drink." But he still had a hand up and it was obvious he was ready for whatever came next. Maybe it was George's fearlessness, or maybe the free drink was enough incentive; either way, the huge guy sat down again and grunted his order at the bartender. I exhaled audibly. George paid for the drink and thanked the bartender and pulled a stunned Jack toward our table.

"I would get out of here before that guy remembers he wants to kill you," George advised.

Jack was mortified, but so grateful. "He was gonna kick my ass, man. Now I owe you two drinks."

"Like I said," George replied, "totally unnecessary. You can get me next time." He plucked my coat from the back of my chair and held it up for me.

I was overwhelmed. George was so steady, so sure of himself, so willing to get hurt to help my brother, who he'd only just met and who frankly didn't help himself. Once again, I didn't know what to say.

We all three made our way out the door. Jack's buzz was visibly killed and he made some noise about heading uptown to find his girlfriend. He thanked George again, hugged me and gave me a look that I knew signified his approval of *this* guy at least. He hailed a cab and disappeared up First Avenue.

I wanted to make small talk, but my heart was in my throat. "That was, um . . . that was really incredibly nice, what you did in there."

"Not a big deal." George shoved his hands into the pockets of his jeans, his jacket under his arm. "Probably really stupid, actually. That guy could have knocked me cold."

We laughed for a second and then got embarrassed again. Then I heard myself say, "So, Jack's out. Can I buy you one of those drinks we owe you? You're running up kind of a Weiler tab."

He looked back up the avenue (and not at me) and paused for a minute.

"Probably not a good idea," he said.

It was like being slapped. This guy had been in my face since the moment I met him and now I was actually offering to spend time alone with him and some alcohol and he was turning me down. Apparently nobody wanted to sleep with me.

"Oh," I said. "Okay, then. Just trying to be ... nicer."

George looked like he was about to say something, but thought better of it and stuck his arm out for an approaching cab. I thought maybe he was going to jump in and speed away, but instead he opened the door for me.

"Heading uptown, right?" he said.

"Right," I responded, too stunned to do anything else. I moved toward the car. George put his hand on my arm, leaned in and kissed me on the cheek.

"It was good to see you," he said.

"Right," I repeated, and dropped into the seat. He closed the door, and the taxi carried me away.

"She puts on a white dress and we're all supposed to pretend she's not insufferable."

CHAPTER 15

I WAS AGITATED FOR DAYS after my run-in with George, but there were still the family to send back home and a perfectly good boyfriend to avoid. And Monday was to bring the start of a whole new chapter: my life as Tabitha's wedding gofer.

She asked me to meet her at her office at the Lower Manhattan Gallery of Female Expression, whose very name made me want to scurry down a back alley and hide. When I arrived, Tabitha was bushy-tailed as ever and already waiting to meet me at the front entrance to the museum.

"Back to the real world, right, Miss Liza?" she greeted me with a cloying grin. "Ooh, you're gonna have to leave that out here," she whispered in the direction of my coffee, "there's no food or drink inside." I reminded myself that I was desperate.

"Sure." I smiled. "Sorry. Just give me one second." I stepped to the curb, slammed my coffee, took a second to absorb the scalding caffeine coursing through my system and turned to face her. "I'm ready," I lied.

The Lower Manhattan Gallery of Female Expression (I

wondered if perhaps there was a similar institution catering to the expressive women uptown) was a two-level boutique museum, meaning it wasn't too big and not too many people knew about it. I don't think they were exactly on the cutting edge of modern art. Tabitha led me past a photography exhibit depicting very old women playing sports and we made our way through a door marked "Employees Only." I somehow expected a buzzing operation—fifteen or twenty people hard at work procuring the latest in vulvular sculpture, but as I followed Tabitha through the door she explained, "We're just a tiny crew here. So much art, so few folks to get it on the walls! And I'll tell you confidentially that they don't pay me what I'm worth." No wonder she was running a rent racket. "Such important work though, don't you think? We need a voice." I assumed that, in Tabitha's case, "our" voice would be shrieking for a bigger diamond and a house in Pound Ridge.

Tabitha led me briskly into her office, which I recognized immediately by the dried-flower wreath on the door. "So this is the nerve center of my personal operation," Tabitha chattered as we entered. "As I mentioned, Tod and I are looking at a September wedding, which gives us just a little less than a year! I'm a busy lady, so you'll be a busy lady, okay?" She didn't wait for my reply. "I'm going to get you started today picking up books from the florists we're considering. There are only eleven of them so it shouldn't be too much running around. Okey-dokey, artichokey?" she asked me.

"Okey ... dokey," I replied reluctantly.

"Well, pull up a chair, silly goose!" she cried, sitting in her own. "Before I send you out, I just need you to sit down and compile my invite list and Tod's into an Excel sheet. We have got to get a sense of our numbers. You can work on my laptop," she explained, pushing her Dell across the desk toward me along with a pile of papers. "Oh, and try to make a note of the ones I've flagged for the engagement party. I told you about that, right?"

It seemed that Tabitha and Tod-with-one-D—or T&T Marriage Factory, as they had come to refer to themselves (don't get me started)—had chosen December 31, the most high-pressure, unfun, letdown evening of the year to have an ENGAGEMENT party. These people are a nightmare. In what foul universe could they possibly dwell to imagine that an obligatory jaunt to their swankety new Upper East Side, overdecorated, overpriced love shack, which is doubtless designed to make the rest of us feel small, would inspire anyone to celebrate the insipid codependence they call love? On New Year's Eve, no less! (Let me just take a moment to say that I realize it is indeed cause for celebration when any two people in the world can find each other and make each other happy. And it's not that I wish Tabitha ill. It's just that somehow whenever I think about her I turn into a third-grader on angel dust.)

"Wow," I commented, "there must be like four hundred names here."

"More like 550," she returned, with a completely straight face. "So let's get moving, huh?!" She smiled and I tried to disguise my distaste.

I spent the next hour or so poring over names and typing until I thought I'd go blind. It didn't help that Tabitha was yammering away on the phone for most of it, or that her cackle pierced my eardrums like an ice pick. The idea of visiting eleven florists was just starting to sound appealing when I saw a name that stopped me cold. I must have been frozen for several seconds, because Tabitha actually looked up from her monitor.

"Something wrong, Liza? I don't hear clicking!"

"Huh?" I looked up. "Oh, sorry, I just...how do you know George Doren?"

"Who?" she asked, tearing the page from my hand. "Oh, this is Tod's list. I don't know half these people. Probably somebody from Turnbull-Prince, where Tod used to work? Make a note that he should be second-tiered for the engagement party. We're only doing nearest and dearest for that."

She handed the paper back to me and picked up the phone to plague an unlucky receptionist somewhere. Suddenly I felt sick.

"Hey, Tabitha?" I whispered. "I'm gonna go do a florist run. I'll finish these this afternoon." I motioned that I was leaving and she nodded without interrupting her conversation. When I was almost out the door, I heard, "Oh, hang on a sec, Marlene. Liza!"

I turned back.

"I almost forgot to tell you—love that new fella of yours. What a catch! I have no idea how you hooked him, but *that's* the kind of guy you marry. Don't screw this one up!" She giggled. I restrained myself from throwing a geode paperweight at her. I was not about to consider seriously the opinion of a woman who owned a hot-pink vibrator that she'd named Sergio.

I managed to hit four florists that day before heading off to rehearsal. The theatrical process was not getting any easier. What had seemed like a biting and perhaps moving drama when I'd first written it now promised to rival a Tori Spelling movie. At first I'd tried to save my comments for private moments off camera, but it grew more difficult as time went by. Will was falling in love with himself as documentary subject and got more into his role every day. Instead of just answering an actor's question, he would crouch and lean on one knee, screw up his forehead and stroke his nonexistent whiskers. He would say something like "Let me feel that out for a minute," or, "I'm visualizing. I'm dreaming it. Okay! I see it." I wanted to vomit. And the actors actually seemed to get worse instead of better. I was losing my grip.

Will also worsened when our rehearsals moved onto the set. Being in a real theatre seemed to spur him on, and he refused to have any discussion with me that wasn't on camera. He kept interrupting my notes to say things like, "I think we need a rewrite, Liza. I feel the need for something more visceral in this scene."

"Will," I seethed, "say something that means something, anything, so I have some idea what the hell you're talking about."

"It's just . . . I don't know . . ." He stroked his beardless chin and tugged his wallet-chain. "I feel like I want to turn these people inside out! I want to put the subtext on the outside! To reveal all of the roiling pain and pathos and really just flip it and reverse it!"

Missy Elliot would have smacked him; I merely considered it.

"Right, but the whole point of this play is the tension between what these people actually say and what they want to say. If they just say it, the play will be five boring minutes long."

"I don't know. . . . I don't know, I don't know. . . ." He paced the stage. The actors looked on, awestruck. I sensed that perhaps the taller Graham wasn't buying it, but I couldn't catch his eye. "I just want to call upon Brecht, you know? Or Artaud," he continued. "Really stir things up! Meyerhold!" Will rattled on with his list of theatrical rule-breakers. He was grinding a tack into one of my pet peeves: if you're going to attempt to help the play, don't tell the writer she should have written something she didn't—work with what's there.

"Look," I snipped, "I'm not Brecht or Artaud or Meyerhold. If you picked up this play because you thought it was edgy and cool and you wanted to exercise some sort of twisted vision with this for a canvas, I suggest you rethink, pronto."

He wasn't listening to me. He kept pacing and I could feel myself reaching a boiling point. I sensed that the camera crew was particularly interested, but I didn't care.

Suddenly Will stopped pacing and threw his hands out in front of him. "STOP!" he shouted. "I have it! We cut the third scene in the second act out COMPLETELY! That makes the ending so much more shocking! We don't see any of it coming—we just get SMACKED right in the face with it!" He actually mimed smacking himself in the face.

"You have got to be kidding," I muttered.

"This is brilliant," he ranted to himself. "This is fucking brilliant."

"Will," I said, in a low, quiet voice that meant business. He ignored me.

"WILL!" I shouted. "Stand in one place for ONE second and listen to me! There is no way in hell that you are cutting one-third of the entire act! Nothing will make any sense! Georgia Allen will leave town and we will have no idea why! You'll completely destroy the arc!"

"That's the point, Liza!" he returned. "It'll be shocking! Completely unexpected!"

He wasn't hearing a word I said. I lost it.

"IT WILL BE A PIECE OF SHIT! IT'LL BE NON-SENSE, WILL, which frankly it's dangerously close to being right now. Everyone here is doing their damnedest to follow your completely incomprehensible direction, but you don't listen to anyone! You're a pretentious, arrogant poseur, and you're more concerned with your fucking television appearance than with actually directing this play, and I HAVE HAD IT! I'm done! Do whatever the hell you want with the play. Cut it in half if you want. But put it in the fucking program that it was your doing and not mine! I'm outta here."

I called Parrot. It was the middle of the afternoon and too

early for cocktails, even for the two of us. We went the other way and nestled ourselves comfortably on a sofa at Starbucks, where we sucked down venti Mocha Frappuccinos and a modest pile of baked goods.

"I'm so over this whole crappy writing life," I whined.

"You are so not you love it you're just having a bad day," she told me.

"Week. Month. Year." I was gloomy and inconsolable.

"So you'll go back tomorrow and say you're sorry for being a nasty bitch but he's not gonna ruin your play and that's it otherwise I can make some calls and we can have him whacked I mean I would do that for you are you gonna eat that last bite?"

"Oh, no," I told her. "I'm not going back there. I meant what I said. He can wreck my play but he's doing it without my help. I'll go see what the hell he's done with it when it's running. Probably." My only consolation now was that at least there were cameras to document everything. At least everyone in America would get a chance to see how thoroughly I'd been fucked over.

"So then you'll have more time to work for Tabitha ...," she noted.

"Oh, God, I hadn't thought of that. I'll have no choice. I can't win. I'm gonna run away and become a hooker," I lamented.

"Okay fine but can we talk about something else?" she asked.

"Sure. Distract me."

"How come you never told me you saw George last week?"

I had meant to, initially, but after the way he blew me off at the end of the night I was honestly too embarrassed to say anything.

"Oh," I lied, "I completely forgot."

"Well you suck because I totally would have wanted to

know that I mean I totally think he has the hots for you don't you?"

"What? Wait," I blustered, "how did you know I ran into George?"

"Well he told Kirk and Kirk told me and get this apparently George went on about how you were seeing some guy and it sounded like he didn't appreciate you or something and he thought it was a complete shame because you're so awesome and he probably said hot too although Kirk didn't say that but I'm sure he did my God what were you saying about Tim?"

Suddenly it made sense. Of course George didn't want to go for a drink with me. I'd just gone to great trouble to tell him I was seeing someone.

I couldn't bear to tell her. "Nothing. God. Why would he say all that?"

"You like him."

"I do not."

"You do you like him, I really think you do."

"P, you are out of your mind. Dr. Tim is fantastic and I am completely happy and George is an ass. I'm serious. He's one of those guys every woman knows to avoid because all he'll do is use you and probably dispose of you in the most humiliating way possible. And I'm sure he only dates incredibly hot girls, anyway."

"You're an incredibly hot girl!" Parrot protested.

"Thank you, I love you, but no, I'm a normal girl. Yes, I pull it together pretty well, but I'm not one of *those* girls. You know what I'm talking about."

She didn't. But she moved on.

"Really because we were thinking it would be so fun to go out the four of us maybe on a night when Dr. Tim is working late so it wouldn't be like a problem or anything and ohmigod I so wanna double-date with you!"

I explained to Parrot in no uncertain terms that the only person I would be double-dating with was Dr. Tim. She pressed the point for several days afterward and I finally had to send her an e-mail explaining that I was completely disgusted with George in general and begging her not to put me in the same room with him ever again.

Whatever it was that came over me when George was around, I didn't need to feel it again. Better to be missing a piece than to lose yourself completely.

"People don't go to the theatre anymore because you can turn television off."

CHAPTER 16

LIKE A DATE with the hangman, the early-December opening of *Georgia Allen's Window* was upon me before I knew it, and I sure as hell didn't feel prepared. I hadn't attended a rehearsal since my confrontation with Will. My confidence in what was about to transpire was not exactly running high.

Though I'd left a message on Will's cell phone a week after our tiff, apologizing and asking if we could discuss the changes he'd proposed, I hadn't gotten a call back. To say I was dreading the performance would be an understatement.

Dr. Tim, on the other hand, could not have been more excited. We had a reunion date after my Thanksgiving "trip" and it was all he could talk about. He had TiVoed the Macy's Thanksgiving Day Parade for me. We watched it over rotisserie chicken and that pecan pie I'd nicked from Aunt Fran's.

"I'm so excited," he said. "My girl's words on stage for all the world to see."

"More like public humiliaton. We are talking about Will

Atherton, artiste extraordinaire. God knows what he's done to it."

"Liza, it's so natural to be nervous. You're offering your naked soul to the whole world. It's your endless wealth of angst that drives you to do great work."

"No, really, I think it's going to blow goat balls."

"I think you should let the audience judge for themselves." He beamed with reassurance. It was like he was breathing different air than I was. It didn't matter what I said; nothing could deter him from his utter faith in me.

Come opening night, even that wasn't enough to keep out the chill I felt standing alone in front of the theatre. I delayed going inside for as long as I could. Someone must have alerted the illustrious director to my presence, because eventually he emerged and discovered me cowering on the sidewalk. Sporting a black suit with a black T-shirt and patterned sneakers, Will made me hope someone else had done the show's costume design. He strolled toward me with camera crew in tow, obviously more confident with his filming entourage than without.

"Liza," he greeted me coolly.

"Hi, Will." I tried to sound gracious. "Did you get my message?"

"I did," he replied. Obviously my attempt to calm troubled waters had been less than successful. "I regret that it's been such a painful process for all of us," he said.

"Well, yeah ..."

"I've taken some liberties since you were no longer interested in being part of the work. I hope you'll realize when you see the piece tonight that theatre is a collaborative art form, and that my contributions as an artist had value." The camera had swiveled around behind me to get a better angle on Will's speech.

"Okay, well, I hope so too," I said. I wished he would just go inside, which in fact he did, turning on his heel and striding away as though he'd vanquished his nemesis. The cameraman scuttled after.

I stopped backstage to thank the actors, who amazingly seemed to bear me no ill will, and headed into the lobby to wait for Dr. Tim and Parrot. (She had promised to hold me down in case I tried to make a break for it during the show.) Since Jeremy was under a dissertation deadline, I'd told him not to bother and thankfully Aunt Fran was shooting a movie in Prague. I don't think I could have stood her particularly straightforward brand of criticism. Dr. Tim, of course, arrived ten minutes early, wearing a J. Crew tie and holding a bouquet of red roses.

"Couldn't let my girl's big night go by without letting her know how proud I am."

I tried to appreciate the gesture but I just couldn't. My only hope had been to get through the evening without anyone in the audience deducing that I had something to do with the drivel onstage. Carrying a big bouquet of red roses says nothing so much as "I contributed to the ruination of your evening. And I'm proud of it." There was, of course, no way to explain this to Dr. Tim. His formidable self-control might have been killing me in the bedroom, but it was going to be my saving grace when it came time to hear what he thought of the performance. I knew he would stand by me no matter what. Grateful to have an ally, I kissed him and held his hand while we waited for Parrot.

And waited.

Parrot would help me move a body, but damnit she is absolutely incapable of being remotely on time.

"She should be here by now," I muttered.

Dr. Tim squeezed my shoulder and looked around. "Yeah, where is Tabitha?"

I just looked at him. "Tabitha?"

"I figured she'd be here. I was kind of looking forward to chatting with her."

"She couldn't make it." I attempted to keep the disgust out of my voice. She couldn't make it because I made a big ol' point of not telling her a damned thing about it.

Eventually we had to go in; it was either that or miss the curtain and Dr. Tim wouldn't entertain my suggestion that we just find a bar and get hammered.

We scooted into the second-to-last row on the end and I tried to shove the roses under my seat without him noticing.

"You want me to hold those, babe?" he whispered as the houselights went down.

"No, no, I'm fine. They're perfect here. I love them."

Will turned and gave me a gratuitous dirty look from his front and center perch. As a general rule, good directors sit in the back of the house. Hell, even bad directors sit in the back of the house. Everyone sits in the back of the house! Trustafarians who wring the life out of people's decent, credible plays, these are the assholes who sit in the front row. Just FYI.

The houselights dimmed and still no Parrot. I was going to pluck her the minute she arrived. She did, only a moment before the lights went up onstage. If there's one thing Parrot has always had down to a science, it's making an entrance. A flurry of giggles preceded her yanking open the auditorium door with a distracting screech of metal, followed by an embarrassed gasp as she realized that fifty-eight people had just spun around in their seats to look at her. She whispered an apology and I tried to convey my silent aggression while beckoning her to the seat I'd saved. But Parrot shook her head and continued to scan the room, finally picking her way to a half-empty row on the other side of the theatre. This was when I noticed that Parrot wasn't alone. Kirk, suddenly ubiquitous Kirk, was with her and some other guy . . .

How could my best friend in the entire world have betrayed me so? It was one thing to bring Kirk after I specifically asked that we minimize the number of people in the audience that I would ever have to speak to again. But in the midst of what foul delusion had Parrot determined that it would be acceptable TO BRING GEORGE??? I slid down in my seat even farther, so much so that Dr. Tim shot me a quizzical look. I tried to smile even as I felt my intestines turning to Jell-O. George had seen me. And he'd seen me seeing him and he'd flashed his patented smirk/ogle all the way across the room. I was just praying Dr. Tim hadn't seen it.

I couldn't help glancing down the row every few seconds, but Parrot kept trying to catch my eye and I was not in the mood to engage in a silent, across-the-room conversation in which she would apologize for being late and I would try to ask her what the hell kind of ganja people smoked on her planet that made her think it was okay to bring George to my shamefest.

Dr. Tim squeezed my knee to alert me that the play was starting. I held my breath and waited for the awful mess to begin. It took only a moment, after the lights went up, to realize that by walking out on rehearsals, I had ushered in the demise of my own play. I had done it wrong, from start to finish. I hadn't asked for cast approval, hadn't insisted on a read-through before agreeing to the production. In a desperate moment, I'd basically signed away my rights to protest in exchange for the fleeting belief that somebody might give me a break.

Will had taken some liberties I never could have imagined possible with my naturalistic living room set. What I was looking at now was four milk crates in front of a twelve-foot-by-twelve-foot silkscreen of a vagina. A very naturalistic vagina, I'll grant him. What the hell could a gigantic vagina have to do with the perils of neighborhood politics? Hmm? NOTHING! NOTHING AT ALL! So distracted was I by the vaginal wall, that it took me a good minute or two to notice that the actors were stark naked. Not a stitch of clothing on a single one. I had expected to be dissatisfied, not rendered suicidal.

I looked at Dr. Tim. He was grinning. He couldn't think I'd intended *this*. Surely he was just putting on a brave face, to make me feel better. This is what good boyfriends do. Unlike certain other people, who just want to antagonize you and drive you into a sanitarium, good boyfriends are kind and sweet and loyal and they try to make your life better. And you appreciate them for it. You try your damnedest to appreciate them. You try not to slap the stupid grin off their face because you know that that would be completely inappropriate.

I was ramping up to a nervous breakdown, but once the full horror of the situation had sunk in, I began to watch the play and to get really, genuinely sad. I had liked this piece when I'd written it. It meant something to me. It was my first attempt to pour my real self into a living, breathing drama. I'd believed in it and I'd been so thrilled to think of it seeing production. I crouched there and peered at those barely post-pubescent actors emoting my lines with all the pathos and gravity appropriate to an episode of *Saved by the Bell,* and I knew they weren't to blame. Even Will, with his hipster footwear and twisted sense of metaphor, had only been trying to make an impact, to stand apart from the crowd. We're all told you have to distinguish yourself enough to get noticed or you die in this business. It's not enough to do solid work; you have to break new ground just to get a freaking job. It's a constant quest for approval that will most likely never come and it's humiliating. Every minute that most of you is in the ring, fighting to prove yourself, the other part is plotting an escape route. Because you just can't bear to imagine a whole life of this much struggle, just to be noticed. Will didn't understand, couldn't have understood, that no man gets noticed in the face of a twelve-foot vagina.

When I thought I couldn't take it anymore, the play ended. I couldn't even clap. Dr. Tim started to stand but realized that nobody else was rising and stayed in his seat for the rest of the applause. I didn't dare look toward the Parrot contingent. Whispering to Dr. Tim that I wanted to beat the crowd to the bathroom, I fled, blessedly losing a cameraman when his cords snagged on a railing.

Breathing the frosty air outside did something to dispel my nausea, and the homeless man who asked me for change rather checked my prima donna trip for the moment. I leaned against the cold stone of the theatre façade and wished I were a smoker.

At least now, I thought, I had a reason to be grateful for the cameras; when that fucking show aired everyone would see that I'd been swimming upstream against a current too strong and too asinine to reach the shore with any dignity. For now, I'd pull myself together and be gracious. I'd thank the cast for their wonderful work and I'd make up something to say to Will about his energy and devotion to the project.

I took a deep breath and reached for the handle of the door to make my reentry, but it sprung open before I could grab it. There was George, caught in the act. God, he was handsome when he looked guilty. The suit didn't hurt either. We were both silent and mortified for a moment.

"Nice ... vagina?" he tried.

"How about I didn't see you and you didn't see me and we both go on our merry way?" I ventured. The last thing I wanted was to be sheepish and apologist in front of him. "I didn't write any of that, in case you were wondering. I mean, I wrote the words but..."

"Hey! I..." George wasn't the sort of person you expect to be at a loss for words. I felt my ears redden.

"Really. I don't blame you. I would duck out if I were you. Of course if I were you I would never have come in the first place." My only hope was to let him off the hook and get him to disappear from my evening as soon as possible.

"Why is that?" he questioned.

"Um . . . this is starting to sound like a conversation and clearly you were in the process of leaving without seeing me so . . . go about your business!" I attempted a chuckle but I sounded like some sort of choking waterfowl.

"I, um . . . Sorry about that."

"No, really, like I said. Who can blame you?"

"No," he said, "I'm sorry about your play. They really . . . they murdered it a little, didn't they? I can only assume you didn't intend to stage the First Annual Genitalia Festival?"

When you fail and you know you've failed, most people try to ease the suffering by telling you it wasn't so bad. As if somehow your own memory of events will be amended by the encouragement of people who care about you. That's what Dr. Tim would try to do, what Parrot would do. George probably didn't even have the capacity to lie to me like that.

"Yeah. Um, yeah . . . they did."

"Man, that must be frustrating. No matter how good a job you do the product always depends on somebody else. I couldn't do that."

"Oh, sure you could. I'm sure your job—"

"Nope. That's one of the reasons I do it. Bit of a control freak, actually."

"I would really have preferred that you not see this tonight."

"Hey, I'm a cultured guy. I come to the theatre on occasion. The ballet. The opera. It's not all dwarf bowling and monster truck rallies."

I laughed. "I'm sure."

"Well, mostly it is."

I laughed again. I hadn't expected to feel good for the rest of the night.

"It's a hell of a piece," he said.

"Yeah, right. You're referring to the set, no doubt."

"No, I mean it. If you closed your eyes and just listened to the words without paying too much attention to the actual actors you could still hear it. You're good."

And then all of a sudden neither of us knew what to say. I found it hard to believe this was only our third meeting. I wanted to say something about the other night and the incident with Jack, but I remembered the end of that evening and couldn't bring it up. George pressed on.

"Well, anyway, Kirk mentioned he was heading over here from the office, so...spur of the moment. So that's the guy?"

"What guy?" I'm ashamed to say I really had no idea who he was talking about.

"Tall, glasses, falling all over you. Ring a bell?"

Oops.

"Oh, yeah, of course! Tim! He's um, he's a ..."

George looked at me askance. As well he should have.

"The, ah...*friend* you mentioned the other night?" he suggested.

"Yeah, well. Yeah." I had to look away, but I thought I caught a flash of that grin.

"So now that you've been forced to tell me what you thought and you don't have to skulk away into the night, come inside for a glass of wine? Watch me castrate that little fuck who ruined my play?

"Unless you have to run—" I added. I looked back and he wasn't smiling anymore.

He didn't hesitate. "I do actually."

"Hot date?" Aunt Fran always says you should never ask questions you don't want the answer to.

"We'll see. She was pretty hot when I met her."

I had no right to be bothered by this and I knew it, especially with my own date standing inside probably wondering where I was by this point. But it felt like a rabbit punch.

"Oh, of course," I shot back. "Hate to keep the ladies waiting."

"Yeah, well. You know how it is," he countered, secure that he'd gained the advantage.

"Oh, George, I'm sure I couldn't even begin to imagine. Thanks for coming." And with that I flung open the door and flounced inside.

Dr. Tim was standing with Parrot and Kirk by the cheese platter, holding a hunk of gouda on a toothpick and looking anxious. He was only beginning to grow accustomed to Parrot.

"Hey, honey! My God, that was great! I had no idea I was dating such a talented girl!" He kissed me.

"Oh, no?" was all I could manage.

"You really undersold this one, Liza. I was expecting something awful," he whispered to me. "There were so many layers to dissect. I'm really impressed!"

"Tim, there was a big pussy in the middle of my play. I didn't write a big pussy and I didn't write naked actors and I sure as hell never imagined that what I did write could incorporate those two frankly unforgettable elements."

"Hey, hey, I read the director's note in the program. I thought Will was very straightforward about the stuff he added and how he thought it made your points stand out more starkly. Baby, I loved it." He was still holding my roses. I must have left them inside when I escaped. I took them back.

Parrot hugged me and said, "Can I tell you something I totally didn't get any of that but I love you anyway," a little louder than I would have suggested. Kirk called me "Eliza" and asked me if I'd always been a radical feminist. I really had no idea what Parrot saw in him except that he followed her around like a dog. Dr. Tim kept gazing at me, his many-faceted, tortured, untamable, artist girlfriend, with only love and support. I could not have felt less deserving.

I couldn't shake the uneasy feeling that I'd been rude to George for no reason.

"So here's what I think we should do I think we should go to a bar and get shitfaced and then we'll go to that fucking director's apartment and like leave him some flaming dogshit or something and then go get pancakes is that a new sweater?" Parrot is proactive in even the most awkward situations.

"I've got an early shift," Dr. Tim spat out so fast I knew he'd been waiting to say it. He looked to me for backup. I realized at some point I was going to have to find a way for my best friend and my boyfriend to get comfortable with each other, but I had no idea how to make it happen.

"Yeah, P, thanks for the offer but I'm a little beat." I would much have preferred to follow Parrot to a bar but I knew I owed Dr. Tim this one.

"You're no fun but I love you anyway come on Kirk we're leaving!" She hugged me and they disappeared.

Dr. Tim put his arms around me. "What do you say we get out of here and go somewhere where I can congratulate you formally?"

I looked at him. "You mean like ... *really* congratulate?" I asked. That he would choose this evening, the moment of my greatest humiliation to finally suggest sex was jarring enough. But the too-fresh sensation of standing out in the cold with George was still in my bones and all of a sudden everything seemed wrong.

"I mean like really." He smiled at me. Apparently staring at an enormous vagina for an hour was exactly what Dr. Tim needed to get over the physical intimacy hump. Who knew?

If I had said no at that moment, if I had tried to tell him

that suddenly I was confused . . . but I couldn't. It would have meant saying too much and for once I didn't want to let the words just fall out of my mouth. What the hell, I thought, I deserved at least a little congratulating. Just for living through the evening.

"As I tell my agent, for God's sake, some things are not negotiable."

CHAPTER 17

W E HAD THE SEX.
   Finally.
After six weeks.
And it was ...
Fine.

It was fine. No, it was good. It was decent. Dr. Tim was a moaner. He had a great time.

I couldn't say exactly what the problem was. I mean, we both knew what we were doing. We hit all the necessary marks. There was plenty of foreplay. It was good. Lackluster maybe. Fine.

I lay in bed the next morning and tried to analyze it, to work through it logically, to figure out what we lacked, and I concluded that I had to be the problem. I should have explained to him that my utter humiliation had clouded my sex drive, that it wasn't the right time for our first time. But I guess I was kind of hoping it would be so great that I'd stop thinking so much.

I'd been sure that the sex would decide it for me. That our

physical union would catapult me out of my head and suddenly, looking into his eyes, I would be falling. Or that the opposite would be true and I'd know there was no future. One so-so lay later, there I was again with a column full of pros and a con or two that I was too afraid or too confused to articulate. Bad sex I could have used as ammo. But fine sex? What are you supposed to think when the sex is *fine*?

And who's the perfect person to spend all your time with when you're contemplating a troubled romance? A fucking insane bride! Tabitha was making me want to rend my own flesh. I was scheduling her tastings and her site visits and her terrifying florist inquisitions. I have no idea how I became the person she took dress-shopping, but I chalked it up to the fact that every other woman she knew must also loathe her. ("Oh, Liza, Mommy's in Gstaad so if you don't come, who will? It's okay that you don't know anything about clothes.") If you'd asked me in November, I would have said you couldn't pay me to visit one of those ghastly bridal emporiums with six million dresses and throngs of heaving, ecstatic women trying to accidentally smack you with their rings so you'd know exactly how many carats they were toting. Turns out, you could pay me.

Tabitha had made an appointment with an obsequious, zaftig woman who set up three good-sized racks of dresses, all of which looked like they'd been run through an explosion in a frosting factory. Tabitha commenced the interminably tedious process of trying on every ugly dress in the world and exchanging fashion terms with the saleslady and I tried to say as little as possible, all the while feeling like Masha in the second act of *Three Sisters*.

"You know, Liza, you can be honest with me," Tabitha told me as her head emerged between two enormous tulle poufs.

"I'm being honest, Tabitha. That one makes your head look small."

"No, not just about the dresses, silly! I mean, you can tell me what's going on with Timothy!"

"Oh, he doesn't really go by Timothy. It's just Tim."

"Well, I call him Timothy and he never corrects me." She preened and the saleswoman nodded her approval. "We had such a nice chat while you were in the shower the other night. He's very serious about you."

The idea of the two of them discussing anything to do with me immediately made my skin crawl, as did the forced intimacy of spending two hours with Tabitha in her underwear.

"Well, that's . . ." I had no idea how to respond. "He's a great guy," I tried.

"Something tells me I might not be the only one wearing a ring soon," Tabitha cooed, and she flashed her enormous rock at the saleswoman, who managed to seem appropriately awed.

"That's really jumping the gun, Tabitha," I said, wishing I had one.

"I don't know," she singsonged, "don't tell him I told you this, but Timothy told me that he can really see himself with you. *Long term.*"

"What, he said that to you? He said 'long term'?"

"Yes, he did. And I know that he's very interested in getting married. His career's on track, he's really getting into those thirties . . . plus he was so burned by that ex-girlfriend."

I had heard nothing of an ex-girlfriend. Come to think of it I had heard nothing about Dr. Tim's alleged interest in getting married.

"He told you all this while I was in the shower?" I demanded.

"No, silly! Some of it then, some while you were in the bathroom, some while you were napping."

It was like they had formed some secret society that met every time I turned my back for three seconds. What had first seemed like a high threshold for shrillness on Dr. Tim's part was beginning to look pathological. I imagined the satisfaction of gagging Tabitha with a fistful of rickrack.

"Look." I tried to sound neutral. "I'd really appreciate it if you wouldn't speculate about my personal life. There's nothing to share, at the moment, but if there ever is I'd really like to share it on my terms."

She let a satin halter fall around her waist. "Oh, Liza. Oh, are you two not doing well? Oh, Liza, don't screw this up. You do not attract men like this in general, and I would hate to see you let him get away."

Now even the saleswoman seemed interested in the future of my relationship. I wondered what she would say if I explained the so-so sex. The fact that even Tabitha, shallow, presumptuous, sheltered Tabitha standing there in her strapless bra, was telling me I should be head over heels for Dr. Tim made me stark raving bonkers. I wanted to scream that I knew! I got it! He was the perfect man—he was king of the perfect men! He was the kind of man who would build you a house with a special room for your porcelain fucking ponies, if only you were the kind of woman who wanted it.

This, I realized, was exactly why I hadn't introduced him to my mother.

"We're doing great," I told Tabitha. "Right where we are. We're both just . . . happy!" I smiled until my jaw hurt.

"Of course you are," she said. "You've finally got it right." And she leaned down from her pedestal and brushed the hair out of my eyes. With that, Tabitha turned her attention to the next fairy princess costume. I didn't know what to do. Finally gotten what right?! Nothing felt right!

Too many of my pieces didn't fit. I hated that I spent every day trailing after Tabitha with a Dyeables catalogue, listening to one band after another cover Peter Cetera songs. I hated that in yet another feeble attempt to get somewhere professionally I had wasted my time and been utterly humiliated. I hated that the only occasions in the past few months when I'd felt any electricity were all centered on George, a person who should never have been of any consequence in my life, a person who mostly just made me anxious and angry. And most of all I hated the fact that I was the only woman in the world who could manage to find Mr. Right and fail to feel all of those things that I *know* you're supposed to feel. I hated being the only one who'd never felt them, and I hated waking up every morning and just wishing that I could be softer or sillier or *something*... I am not a person who sits around and agonizes. I take action, I fix. Except at some point when I wasn't looking, my life had become a pile of square pegs, and I was just sitting there and wondering at them.

Love at first sight is probably bullshit, right? It takes time to love someone. So how long are you supposed to wait before you decide that it's never going to happen?

*"The only real bargains in this world involve
selling your soul. I'd rather just pay retail."*

CHAPTER 18

T HANKFULLY, we were well into December, and the
onset of a frantic holiday season would keep me from
sitting around and dwelling. Tabitha finally moved out, leaving us a fruit basket and a renewed faith in the miracle of
Christmas.

With the right interfaith parents, a kid can get all the perks;
I, for example, am a Jew who loves Christmas. Yes, Jack and I
went to Hebrew school at our convert mother's insistence,
but Peg never could see a menorah replacing her beloved
Christmas tree. Perhaps because of the unadulterated joy it
elicited from my mother once a year, I learned to start antici-
pating Christmas's splendor around the time the Halloween
costumes hit drugstores. There's just something magical
about the holiday season, especially in New York. I flit about,
feeling as though something wonderful is going to happen
the minute after next, and I generally maintain this sense until January 2. Then there's a major letdown, but that's not the
point. I love the holidays.

I do not, however, love any gift obligation that arises

within the first three months of a relationship. This is a terrible, horrible imposition and is likely to catapult even the coolest of customers into a full-blown panic. For one thing, it is always difficult to buy gifts for people you don't know well. Even if you have a general fix on the recipient's likes and hobbies, it's very hard to know what someone is looking for in a gift. For another, the early relationship gift needs to strike the perfect chord. Usually something like "I'm very interested in you, but I know we've just started and my expectations are reasonable. Also, I'm a genius." Or in my case, "I'm full of uncertainty and guilt. Merry Christmas."

Dr. Tim was no help at all. So focused was he on my needs that he seemed almost unable to provide guidance during my period of subtle probing. Over frozen hot chocolate at Serendipity one Saturday afternoon, I casually asked what Santa would be bringing him. He told me Santa had come early and that he was sitting across the table from his perfect gift. Technically, he was sitting across the table from my coat, but I didn't quibble. I spent a late morning poking around his apartment after he'd gone to work, trying to find holes in what seemed to be his perfectly ordered existence. No go. The best I could come up with was that robotic vacuum cleaner that sweeps under your couch while you laze in front of the TV, but that didn't exactly scream, "I'm hot for you!" and it was two hundred dollars. I even tried to squeeze one of the hospital residents, but the best he could tell me was that Dr. Tim kept a really neat locker and suffered from mild but chronic back pain. I considered a heating pad but it seemed too geriatric.

The nights were getting frostier, though, and time was a-wasting, as they say. Harried Jeremy and I were making a concerted effort to accomplish all of our shopping early in the season so that the later weeks could be squandered slathering ourselves in eggnog and Christmas cheer. Jeremy is the eldest of four boys and gift-giving is an art in his family. He's actually one of the few men I know who thinks about this sort of thing in advance. It was at his urging that we stumbled into Banana Republic one blustery evening.

I'd already picked up a pair of adorable zebra-print rubber rain boots for Parrot and helped Jeremy to score a blue cashmere V-neck for his mother, on sale, and a handsome leather photo album for his middle brother who'd just been awarded a Fulbright. For my parents, though I'd gagged slightly while placing my online order, I had already gotten a couple's massage at a spa in Chicago, so the only family member left on my list was Jack, who would always accept DVDs. Jeremy and I were feeling festive and accomplished, but I'd had no luck finding that elusive *cadeau parfait* for Dr. Tim.

"How 'bout a massage?" Jeremy questioned as we combed through a rack of corduroy pants for his father.

"Too impersonal," I replied. "If I were him I'd just wonder why I wasn't willing to do it myself."

"Make him a really fabulous dinner."

"But he spends so much money taking me out. I would feel like I wasn't doing enough."

"Jeez, L-Train, why don't you just get yourself some sassy lingerie and treat him to a little fashion show?" He chuckled loudly, very pleased with himself.

"As if I needed an excuse like Christmas," I joked, because I didn't know how to explain that Dr. Tim was just not the kind of guy you do that with. "Would you be helpful, please? I know he's gonna do something really nice for me and I'm gonna be standing there holding a book or a pen or some other unimpressive and totally inadequate excuse for a present. I have to find the right thing."

"Helpful. You got it," he promised.

"I kind of just want to pick something and give it to him, you know? Just whatever. Just get something nice and if he doesn't like it, tough."

"That's pretty romantic. I'd be really blown away if a girl felt that way about me."

"That's not how I *feel* about him!" I protested. "It's just too early to be buying gifts. It's too much pressure and it's sucking away my holiday fun."

Jeremy made a face at me.

"What?" I asked, refolding a pair of jeans.

"Nothing," he demurred.

"This," I said, "will be perfect," pouncing upon a gray scarf with a black stripe down the center.

"It's a scarf," he said.

"Yes! It's a scarf. And it's very soft—ooh! It's cashmere."

"How much?"

"Seventy-eight on sale for thirty-two. I'm getting it."

"This is it? This is the gift you've been desperately searching for for a month? A gray scarf?"

"A gray *cashmere* scarf. What's wrong with a gray cashmere scarf?"

He laughed. "Nothing. Absolutely nothing."

"Are you not saying something you'd like to be saying here?" I demanded.

"You've been freaking out for a month about the perfect gift for your perfect boyfriend and it turns out to be a gray scarf on sale. Just interesting, that's all."

I narrowed my eyes and glared at him.

"He'll love it. It's an inspired choice. I meant nothing." If there's one thing about my roommate, it's that he always knows when to back the hell off.

I bought it. A gray cashmere scarf is a very nice gift.

I knew that Dr. Tim was going to deliver some sort of Christmas romance, especially since I'd still been relatively depressed in the wake of my great theatrical belly flop. I had a feeling there was a big gesture in the works. Dr. Tim was a great fan of a big gesture.

Sometimes it sucks to be right.

One evening, having braved freezing sidewalks and

packed subway cars, I made my way through the museum to deliver Tabitha's save-the-date cards to her office. (There was confetti in the envelopes, so Tabitha's nuptial announcement provided each wedding guest with his own personal mess on the floor.) I was more than a little surprised to find the assistant curator absent from her lair, as she never left the office before six-thirty, but I left the cards on her desk and turned to go. Just as I was about to exit into the gallery, someone caught me around the waist. Before I could scream, a pair of dangling white skates appeared before my eyes.

"Merry Christmas, pretty girl," Dr. Tim breathed into my ear.

"What the hell are you doing?" I shrieked, relieved that I wasn't being mugged, but still freaking out.

"I'm sorry!" He laughed. "I just wanted to surprise you!"

"Oh my goodness!" a little voice twittered from the corner as Tabitha emerged from her hiding place behind a filing cabinet. "This is so romantic!"

"I don't even know what *this* is," I said through clenched teeth.

"This," Dr. Tim answered, "is your Christmas celebration. Since we won't be together on the actual holiday, I thought we could do a little special Christmas of our own. Tonight."

"When he told me what he was planning I just thought that this would be the perfect place to catch you unawares!" She giggled some more and rubbed Dr. Tim's arm.

"What do you say?" he asked expectantly.

I wanted to say this was never going to work, that I could not possibly continue to date someone who would even think to conspire with Tabitha in giving me a Christmas surprise, but I would not, *could* not, let her see me crack.

"I say you're too good to me," I said, resolving to bring up later the fact that it's never a fun surprise for a woman to think she's being attacked in a deserted office.

"That's what I said!" Tabitha enthused.

"No such thing," Dr. Tim argued. "Come on. Wait'll you see the tree I got you."

We walked hand in hand to Rockefeller Center, sans Tabitha, and fought through the crowd to find bench space to strap on our skates. Never particularly coordinated to begin with, I was especially ill at ease when asked to navigate slippery surfaces. I felt certain that Dr. Tim was aware of this, as my awkwardness had actually brought us together.

"Are we sure the recovering ankle can take this?" I questioned as he knelt in front of me to lace up my skates.

"That," he assured me, "is taken care of." He pulled a roll of athletic tape out of his pocket and proceeded to truss me up. "You could not be better supported," he told me.

"Well, at least you'll be close by when I sprain the other one," I joked.

He kissed me very suddenly and then leaned back and gazed at me for a moment, as if I were a Hummel figurine.

"You're beautiful," he said. "You amaze me."

I blushed. "You're not so bad yourself. I can't believe you thought of this."

We skated for nearly an hour and Dr. Tim held my right hand in his and kept his left on my back the whole time. Around and around we went. I couldn't have fallen if I'd tried. It was the enchanted New York scene I'd always imagined. Afterward we sat in a Starbucks on Fifth Avenue drinking hot chocolate. Dr. Tim looked rosy-cheeked and content.

"I have something for you," he said.

"More?" I thought guiltily of the scarf, which was still sitting, unwrapped, in a plastic bag on my dresser. I quickly considered pleading Judaism and insisting that we dispense with gifts altogether, but that would have meant being denied my own gift and I admit I couldn't bear not to find out what he'd gotten for me. Besides, sale merchandise wasn't returnable.

"It's just a little something," he insisted, reaching into his inside coat pocket and producing . . . *a little blue box.*

Most women dream of the Tiffany box. I panicked. Immediately. All I could hear was Tabitha's voice in my head saying, *"LONG TERM . . . finally got it right . . ."* I could feel myself turning green.

Dr. Tim must have seen the fear in my eyes.

"It's not a big deal. Really. It's little."

I didn't reach for the box. He took my hand, palm up, and forced it on me. I just held it and hoped it might crawl away.

"Liza . . . are you going to open it?"

There was nowhere to go. "I . . . of course! Yes! I'm just . . . this is so . . . you really shouldn't have."

"It's not a big deal," he said, "and I wanted to. You make me want to."

So I opened the box, shaking, barely looking inside, but feeling my fingers come to rest on . . . a keychain.

"It's a keychain?" I didn't mean it to be a question.

"I didn't know what you'd like, but . . . you have so many keys . . ."

It was sterling, of course, and engraved with my initials. Not too personal, but it came in the blue box, which was obviously the point.

"I just wanted to do something special," he said. "This way I figured it would be close to you every day and . . . that store's really intimidating."

I was so relieved I could have cried. I looked away from him for a moment to take a deep breath, and I caught the eye of a teenaged girl sitting two tables away. She was maybe fifteen, awkward in the way of certain teenaged girls who don't yet have any idea who they might become. She sat with her two pretty friends and their boyfriends, who barely noticed her, and she'd been watching us. She'd been watching a handsome man offering a blue box to a lucky, lucky woman, a woman who was made graceful and beautiful by his very attentions to her. She smiled at me, and I could not, I would not, tell her that it wasn't real, that some of us weren't made to play this part. So I smiled back.

"It's beautiful, Tim. Thank you."

Because it felt good to be that woman.

"You really like it?" He was so sweet. And he wanted so much to please me.

"I really love it. You're the best." I kissed him. I took him back to my place and made him wait in the bathroom while I wrapped his scarf. And then I put on fancy underwear because I felt bad for making him wait in the bathroom, even though I'd just cleaned it.

I was right; he loved the scarf. At least he said he did. Actually he said, "Liza, I love ..." and then he paused, ominously, before adding, "this scarf. I love it." I threw myself at him to avoid further conversation on the subject of things we loved.

Sometimes we all just need to be reminded of our lines.

"Think of it this way: if it's the end of the world, they won't have time to write about how you screwed up."

CHAPTER 19

PERHAPS SOMEWHERE INSIDE my brain there is a defect, an imperfection, that makes me work against my own joy. This New Year's Eve was supposed to be a departure from the traditional regret-generation festival I create annually. Why? Because all the parts of myself that I depend on, the parts that are independent and stubborn and uncompromising, had been wrestled to the ground by the part that jumped up and down and giggled that I had a boyfriend. Supposedly, when you have the rare boyfriend, all of those awkward, unbearable social obligations that usually make you feel dull and inadequate become opportunities to capture Kodak moments. Even if you won't recognize yourself in the pictures.

I had convinced myself that, all my doubts aside, Dr. Tim's mere presence as my New Year's date would make the evening delightful. And then he had to work.

Still, I was okay. My boyfriend had to go save lives; how could I bitch and moan about that? I would snag a couple of friends, a little cheap champagne and some ice cream, sit in someone's apartment and have ring-in-the-new-sex when

Dr. Tim got off work, just so I could say I had. But no, too easy. Useless Jeremy was planning to ignore the holiday completely, and Parrot, who was by this point preparing Kirk for introductions to her family, had committed her New Year's Eve to him. I was out of options. Then an invitation arrived.

Maybe my work had made a good impression or maybe it was Dr. Tim who prompted her, but Tabitha had invited her two old roomies to the awfulest New Year's party in New York. How was this possible? Did she not have any friends? Or was she just inviting everyone she knew so she could show off her fancy new apartment? Jeremy and I immediately disintegrated upon receipt of our engraved invitations. I flew to the closet to summarily dismiss all of my clothing as inappropriate, while hapless Jeremy sat on the couch hugging himself and muttering things like "We'll tell her we have Ebola. We wouldn't want to infect the other guests. Yeah, that's it." But of course we knew she wouldn't buy it. We'd just have to go.

I called Parrot to arrange an emergency Anthropologie expedition.

"Liza this is fucking amazing do you even have any idea how cool this will be?"

"Clearly I do not."

"Ohmigod do you not realize that Kirk worked with Tod at that money banking thingy until Tod got totally fired which I guess is so sucky and that this is the party we're going to I am so glad you're going because I was thinking it was going to suck because who are these people I mean Tabitha sure which only confirms that it's going to suck but now you're going and you can bring Jeremy and we can all get completely fucked up and trash their place I mean I was thinking I would have to take Kirk up to the roof and have sex just as the ball was dropping in order to amuse myself but now I won't even have to."

It's really the simple pleasures for Parrot.

Nonetheless, we hit the stores and I acquired an absolutely devastating cleavage-baring black dress that would nicely highlight both Tabitha's sizeable ass and Dr. Tim's huge regret at working on New Year's Eve. Parrot ended up trekking to Barney's for a blue sparkly thing that barely covered her ... well, anything, and we began to prepare ourselves for the social ambush that would be our holiday.

Oh, what an ambush it was.

I would be lying if I said the place wasn't humbling. Tabitha had managed to sink her claws into a man who would keep her in the style to which she was accustomed. As long as Tod-with-one-D didn't squander his sizeable trust fund at the track, I had no doubt they would be very happy. It's amazing how grown-up an apartment can look when your coffee table is made of wood and your drinking glasses aren't from a Sunoco football promotion circa 1987. Jeremy and I couldn't help but be slightly ashamed of our humble abode.

T&T Marriage Factory had actually shelled out for caterers, liquor included, and though we felt horribly out of place and slightly depressed from the word go, there were some perks to this shindig. Lonely Jeremy got buzzed early and I would occasionally spot him fumblingly flirting with some of Tabitha's gal pals from the museum (I tried to impress upon him the horror of waking up with one of Tabitha's friends, but alas ...).

I spent most of the evening drinking, glued to Parrot's side, quietly regretting my decision not to fake my own death the day before and deflecting the rare advance from men who looked wrong in casual fashions. Tabitha, glorying in her newly elevated status as a non-single woman, spent the entire night sweeping through the party, giving a disingenuous pinch to every arm she passed and only occasionally bothering to talk.

"Liza! Parrot! Kirk! Fabulous! How are you! Don't you love this! It's such a fabulous opportunity to reflect on how lucky we all are! Liza! Where's your doctor friend?!"

I explained that he had to battle death for the sake of the innocents that evening.

"Too bad! That's okay though! Being a good partner is about making sacrifices! Just don't you let him get away!"

The thought that I was depending on her for my livelihood made me start on my third glass of champagne.

At about eleven forty-five, Parrot abandoned me to pull Kirk into the bathroom, whiskily whispering the words "blow job" as she breezed by; apparently she still intended to ring in the new year with a bang of one kind or another. So I had still managed to be standing alone at a lousy party on New Year's Eve.

Briefly.

"Well, look who it is. Did somebody order a Vagina Monologue?"

Pure dread shot through my entire body as I realized that apparently the second tier had made it to the engagement party after all ...

"George."

When, oh when, would I learn this damned formula? It was like his mission in life was to prey upon every vulnerable moment I had.

"You remembered my name."

"I remembered your smirk."

Just what I need. Standing here alone. Damn you, Parrot, and your blow jobs too.

"You're looking festive," he said with a sweeping glance that felt surprisingly like being groped.

"Is that a compliment?"

"Let's say yes."

"Aren't I flattered."

"Aren't you?"

Why? Why did he have to be there? Why could I not just

enjoy a lonely, awkward New Year's without him sneaking up on me in his nicely tailored and very flattering striped shirt?

"I'm surprised to see you here. This doesn't seem like big enough fun for you."

"It's not, actually. But I was told there would be a lot of hot women."

"I trust you're not disappointed."

"Enh."

What does that mean? WHAT DOES THAT MEAN? I waited for him to revisit the Night of the Enormous Genitalia or having to save my bigmouth brother from being pulverized, but he went another way.

"So how's the ankle? No limp?"

"No, but the night is still young. You could always try to hail me another cab."

"Sorry, doll, that one was all you."

DOLL??!! What were we, in some sort of teen gangster movie? I looked around for Richard Grieco.

And George was right, which naturally made me want to die. The worst part of sitting with him in the emergency room for three hours had been the nasty unflattering redness that wouldn't leave my face. I suddenly began to panic, wondering what sort of fool I was going to make of myself this time. Fate can be cruel.

"What can I do for you, George?"

"I didn't know you were interested in trying. I haven't given it much thought."

Ever since he'd learned about Dr. Tim, there had been a sharpness in his tone. As though he wanted every barb to sting a little. This would have been a really good time for me to keep my mouth shut until I figured out how to gain the upper hand. A really, really good time.

"You know, actually I should thank you. I met the guy I'm seeing the night that you left me at the hospital."

Hah! And it just came to me. Did his ears just redden or did I dream it?

"Mental patient?"

"ER doc."

"How NBC. Guy at your show, right? So where is he?"

Shut up.

"Oh, he's working tonight. You know, emergency rooms get really busy on holidays."

"Sure."

"It's too bad. You should really meet him."

"Why is that?"

Good point. Why is that? So you'd leave me the hell alone. So you'd be jealous. So the two of you could have a really big fight over me. Because I hate you. Is it possible to go insane very, very quickly?

I noticed Tabitha flitting about making sure everyone had champagne. "Almost midnight!" she chirped.

"Liza?" George asked.

Midnight.

"Hello? You in there?"

Not really. *Get away,* I thought. *Get away now. Don't be standing here at midnight.*

"Oh, yeah! I think—it's really hot in here. I'm going to go get some air."

I moved toward the balcony off the living room.

"I'll go with you."

Don't. Oh, please don't.

I slipped through the glass doors. It was surprisingly quiet outside, which didn't make things any less awkward. I kept reminding myself that across town a very sweet man was busy trying to medicate people and thinking, ostensibly, of me. So what was I doing on a balcony uptown with this guy I couldn't stand?

George stood next to me, leaning on the railing looking toward the East River.

"New Year's is really hard," I said. Great. I was simpering.

"That thing people always say about how you should spend the stroke of midnight doing whatever you want to do for the next year," he humored me.

"I hate that."

"Me too."

The glass muted the beginning of the countdown, but by eight we could hear them chanting.

"Five! Four! Three!"

We stood there. Silent.

"Two!"

Oh, no.

"One!"

I kissed him.

"HAPPY NEW YEAR!"

I kissed him.

He kissed me back. Like I hadn't been kissed in a long time.

Oh. No.

My cell phone rang three times before I noticed it.

I broke away and fumbled through my tiny little evening purse to get it.

"Hello?" I was sure I sounded panicked.

"Happy New Year, babe!"

Oh, no.

"Tim!"

"You having fun?"

"Yeah. Yes."

"It's busy here, I can't talk. But I miss you."

You do?

"Liza?"

"You too." It was all I could manage.

"I'll see you tomorrow."

"Okay."

"You sound a little drunk." He laughed.

"I am, I guess." Not drunk enough, though, to justify what I'd just done. George was looking down toward the people shouting on the sidewalk.

"Well, go have a good time. And here's to being together this time next year. G'night, Liza."

"You too. Night." I snapped the phone shut as if Dr. Tim could actually see me through the display screen.

George looked at me. Without the swagger this time.

"Happy New Year," he said, and then he got that slightly amused look again.

"I have to go." And I bolted. I just left. Maybe he chased me and maybe he didn't. I was in a cab in what seemed like seconds and I didn't look back.

It was nothing. Yes, there was a rush. It was exhilarating kissing George, the way it is when you jump out of a plane. But there was just as much potential to crack my head open on a rock. Dr. Tim was like a soft place to land. No sharp edges. No risk. You just don't throw someone like that away.

*"When the smoke cleared the next morning,
we realized it had been a wonderful party.
They rebuilt the house."*

CHAPTER 20

New Year's Resolutions for Elizabeth Weiler
1) I will go to the gym at least four times a week.
2) I will clean the bathroom on a regular biweekly
   schedule.(Resolution long overdue.)
3) I will do all that is in my power to merit Dr. Tim's
   overwhelming affections.
4) I will finally discover and take the necessary steps to
   make my career take off.
5) I will not kiss nasty, arrogant misanthropes.
6) I will not have impure thoughts about infantile but
   well-dressed overachievers.
7) I will not fuck this up. I will not fuck this up. I will
   not fuck this up.

WHY DO I EVEN BOTHER to write these things
down?

The sex with Dr. Tim was definitely improving. Sort of.
Yes, I was slightly thrown by his unwillingness to do it anywhere but the bed. Yes, I thought his three-position reper-
toire could use some work. Yes, he developed a weird, giant

grin during the big moment. But so what? It wasn't bad. And besides, relationships don't always start with great sex. Sometimes that takes time. I read that somewhere and it sounded totally believable.

Certainly it was unacceptable to be comparing the sex I was having with Dr. Tim to the sex I was imagining having with George. I would be lying if I said guilt played no part in my renewed commitment to making it work where I was.

Especially when I remembered how incredibly soft George's lips were. When compared with his incredibly hard chest. Oy.

On the upside, like manna from heaven, Aunt Fran had landed in New York again.

"Lock up your boyfriends," she croaked into my phone. "I'm back." I would have rushed to her apartment uninvited had she not sensed something in my voice and immediately arranged for our usual table at Café des Artistes. The sight of her gold-plated Zippo on the table told me that one way or another, help was on the way. Somehow, Aunt Fran is the only person still allowed to smoke indoors in New York.

Beneath the comforting murals of frolicking wood nymphs I explained the situation. Everything. Dr. Tim. George and the kiss. My embarrassing position with Tabitha and the mockery and demise of my first real play. By the time I finished ranting I had downed a good two-thirds of the bottle of Red Zin we'd ordered. I think Aunt Fran gets me drunk to lower my resistance.

"Liza, what have I always told you?" she demanded.

"The best way to get over a man is to get under another one?"

"Yes, and thank God you listen when I talk. But not what I'm thinking of. Men are like pasta. You're supposed to throw them up against a wall until one sticks. You made a rookie mistake. You allowed a novelty fuck to turn into a three-month commitment. You don't want to marry the doctor.

You want to screw the doctor in the hospital supply closet. Which you should do. But good Christ, get the idea out of your head that you're supposed to light your own pilot. You should be running through the streets of New York rubbing up against as many men as possible until one of them generates a spark. Learn from the example of your friend Cockatoo. Not a brain in her head but she's got tits and instincts."

Parrot and I got drunk with Aunt Fran once, or, more to the point, Parrot and I got drunk and Aunt Fran defied the laws of nature, failing to be affected by seven G&T's in a three-hour period. (Don't try this at home unless you're a leathery old crone who once peed on Jackie Onassis's petunias during a garden party.) Needless to say, they bonded.

"You know what your problem is, Niece?"

"Tell me. Please tell me."

"You think too much. Liza, my dear, life is all about what you want and what you do to get it. Do you think I gave careful consideration to going home with Gregory Peck? LBJ? The '67 Dodgers? No! I went! I flew! I followed my heart and my loins and my raging passions! And look at me now; I'm 116 years old and not a regret in the world."

Aunt Fran is miraculous, but she has no understanding of the average human being's insecurities. "Aunt Fran—"

"Liza, you're my favorite member of the family. And you're flushing your finest years down the toilet. It breaks my fat, black heart to see you squandering your youth doing piecework in sweatshops and squeezing your great soul through the cheese grater of one forgettable affair after another."

"It's temp work, Aunt Fran, not piecework, and right now it's not even that—"

"Whatever it is! It's sucking your glorious life away! Now, what the hell are you going to do about the doctor?"

"I don't know."

"Get rid of him."

"Aunt Fran, you don't understand—"

"Believe me, my girl, I understand men. I understand that he's sweet and he's kind and he's going to make somebody a fine, safe husband, but do you know who she's going to be, Liza? Someone who stays at home and makes soup while the men go off to battle. You're a warrior, Niece! You want to run into the fray with your spear in your hand and the man you love screaming alongside you with his face painted blue and his hair streaming in the sun!"

I prayed that she had just been sent a script for the *Braveheart* sequel and had not finally begun to crack up.

"Have you ever considered the possibility," I asked quietly, "that that's you and not me?"

"No!" She slammed her fist onto the table and I jumped with the silverware. "No, my young friend,"—she stared me down—"I have *never* considered that. But as long as you do, you'll be a slave to your fears. You need to live more like you write, Niece. Like Georgia Allen."

"Georgia Allen gets wiped off the map because she makes stupid decisions."

"Georgia Allen gets real, wild love, even if it's only for a moment. If you could be half as naked and exposed as those people you put onstage ... You think getting your heart broken is the greatest tragedy in the world? Try going through life without ever letting anybody touch it. You'll reconsider."

Her expectations were so unfair. I shouldn't have been less of a person for being cautious, for not acting like I was some kind of damned superhero. I didn't want to discuss it anymore. We sat in silence until I couldn't take it. Her disappointment was too painful.

"I sent the play out," I finally said. "To the New Manhattan Playhouse development series and a couple of other places." When I'd finally begun to pull out of my post-disaster shame, I realized I had a choice. I could either accept defeat, or I could try to get *Georgia Allen's Window* done again, and done right.

"That's my girl!" She brightened immediately. "Courage! The universe rewards bravery, Liza, in ways you may not expect."

"I don't know what's gonna happen . . ."

"Something will happen, Niece. Even if I have to swoop in and change your world like the fairy-fucking-godmother I am."

"You're not my fairy godmother, Aunt Fran."

"You'd better hope I am, Niece. Frankly, you could use it."

*"Just once, do something truly stupid and
then roll around in the consequences."*

CHAPTER 21

P ARROT CALLED the following Wednesday, hysterical over a cut in her allowance. Parrot is one of the
few people over the age of eighteen who still receive an allowance.

"You know when you just have to have something or
nothing will ever be the same so I went in and I tried them on
and the salesman was hitting on me but I told him to go fuck
himself it was totally not appropriate because he wasn't even
cute and was like completely middle-aged but anyway I gave
the woman my card and she freaking cut it up!"

"Jesus, P. Have you been paying the bill?"

"Ohmigod I don't even get the bill my father gets the bill
and I called him and I was like what the hell and he goes you
ran over your limit again and I was like what limit you never
told me what it was and how was I supposed to know it's not
like I spend that much."

We were watching a hockey game downtown the other
night, and Parrot bought a round for the *entire* bar when the
Islanders won. Infamous for her senseless acts of frivolity,
she had our dorm re-carpeted sophomore year because the

pile made her toes itch. Though she picks up the occasional print-modeling gig, I've never known her to hold down a real job. She mostly goes to the gym and redecorates her apartment over and over. I have to admit, this is a huge obstacle to the harmony of our friendship. I could spew my romantic woes at Parrot for three days straight and she would never tell me to shut up, but being low on cash or needing to pay the rent are foreign concerns for her. She'll just change the subject to something she finds more interesting, like the resurgence of leggings or where ylang-ylang comes from.

The thing is, though, she's like a human roller coaster; yes, sometimes you feel a little sick to your stomach, but if you just throw your hands up and scream it's more fun than almost anything else. And she gets me. All the things I don't put on display, Parrot somehow sees. She can cut through my bullshit, size me up and explain me to myself in ways that almost always make me feel like I'm going to be okay. A friend like that you just have to humor once in a while.

"Do you think maybe you should start paying attention to money, Parrot?" I ventured.

"Oh I so completely do so I was talking to this girl in my building and she was saying how she works at the Rainbow Room and lots of offices have their Christmas parties in January because you know December gets so busy and everybody's having parties like I totally went to sixteen of them or something this year so anyway a bunch of girls quit after the holidays but they still need people and it's just a couple of nights a week and all you do is check on people's coats!"

"You mean check them? You're talking about working coat check," I suggested.

"Whatever you get all dressed up and it's super-easy and you make like three hundred dollars a night do you want to do it with me?"

An extra three hundred dollars a week would allow me to cut my Tabitha time in half. Although a part of me wondered if I'd be able to swallow being treated like the help by much more successful, better-dressed people my own age.

"This girl said sometimes you get free champagne!" Parrot added hopefully.

On the one hand, I knew I was going to resent it. On the other hand, three hundred dollars for a night's work hanging out with my best friend. Not surprisingly, Parrot and the three hundred dollars won. I told her to count me in.

By the following Wednesday, the Rainbow Room had two plucky, new coat check girls. Penny, our supervisor, met us as we stepped off the elevator. Penny was short and slightly dumpy and gave the impression of teetering constantly on the edge of total breakdown. Parrot immediately rubbed her the wrong way with too many questions about pee breaks and free drinks. We were stationed in a largish, carpeted room with four enormous banks of hangered racks and a big paneless window that looked out onto the corridor. It wasn't exactly my dream job, but I have to admit it was a little thrilling to glide across the ballroom and over the revolving dance floor. Even if we were just on our way to the coat check room. We pretty much laughed our way through the evening and walked with enough cash to buy Parrot some more shoes.

Back at my day job, Tabitha had put aside misgivings about "your slightly odd proportions" and assigned me to try on seven different bridesmaids' dresses, take photographs and bring them back to the hive for her to peruse. Apparently the bridesmaids all had more important things to do. Some days I just felt like the rent-a-friend. I enlisted my reluctant roommate to tag along with the digital camera.

"Am I suddenly your woman-friend?" ruffled Jeremy demanded. "We actually had sex once. When did I become your shopping buddy?"

"Please, J-Dog! Please, please, please! I've barely seen you lately! It'll be fun. And I could probably be convinced to use some of my coat check money to take you out for Cuban food afterward ..."

"I can't believe you're using food against me. Fine. Sold. This is why I never get laid."

Jeremy helped me to brave three highly intimidating midtown bridal salons and bore up stunningly well under the lacerating gazes of various shopgirls. They had probably never seen a zip-up hoodie before.

It was a painful and boring exercise, trying on seven ugly pink dresses, and I thought sadly of the women who were going to have to shell out hundreds of dollars to wear them for one night. Then I realized they were Tabitha's friends and probably deserved worse.

"So how's the lurve doctor?" Jeremy asked me later that afternoon. We were strolling along Houston, happy to be back on the Lower East Side, where no one looked at us funny.

"He's fine," I said. Jeremy seemed to be waiting for something more.

"Just fine?" he pressed, and gave me one of those I-know-what-you-did-last-summer looks.

"Don't silently judge me. You know I hate that."

"I'm not judging. I'm suspecting."

"Suspecting what, exactly?"

"You spent months mooning over this guy and telling me how terrific he is ..."

"Yeah, so ..."

"So now you're all official and couply and I'm getting radio silence."

"Well." I felt instantly defensive. "You know how it is. In the beginning it's really exciting and scary and then you just kind of settle down and live your lives. Anybody in a long-term relationship will tell you that."

"You've been dating for less than three months."

"So?"

"So, nothing. Tell me more about this George kid."

"Like what? There's nothing to tell. George is an arrogant bastard who once took me to the hospital."

"And came to your show and spent an evening following you around Tabitha's party."

"Who told you that?" This made me nervous.

"You told me." He laughed. "Have you not noticed that you bitch about him all the time?"

"Well, it was really irritating. *He's* really irritating. I'm just hoping I can avoid him."

Jeremy sputtered an incredulous laugh.

I stopped walking. We were standing outside Katz's Delicatessen at the exact spot where the sidewalk smells like pastrami.

"Why don't you just take a dried salami and beat it out of me?" I asked.

"I don't think I have to." He smiled. "Wanna get a drink?"

"Let's make it three."

We sat down in the afternoon quiet of a little bar on Ludlow Street and I told him the sordid tale of the party and the kiss. (Though perhaps I suggested that George had initiated.)

"You didn't sleep with him, Liza."

"But it's cheating! It's extracurricular necking and it's wrong! Do you know how angry I would be if Dr. Tim kissed some other sprained patient?!"

"How angry?"

Good question. I tried to picture it. Dr. Tim and someone else. Kissing. Groping. His hands all over her. It made me feel . . . not much of anything, really.

"You're a guy," I said. "How would you feel if you were dating a girl and she kissed someone else?"

"I'm sure I'd feel pretty shitty about it. If I knew."

"You don't think I should tell him, right?"

"Of course not. Absolutely not. My point," he continued, "is that you really haven't done anything so, so bad. It's a kiss. And as you've said, you never want to do it again. So what's the problem? You were drinking, he was drinking. He kissed you!"

Not exactly.

"What if I kissed . . . back?"

"So you kissed back," he went on.

"What if I kissed front?"

"Liza."

"Yes?"

"You kissed a guy who isn't your boyfriend," he recapped with a withering glance. "You're a grown-up. It's not the kiss."

I took a giant swig of Pinot.

"It's not?"

Of course even I, master of self-deception, was starting to feel forced to accept the fact that this wasn't about the kiss. It was about the dreams—every other night I was rolling around with George even as I slept next to Dr. Tim. And the waking fantasies, the ones where I ran into George and he was compelled to kiss me again and maybe we wouldn't be able to stop and then maybe I'd have to break up with Dr. Tim because it would be only right.

Jeremy downed the last of his Yuengling. "You'll do the right thing, L-Train. You always do."

Jeremy is an extraordinary friend, and I sometimes regret the fact that we're not more attracted to each other.

Dr. Tim stayed at my place that night, and as we were getting ready for bed he noticed the dress I'd worn on New Year's Eve hanging on my closet door.

"Doing a little shopping?" he asked.

"Oh, no, I just picked it up from the dry cleaner's." All the perfumes of India, etc.

"When did you wear that?"

"That New Year's party." I kept my back to him while I took off my watch.

"Wow! Now I'm really sorry I missed it."

I laughed weakly.

"So why don't you model it for me?" he asked. I was down to my bra and underwear. "Do a little runway show." He chuckled.

"No, it . . . it needs a special bra and I don't even know where it is. It won't really look right."

He smiled. "You women. You crack me up." Who says things like "You women"? If we got married, would he refer to me as "The Wife"?

We got into bed and I tried to find the place I'd left off in *The Power Broker.*

"I'm going to get you a bookmark," he said, and he slid his hand up the outside of my thigh.

"I don't like bookmarks."

"Yeah, but that's an enormous book. How do you remember your place?"

"I just do."

"Yeah, but sometimes—"

He pulled back the sheet, leaned over and began to kiss my stomach.

"—it helps—"

More kissing.

"—to be reminded of where you are."

He lifted his head and knocked the book out of my hands and onto the floor, where it landed askew with a thud.

"Shit," I said, and lurched to retrieve it.

"Sorry."

"The cover's all mucked up now." It was bent in half.

"It's not so bad."

"I borrowed this." It was just Jeremy's and already ferociously abused.

I was clearly doing a seriously poor job of disguising my annoyance, and Dr. Tim looked confused and wounded.

"I ... I'll replace it if you want," he said.

I felt guilty.

"No. No, it's fine."

"You just looked so cute sitting there with your little glasses on your head."

He grabbed me by the hip and pulled me closer. I extracted said glasses from my head and put them on the nightstand. He looked deeply into my eyes and said, "You know, for a time there I was starting to wonder if I'd find a lady I really wanted to be with. Now I don't have to wonder anymore."

He kissed me, softly, gently and suddenly ... I wanted to get the hell out of there. There was the *"long term"* again, stretching interminably before me like some kind of passionless purgatory.

That night, let's just say Dr. Tim was coming and I was going. To tell the truth, I was already gone.

"Nobody said it would be easy,
but they did say there would be an open bar."

CHAPTER 22

J ANUARY WAS DRAWING to a close, and Parrot and I had our last coat check gig on the thirty-first. I guess nobody could justify throwing a holiday party in February.

I stepped off the elevator that night in my customary little black sheath and heels, trying to compose in my head the speech I would make to explain to Dr. Tim why we couldn't have a happy ending. Miraculously, Parrot had beaten me there and was already in the coat check room chatting animatedly with Penny. I had only an instant to wonder what the problem was before I noticed a stack of table tents in Penny's hand. I had to blink to be sure I was really reading the words *Turnbull-Prince*. My stomach lurched. This couldn't be happening. This could not be George's company Christmas party.

Parrot noticed me and motioned me over. "My boyfriend's with the company that's having the party," she was explaining to Penny, "and he's kind of an important guy so I might need to leave the coat check room to go be with him if he wants to like show me around and introduce me to some people, okay?"

Penny looked Parrot up and down. "I'm sure your gentleman friend will be empathetic to your working conditions
and not try to take you away from your station, Miss
Piccione."

"I'm just saying if he does—"

"I'm sure it won't be a problem, Parrot," I interjected, desperate to change the subject and explain to Penny that I
wouldn't be able to work that night because I was about to
hyperventilate. Just as I opened my mouth, a loud crash
sounded in the other room and several of the busboys began
to curse. "If they broke more fucking dishes!" Penny shouted
and bolted for the kitchen.

I wheeled on Parrot. "Did you know about this?" I demanded.

"No I mean I knew Kirk had his party tonight but I didn't
know it was here isn't it totally completely crazy aren't you
excited?" she shrieked.

Excited? I was ready to heave. No, this had to be a bad
dream. Yes, I had imagined a thousand different ways of running into George, but not one of them involved my handing
him a plastic number and hanging up his probably delicious-
smelling coat! I had to get out of there!

"Can you believe she talked to me like that?!" Parrot had
clearly not registered the magnitude of humiliation that was
about to shake my world.

"Parrot Irene Michelina Piccione, do you realize what is
about to happen here?"

"What?" she asked. I couldn't believe she could be so very
inattentive to detail.

"What?" I mimicked. "What? Who is coming to this party,
Parrot?"

"Big suity money people and my boyfriend."

"Who else, Parrot? Who else? Who else is coming to this
party? I'll give you a hint: nothing to do with you and a shit-
load to do with me!"

"I don't know what you're—ooooh!" She got it. "Oh you *do* like him and you're gonna see him tonight and we're trapped in a cage and that's a problem right?"

"Right."

"Right." Finally she looked appropriately sheepish. "Sorry."

"I can't see him like this, P. I cannot be his coat check girl. I need an ounce or two more dignity than that. Why didn't you warn me? I have to get out of here before he sees me."

"That's a really good point oh Liza I'm so sorry I didn't think about that and now you're stuck in here and you're going to be totally humiliated and it's all my fault I just only thought about myself again I always do that my father is always telling me I shouldn't do that damnit I'm so really really sorry what can I do to fix it?"

Just as infants are born cute so that we'll feel compelled to nurture them, Parrot has an unbelievably endearing pathetic quality when she is truly contrite. I find it almost impossible to stay angry at her when she gets the puppy-dog eyes.

"It's not your fault," I told her. "I'm just freaking out. Tell me you'll forgive me if I leave you here to do this by yourself?"

Like a perfect sound cue, we heard the ping of the elevator as a car approached our floor.

"Hide!" she squawked at me.

"Where, exactly?" I hissed.

We scanned the nearly bare room.

The doors began to open and Parrot leapt to the window and kicked me behind the knees. Before I knew it I was on the floor.

"Happy belated holidays!" she tweeted, clearly pleased with her brainstorm. "Can I take your coat?"

I rubbed the back of my knee where she'd caught me with her pointy toe. She totally missed the slightly resentful stare I was shooting up at her.

"Not him." She smiled down at me when our first customer had moved on.

"Great," I replied. "I can just spend the entire night on the floor and everything will be just fine."

"See?" she squealed. "I told you I'd fix it."

There was nothing to do but wait; I couldn't risk running into George if I tried to leave. A steady stream of guests was already starting to teem past our window. I slumped there for half an hour as Parrot plucked coats from a torrent of dressy investment bankers. No sign of Kirk or George, and thankfully no Penny. It was quickly becoming clear, however, that if I didn't get off the floor soon I would have carpet marks for a month. This was not a permanent solution. I prayed that he would just get there already and end my misery.

Though I despaired, Parrot's little brain was virtually smoking with her efforts to brainstorm me out of certain humiliation.

Finally, as she was determinedly applying a very heavy and very expensive-looking beaver wrap to a hanger, Parrot squeaked and briefly became airborne.

"Okay I know what to do!"

I was skeptical. "Go ahead. Thrill me."

"I'll go tell Penny that you're allergic to fur and that with all these fur coats you're breaking out in hives so she better take you down the service elevator or it'll look really unprofessional!"

"That's very sweet, P. But I don't think she'll buy that."

"No no it'll totally work I promise I'll just be a sec."

She began to trot for the door, but I caught her by the ankle.

"PARROT," I hissed. "What exactly am I supposed to do while you're off busting me out of here, huh? What if somebody, *somebody*, comes to leave a coat? What exactly will I do then?"

"Just pretend you're not here I'll be back so quick they'll only have to wait a sec and besides I wanna see if Kirk is here yet I'll be right back!" She thrust the check stubs she was holding into my free hand, shook me off and slipped out the door.

"Parrot, wait!" I called after her. This was just like Parrot, just like her to get me into a situation and to run for the hills exactly when I needed her. I crawled to the door and poked my head out in hopes of retrieving her before she got too far, but she was already out of sight. Feeling vulnerable and alone, I had just begun to shimmy my way between the now-crowded racks toward my "post," when I heard him. There was no question it was George. My heart began to beat too fast and I ducked into the middle of a rack between a hand-some double-breasted camel and a navy cashmere.

"Hello? Is there anybody in here? Coat people? Hello?" It was Kirk.

"Good help is so hard to, ah ... find." George chuckled.

Shit. Shit. Shit. Shit. Shit.

I was trapped. I could not have been more trapped.

"Right, yeah. I think I'd really like to leave my coat now." The stakes always seem so high for Kirk.

"Anybody there?" George called. "Anybody at all?"

"Okay, so what do you think we should do?" Kirk asked.

"I don't know what you're going to do, but I'm going to hang up my coat," George answered.

What was he talking about? What the hell was he talking about? How was he planning to hang up his coat when there was nobody at the damned coat check?

This was when I heard the unfortunate sound of a manly, tuxedoed form hoisting itself onto the ledge of the coat check window. And a pair of handsomely shod feet dropping to the ground *right in the room with me.*

I tried with all my might to avoid breathing.

"Oh, George! What on earth are you doing?"

Woman's voice. WOMAN'S VOICE! WHO THE HELL WAS THIS WOMAN? WHO THE HELL WAS THIS WOMAN AND WHY WAS SHE WITH GEORGE? WHAT EXACTLY WAS GOING ON HERE?

More importantly, why was I not focusing on the immediate problem of my imminent and humiliating revelation in the coatrack?!

"Let's see ... hanger, hanger, free hanger ..." I could hear George's footsteps moving down the aisle toward me.

"Crowded in here," he mused. "Come on, I just need a couple of—" He stopped. He was so close I could hear him breathing.

For one agonizing moment I thought maybe I would get away with it.

*"If you're going to have a public tantrum, do it
in a ball gown. And preferably in black and white."*

CHAPTER 23

WELL, WELL, not so empty in here after all," he said
cautiously.

Then he yanked the coat out from in front of me.

And began to laugh. Hysterically.

"Oh," I said. "Hi."

"What in the hell are you doing here?" he choked through
a chortle.

"Just . . . hanging out?" I ventured.

"This is the funniest thing I've ever seen." He couldn't
stop laughing.

This was just exactly the reaction I would have hoped for
upon being spotted. Uncontrollable laughter. I am truly a sex
symbol.

"Please complete my evening and tell me you're the coat
check girl."

I looked down and realized I was still clutching the check
stubs. There was no way out.

"No, I'm a coat."

He chuckled, but the old smirk had settled in.

"And a lovely coat you make. That's quite a dress."

"Thank you." I prayed for the aliens to come and take me away.

"If I throw you over my shoulders will you keep me warm all night?" He was clearly so proud of himself for this one.

From outside, the woman's voice again: "George? What's going on in there?" She sounded pretty.

"Umm, gee. That's a tough one." He grinned at me. "Would you care to explain?"

Before I knew what was going on he had taken me by the hand and was dragging me down the aisle toward the window.

"Look what I found!" he exclaimed. "It's a girl!"

Kirk was standing there looking mildly dazed, as was his wont. And beside him, standing about six feet tall with raven hair (I now understood what people meant by "raven hair") that appeared to be blowing though there was no wind, was the woman with the voice.

She may have sounded pretty, but she wasn't. She was stunning. She was a fucking vision. She was exactly who I'd pictured George with.

"Eliza!" Kirk smiled. "Great to see you! How come you were hiding in the coats?"

"Liza Weiler, Dominique Fahrenstadt."

"Pleasure," she purred, and took my hand.

"Absolutely." I tried to lower my voice and ended up sounding like Bea Arthur.

"Eliza, why were you hiding in the coats?" Kirk had latched on to this question like a mongrel on a veal chop.

I was so red by this point that Penny probably would have believed the whole hives story. (I could have killed Kirk, whose utter inability to add two plus two was to blame for this whole situation. Who wouldn't put it together that his girlfriend was working at the restaurant where his office was holding its Christmas party?) I opened my mouth to answer the question, but George interrupted me.

"Liza left something important in her coat."

This was not what I'd expected from him.

Dominique eyed me suspiciously.

"Wait, Eliza, so is Parrot here too?" Kirk started in again, the engine in his tiny brain whirring into action.

"If you have everything you need now, Liza, we were going to head for the open bar. Care to join us?"

"Sorry, I have to go kill myself" didn't seem like an appropriate answer, so I said, "Sure." In the moment, the fact that I was about to be out a night's tips and very possibly ejected from the party seemed oddly unimportant. I had never seen George in a tux.

Roughly fifteen minutes had elapsed since Parrot had abandoned me, so I was somewhat surprised to see her huddled in a corner with Penny, deep in some serious and obviously heated conversation. Parrot's fists were balled up at her sides, which I recognized as her fighting stance. I gathered Penny cared little for my fur allergy.

George, who had taken Dominique by one arm and me by the other, also spotted Parrot.

"Hey, Kirk, isn't that the ball and chain over there?" he piped up.

Kirk spotted Parrot, in her barely-dressed finery, and made a beeline.

If I had felt relatively attractive when I set out that evening, my ego was receiving a sound check from the head-snapping that Dominique engendered. She reminded me of Kim Cattrall's arch nemesis in *Mannequin,* the one James Spader wanted so much to sleep with. Obviously, she was perfect for him. George, not James Spader.

If everyone on the dance floor was staring at Dominique, I was neglecting the extraordinary city views to steal glances at George. I found myself wondering if everyone saw how handsome he was, or if maybe I was under some unfortunate spell.

"So, ladies," George inquired when we encountered a

waiter, "what are we drinking? Dominique, I know, will have champagne. Liza?"

"Highland Park. Neat," I said, wishing I could just order the bottle.

"That sounds like a fine idea." He looked pleased. "We'll do two of those," he told the waiter, who bowed and scraped toward the service bar.

Dominique kept looking me up and down as though at any moment I might turn to ash and blow away. Which, it seemed, would not displease her.

"Dominique works with me in mergers," George explained.

And we have wild sex on my desk.

"You can't tell by looking at her, Liza, but she's a shark."

Yeah, I could tell.

Our waiter returned with our drinks. "Thank you, my good man," George told him. Christ, he was pretentious. I could have sworn that Dominique growled at him when she accepted her champagne.

"So, Liza, was it?" she purred. "How is it you know our George?"

The possessive was not lost on me and I seemed to detect a hint of an ambiguously European accent.

"We have mutual friends."

"Actually I rescued Liza from a crippling injury and she's been unable to stay away from me ever since." He grinned at me.

"How lovely," Dominique replied. She couldn't have been less moved. "And what do you do?"

"I'm a playwright."

"Really? Again, very lovely." Now I was starting to feel patronized.

Suddenly I saw Penny charging at me from across the ballroom, with a seething Parrot behind her and poor, addled Kirk hot on their heels.

Even from a distance I could see that Penny was half-shrieking and half-muttering, but only when she drew near could I make out what she was saying.

"THE COAT CHECK IS EMPTY! THERE IS NO ONE AT THE COAT CHECK!!"

Ah, yes. I'd forgotten about that. I supposed that was something of a problem.

"Miss Weiler. Miss Weiler! What do you think you're doing? This is not your station!"

Penny's accent had thickened with her rage. I was clearly about to be dressed down in front of George's towering and haughty date, not to mention the rest of the Turnbull-Prince guest list. The people around us were starting to notice.

"I'm sorry, I—"

"I don't want to hear 'sorry,' Miss Weiler! I don't want to hear 'fur allergy,' I don't wanna hear vomiting, I don't wanna hear it! There is one thing I want, Miss Weiler, and that is to see you dragging your overpaid butt back to the GOD-DAMNED COAT CHECK!"

Dominique looked vaguely amused and slightly nauseated. Even Parrot stood helpless and Kirk still seemed to be working on why I had been found in a coatrack in the first place. I could feel my face turning from red to eggplant. This would have a lovely time for the revolving dance floor to speed up and catapult me out a window. I couldn't look at George.

"Excuse me." Apparently he wasn't feeling quite as shy as I was, as I realized he was talking to Penny. "I think maybe you want to think about your tone."

Whoa. What exactly was he doing?

Penny seemed to have the same question. "My *tone?* Excuse me, Mr. Fancypants, but I'm conducting some business here. So maybe you want to think about backin' the hell off."

Oh, this was going nowhere good. Parrot drew closer. Kirk leaned in. I did look at George then, and he seemed as though he might burst into flames.

"You've been very rude to a young lady who is here as my guest, and I think we'd all like to hear an apology now."

"Your guest? Five minutes ago she was my freakin' coat check girl and now she's your goddamned guest?" Penny practically bellowed.

This was all absolutely, unquestionably my fault. Why hadn't I just owned up and checked his coat like a normal person? Who did I think I was kidding? In comparison with my current horror, it seemed like nothing at all.

"I don't know who you think this hooch is, but I'm guessing your money could buy a notch up, you little prick."

Penny had every right to be angry with me, but now she was attacking George. I moved to defend him, but he put a hand on my arm. He wasn't looking at me. His eyes flashed at Penny and he took a step toward her.

"If I were you," he said, so quietly that we'd all have had to strain to hear him, were we not already rapt, "I would be far more concerned with my own funds, because if my friend doesn't hear an apology, you're going to be looking for a new job, Ms. . . ." He bent forward to look at her nametag. "Penny, is it?"

No one spoke. I thought one of them might clock the other, and Penny looked like she'd throw a mean left.

Or maybe she'd just burst into tears and run from the room. Which was, in fact, what she did.

Only a moment earlier I'd been ready for George to flatten her, but now that he'd actually gone and done it, I felt nothing but guilty, stuck and mortified.

The small group of onlookers saw that the show was over and quickly dispersed, leaving me, George and Dominique. Parrot and Kirk attempted to join us, but she saw the look on my face and decided she'd rather investigate the buffet than be dinner herself.

I wondered if I should try to find Penny and apologize.

"Unbelievable," George muttered.

"You certainly handled her." Dominique tossed her exquisite tresses and smiled at him.

Suddenly I was furious. "Tell me why exactly you felt it necessary to do that?"

"What?" George was taken aback.

"Where do you get off decimating a person in public like that?" I felt rage spinning in my gut for reasons I couldn't even explain. He just did this, over and over again, came to my rescue, looked into my eyes and it was like having someone step inside me. And there I was, breaking rules, hurting people, losing control over someone who just thought I was an amusement. Fine for an appetizer maybe, but I only had to look at Dominique to know I wasn't the main course.

"Are you kidding me?" He was shocked, I could tell.

"She was just doing her job," I insisted.

"I was standing up for you!"

"I don't remember asking for your help!"

"You sure as hell needed it!"

"What I needed was the three hundred dollars you just cost me, which is why I was here tonight in the first place!" I couldn't stop.

Dominique stood by looking bemused. This woman's natural facial expression was that of a Victoria's Secret model at the end of the runway. She seemed constantly to be staring down her bra with disdain.

"Oh, right, because you're a starving artist. I forgot. Is that why you were so quick to leave your 'station' and trot out here with me?"

"I shouldn't have come out here with you," I returned. "I should have been working. Which is what I was being paid to do. Some of us actually work for a living."

"Hey, I work my ass off."

"I'm sure you do. And from the way you throw money around, George, I'm sure you're handsomely compensated

for it. I'm sure that accounts for your unthinkably conde-
scending and demeaning behavior toward poor Penny."

"Poor Penny? Poor Penny was standing here calling you a
whore! Next time, I'll just stand back and laugh with everyone else. Would that make you happy?"

"Thrilled!" I spat.

He stepped toward me. "Will you please lower your voice?
And maybe consider just telling me the real reason you're
upset?"

Dominique chuckled.

"You are unreal." I wanted to evaporate. "Maybe you
should be paying some attention to your date, hmm?"

"My ... Dominique? Is that why you're being such a pain in
the ass?" He laughed. I could have socked him in the jaw. "Oh,
my God, Liza, you really have no idea what's going on here—"

"Nor do I care." I had no intention of listening to any
more. I shot my Scotch, turned on my heel and with as much
dignity as I could muster, strode out of the ballroom.

He didn't try to follow me.

I wanted to find Penny. I wanted to apologize for behaving
like someone so completely unlike me and to tell her I was so
sorry that she had been embarrassed in my stead. But the
captain of the waitstaff told me she'd knocked off early. I
scribbled a quick note and left it with Penny's assistant. I
knew I wasn't getting my money, but I hoped she'd at least
know I felt horrible. Not that it would matter.

I had no idea where Parrot had disappeared to and I just
wanted to get the hell out of there. I swung past the coat
check, but another girl was there and happily raking in the
tips. I grabbed my own coat and ducked into the ladies' room
on my way out. Parrot could fend for herself.

Standing at the mirror, applying a fresh coat of glossy
Chanel lipstick which would no doubt leave marks all over
George, was Dominique. She chuckled at the sight of me.

"You were very angry." One minute she sounded German and French the next.

"Yeah. Mostly at myself."

"So you were supposed to be taking the coats?"

This was like the sixth ring of hell. There was no escape. The evening was just going to go on forever.

"Yes, I was supposed to be taking the coats."

"Hmm. Our George, he is a maker of trouble."

"Yes. Your George is."

"You have been ... lovers?" she probed.

"No! No. Never. Definitely not."

"Ah ..." She flashed me a foxy smile in the mirror.

"Really. Believe me. He's all yours." Why was this woman torturing me?

"May I call you Liza?"

No, you exotic bitch, you may not.

"Of course."

"Mm, Liza, I think you do not have an understanding of this. George is my partner in work."

"No, I do understand. What, is it a secret? Don't worry. I wouldn't even begin to know who to tell."

"I think you still do not understand. If I were to find a lover this evening, I would prefer it would be you."

Umm ... what?

"Excuse me?"

"Men are not my interest."

I didn't have a clue what to say.

She continued. "So there is not a reason to be so angry at George. He is very fond on you, I think."

"Of me. And he's not. He's just obnoxious."

"Hmm. Perhaps. But you care very much for 'just obnoxious.'"

"I don't care for it at all, actually. He was very cruel and he had no reason."

"You were the reason, yes?" She snapped her purse shut

and turned to go. "You are a very beautiful young woman. If you ever finish being angry with George, I would welcome you to be angry with me sometimes." She chuckled. "And I know it is not my station to say, but men who are very hard outside I think are very soft inside. Maybe you have been too 'cruel' also?" She growled another throaty laugh and departed.

Grateful to be alone for a moment, I stared at my reflection and tried to take a deep breath. Dominique was right. George had cornered me and I'd been cruel. He just made me feel so transparent, like everything I felt was written across my face. I couldn't let him think that I wanted him.

I gathered what little I could of my wits, and left the ladies' room, hoping I could make my escape undetected.

I should be so lucky. Directly in front of me, coming out of the men's room, was George.

I froze. He froze. Neither of us spoke. Through my shame haze I couldn't help noticing that he still looked incredibly dashing.

And disgusted. Incredibly disgusted. With me.

Without a word, he turned away and started toward the ballroom.

"George, wait!" I said.

He stopped, his back to me.

"I'm sorry. I know you were trying to help."

He turned around.

I wanted desperately to fly through the air and just kiss him. But I didn't.

"And?" he said.

"And ... and I hope I didn't cause you too much embarrassment."

"Mm-hmm," he said.

He didn't look any less angry. I didn't know what to do, but I couldn't leave things this way.

"Look, you and I, we really got off on the wrong foot. I'm

sorry, I get very... antagonistic around you. I owe you an apology for what happened on New Year's Eve, and I appreciate that you think we can be friends, but... I have this boyfriend I should get home to."

He laughed quietly and without smiling.

"You know, I think you've got the wrong idea," he said. "Because I have no interest in unavailable women. I don't need to work for it. And to be honest, even if you were single"—he paused—"you're more trouble than you're worth."

I concentrated very hard to keep the hallway from spinning as I watched him stride away.

"It's very easy for a nice girl to meet a nice boy, and damned difficult for the rest of us to get rid of him."

CHAPTER 24

I AWOKE THE MORNING after the party knowing I had to break up with Dr. Tim. I'd behaved like an infant the night before, embarrassed George in front of his colleagues, and certainly debased myself. But much worse, I could no longer deny that I'd been moving forward with Dr. Tim and all the while I'd been thinking of George.

Dr. Tim was such a lovely man and so good to me. But that thing that happens where you can't look somebody in the eye and you think about them all the time and annoy all your friends by working them into conversation at really inappropriate times ("Speaking of Ebola, Craig is so knowledgeable about antique brass.") . . . it wasn't happening for me. Because I knew how Dr. Tim felt, because I had begun to understand what he was looking for, I knew it was time.

I picked up the phone to call him that morning, hoping to arrange a time for us to meet so I could do the horrible deed.

"Hey, pretty," he answered, sounding all sleepy and sweet. I had a feeling I had awakened him but he would never have told me so. "How was your gig last night?"

"Oh, it was good," I lied. "How was your shift?"

"Not great." He yawned. "But it's a gorgeous morning, huh, gorgeous?" I pictured him lying in bed with the sun streaming through his window, completely unaware that I was about to zap him with a rejection ray.

"It is," I concurred. "So, what are you doing this afternoon?"

"I don't know," he said lazily. "You want me to come over and fix that curtain rod in your room?"

"Uh, no," I fibbed again, "Jeremy already did it. But I would like to see you."

"Well, I'd like to see you too"—I could hear him smiling—"because you know what today is . . ."

The day I secure my seat in hell? I said nothing.

"Today is the first day of February, which is the traditional start-date for the countdown to Valentine's Day."

OH. GOD. NO.

"And since somebody already got somebody a pretty terrific Valentine's Day present, I think somebody should be pretty excited. . . ." He chuckled to himself while my insides shriveled up in fear.

"Gosh," I said, a tiny quaver in my voice. "Somebody bought a present . . . already?"

"Well," he replied, "when you're thinking about *somebody* all the time, that's the kind of thing you do."

Somebody silently vomited on the other end of the line. This only made everything I was going to do more horrible. More insensitive. More ugly. I had to do it immediately, that afternoon. I couldn't wait another minute. I heard Dr. Tim yawn again.

"So listen, sweetie," he said, "if you don't mind, I'm gonna go back to sleep for a while and I'll call you when I get up, okay?"

"Oh," I answered, "of course. Sorry, did I wake you?"

"I just didn't get much sleep. This kid came in last night,

hit by a car. I worked on him forever. Didn't think he'd make it but the kid's a fighter."

Perfect. And when I finish dumping you this afternoon I'll stop and club a baby seal on my way home. Just for fun.

So I didn't see Dr. Tim that day. He was exhausted and not in a great mood and he later decided not to inflict it upon me. When we still hadn't gotten together three days later, I realized I was dangerously close to missing my window. Dr. Tim was bringing up Valentine's Day with nearly every conversation. I had no idea how to respond. I refused to be one of those horrible phone-dumpers, but really what the hell was I supposed to do?! When he had to cancel our date on Saturday to fill in for someone at the hospital, I knew I was screwed. Valentine's Day was less than a week away.

You just can't do that! As if it isn't hard enough to navigate the oppressive pink and red doom that blankets New York City from January 2 through February 14, one cannot be expected to survive a Valentine's dumping. Yes, I was ready to end the relationship, but maybe I was supposed to do some advance atoning. Maybe, I reasoned, I should attempt to give this really good guy the kind of Valentine he deserved. I had a lot to make up for. And then maybe I wouldn't have to feel so low.

All I had to do, I figured, was act normal for another week. Two weeks tops. I see now that this was a bad idea.

Nonetheless, in light of my decision, I was forced to reconsider my usual dismissal of V-Day as an evil plot of major advertising agencies designed to make us all feel lonely and consume horrifying amounts of expensive chocolate. I had to do something romantic, but not too over the top, to make Dr. Tim feel appreciated. (I also got caught up in the math of how long after the actual day I'd have to wait to have "the talk," but decided my head would explode if I thought too much past the fourteenth.)

I considered a visit to Victoria's Secret, but the thought of braving thronging crowds of desperate lingerie-seekers burrowing into enormous piles of panties and forests of negligees made me a little ill. Plus I didn't think it would pay to rub in how much I wasn't enjoying sleeping with him. So instead, I baked a cake. Okay, fine, a heart-shaped cake.

I missed most of the *Six Feet Under* I had On-Demanded while I concentrated on a perfect icing job. It was all I knew how to give Dr. Tim, and as I looked down at that sad, sugar-coated attempt at doing the right thing, I began to panic.

I knew my intentions were honorable, but is it ever fair to lure someone into a false sense of security by being nice? Dr. Tim was an adult. Maybe I was only being deceitful, again, by trying to con him into a day of happiness that I was only going to tarnish days later when I dumped him on his ass.

I called Parrot, who will always tell insert-name-here to roll over and amuse himself when a friend is having a crisis. She is also generally the best person to talk to in a romantic emergency, as she has learned scads from the completely loveless marriage of her parents. As she explained it to me, in 1971 when Nick and Arlene were wed it was really a question of "joining the two families." I never asked a lot of questions after that.

As usual, Parrot had voluminous advice.

"Liza you really need to learn how to relax and have some fun and you also need to realize that not everyone you date has to be like the best guy in the whole world and give you stories to tell your grandchildren but then again what's the point if you aren't crazy about him and he doesn't really get you anyway you know how sometimes you can really really like the idea of eating one of those giant Hershey's Kisses they make but once you're halfway through it you realize it isn't going to get any better and you know what it's all about and you'll probably get fat if you keep going but the point is that you've had enough to know whether you want any more and maybe that's how much you've had."

I was just about to burst into tears when the buzzer rang. I knew Jeremy would probably climb up the fire escape and tap on the window if he forgot his keys. So who could this be?

"P, I gotta go. Thanks for listening. Someone's here."

"Liza!" she said.

"Yeah?"

"Don't sweat it it's only a relationship."

The woman really has perspective. I have no idea what kind, but she has it.

I pressed the intercom and within forty-five seconds Dr. Tim was standing at my door, looking . . . like shit. I felt like Hot Lips Houlihan and here was Hawkeye, who needed comfort after a particularly grueling day of "incoming." Maybe my Valentine surprise was the right idea after all.

"I'm sorry to come without calling," he said.

"It's okay. Come in."

Thank God I had made that heart-shaped cake.

"I just really need to talk to you."

"Okay. Sit. What's going on?"

I get it. Big setup. Make me think there's something wrong and then whip out the Godiva, right?

"We have a problem."

Russell Stover?

"I'm not going to be able to spend Valentine's Day with you, Liza."

Good & Plenty?

"I don't think I want to see you anymore."

Oh, I get it! Dumping me?

"I'm sorry."

Definitely dumping me.

Then he just sat there and stared at me like I was going to burst into song or something. And he sighed. Twice.

"Have I missed something, Doc?" I knew I shouldn't quibble when he was making my life a thousand times easier, but the question was an honest one and I wanted the answer.

"I think maybe I have. I think I wanted to." He paused for dramatic effect. "You're so beautiful, Liza."

This was when I began to get irritated. (Followed by more staring and another sigh.) Yes, he was doing my dirty work, but in that moment I realized that it's always preferable to be the dumper rather than the dumpee.

"Tim, what are you talking about?"

"I think you know."

"No. No, I think I don't. Where is this coming from?"

"I've been doing a lot of thinking this week—I know you've probably sensed I was avoiding you and I apologize for that. Liza, when I met you, I felt like I'd been given a gift. You are so beautiful and funny and alive and you know what you want and you made me feel like something extraordinary was possible."

He quoted A Beautiful Mind*! OH, MY GOD! He quoted* A Beautiful Mind *WHILE DUMPING ME!*

"And I so want to be close to you, Liza, but I feel like I've hit a wall. You just won't let me in. I know that there is something so amazing inside of you, but I can't get to it. I want to be able to talk to you about how I feel and our love...."

Our LOVE? This had never been discussed. Not in any way that would entitle him to link the possessive pronoun "our" with the noun "love." His mention of love allowed me to ignore all of the very true things he said before it.

"Tim! Stop. I want to be clear. You're dumping me because you think I'm so wonderful and you want to be close to me?"

"I'm not dumping you, Liza! I have made ... overtures, in the past few months. You know I'm looking for a commitment, you know how I feel about you...."

"Tim, how is it you know how you feel about me after

only a few months? How could you know that?" I realized I
was asking because I really wanted to know.

"When something is right, Liza, and you're ready for it,
you just know. And I know it about you."

Suddenly I felt sure that what Dr. Tim knew had very little
to do with me. I'd barely let him scratch the surface of me,
and from day one he'd just been in love with the idea of having found someone. I wanted to be angry, except I knew I'd
gone along with it for reasons of my own.

"But you are dumping me."

"I don't like that word."

"I don't like that action." I had to stop myself from arguing
just on principle.

"Liza, I love you."

He looked at me and I knew I was supposed to say something, but I couldn't. I couldn't think of what to say.

"And you don't love me back."

Oh.

"Do you?"

Aiee . . .

"Do you?"

"I . . ."

"I just couldn't go through this Valentine's Day charade
knowing that. And I can't make you love me if you don't."

I felt really, really bad, but I also had to work very hard to
keep from laughing at his apparently unwitting pop culture
references.

He cleared his throat. He stood up. He kissed me on the
head.

"I think I should say goodbye now, Liza."

"Tim."

"What?"

Nothing. Just nothing. I couldn't find anything to say. So
he left. End of scene.

I looked at the clock. It was 12:09 a.m., officially Valentine's

Day. I had just been dumped on Valentine's Day. By someone I was too sheepish to dump *before* the day, let alone on it. This was clearly a new low.

So I did the exact right thing. I ate two-thirds of the heart-shaped cake and got so drunk that Jeremy had to carry me to my bed when he came home. I was single. Yet again.

And probably glad.

I wondered as I lay in bed the next morning with my very own heart-shaped hangover whether George had meant it when he said I was too much trouble. The ebullient hope that made me doubt it was warring with the wounded fearful part that thought maybe it was true. Maybe I was too much trouble.

Then again, who was better equipped to deal with it than the most obnoxious man I knew?

Like Aunt Fran always says, nothing ventured, nothing stained. It's dirty, but she has a point.

*"Some people just won't hold still long enough
to be gagged."*

CHAPTER 25

BREAKING UP WITH SOMEONE is like scoring poorly on the President's Physical Fitness Challenge. When I was in elementary school we had to do this inane annual testing in gym class to see how America's youth measured up. I remember sitting straight-legged with my feet against this wooden box and being told to reach forward as far as I could. Then the gym teacher looked to see where my eight-year-old fingertips hit on these stupid yardstick markings and with this scant information the government determined how flexible I was. Nobody explained to you that the testing really wasn't about you at all and that you were just going to serve as a fraction of a fraction of a percentage point in some weird children's fitness census that no one would ever address in any meaningful way. So you assumed that this was really important and that although you didn't recall using this box-reaching skill in daily life, if the President was concerned it must be important, and why couldn't you box-reach as far as other kids? What was wrong with you? Why were you such a failure?

Okay, maybe I took the President's Challenge too seriously. I can admit that. But the point, and I am getting there, is that when you break up with someone, no matter how much or how little you actually miss them, you just can't shake that feeling that you're failing at something that human beings are just naturally supposed to succeed at. Conclusion: there simply must be something wrong with you.

It wasn't that I missed Dr. Tim. If I felt a void, it was the void left by the lack of void left by Dr. Tim. But once again I couldn't do it. Couldn't make the magic or whatever it is that makes people walk around SoHo with their hands in the back pockets of each other's jeans. Plus, I had to admit to the unpleasant fact that for a short period of time I had become one of those people who would just rather be with someone than be alone, even when it obviously isn't going anywhere; I always swore I would never be one of those people.

To top it all off, my apartment had developed a smell. A weird, horrible, unidentifiable New York smell. A smell so horrific that I actually contemplated knocking on doors to make sure that none of the neighbors were rotting in their living rooms. Jeremy had been AWOL, dividing his time between grappling with the Once-and-Future Dissertation and playing grabass with his new paramour, Natasha, a Russian studies post-grad for whom he'd completely fallen at first sight. I had no one to share in my olfactory horror. What was worse, I believed I'd traced the offensive stench to my closet. Or to be more specific, to the wall behind my closet. Parrot insisted that a small rodent had curled up and died in one of my shoes, and we spent a shriek-filled evening gingerly picking up each boot and pump and then throwing it across the room to see if a carcass rolled out. None did and the mysterious odor remained.

I was completely alone in a stank crib.

For once, the idea of spending time in Tabitha's lair didn't seem so bad. At least it smelled good there. Around lunch-

time the Friday after Dr. Tim and I parted, I gathered my
courage and trotted down to the museum. I knew I had to tell
her sometime and I had prepared a concise statement regard-
ing our separation. I was going to explain that yes, Dr. Tim
was a wonderful man, but no, not all of us are looking to get
married in the next five minutes, and that he would no doubt
be better suited to someone who was seeking a more serious
commitment.

Tabitha was at her desk when I arrived, carrying a stack of
sample menus I'd recently retrieved from the caterer. She
looked up at me as I knocked on the doorframe, and before I
could get a "hello" out she was up and around the desk and
hugging me.

"Liza," she cooed. "Oh, Liza."

"Hi," I said, unsure of the reasons behind the warm welcome.

"I'm not going to say anything," she said, pulling back,
"but I think you know how I feel."

There was only one way she could know, and I really didn't
want to believe that Dr. Tim had called Tabitha for comfort.
But as we sat down to discuss the day's errands, she kept
looking at me like my puppy had died. I attempted to explain
the various menu ingredients and was about to ask her for
dates to set up the official tasting, when Tabitha reached
across the desk and put a hand on my forearm.

"I'm going to stop you," she said softly, still peering at me
oddly. "You don't have to be brave. I know. I know everything. He's very upset, Liza. If you want to salvage this thing,
now is the time."

He had called her. DR. TIM HAD CALLED FREAKING
TABITHA!

"Are you kidding?" I said, more to myself than to her.

"I'm not kidding," she answered.

"Tim called you to talk about our breakup?" I asked, still
incredulous.

"He needed to talk to someone, Liza. He's been struggling with this for some time and I have really been trying to diffuse the situation. Timothy is very ready to be married; he knew that I would understand and he knows that you and I are close."

OH, MY GOD. HOW WAS THIS POSSIBLE? He had been talking to her BEFORE we broke up?! What, did she help him plan it?! My outrage was immeasurable. I had to fight to control myself.

"Can I tell you something, Liza? It's okay to be afraid. And I know that you're terrible at relationships. But running away from a good man, the first good man I've ever seen you date . . . that's the wrong answer."

I stood up very suddenly and Tabitha's wedding binder slid off my lap and hit the carpet with a thud.

"Tabitha," I stammered, "I'm not discussing this with you."

He thought we were close? How had the man dated me for months and decided that Tabitha and I were close, HOW?

"I'm just saying," she continued, pitying me with every word, "that I don't think it's a lost cause! Now listen, I'm having lunch with him today, and I think I can lay the groundwork—"

"YOU'RE HAVING LUNCH WITH HIM?!" I hadn't meant to raise my voice.

"He needs me right now, Liza. He's just lost his best friend and he needs a female perspective. He's coming to pick me up—"

"Oh, my God," I said. "Oh, my God, I can't believe this. Oh, my God! I have to get out of here. Excuse me! I have to get out of here!"

"Liza! Liza, don't run away again!"

I fled from the echo of Tabitha behind me, begging me to stay and talk it over. If I'd had to sit there for another second,

I think I would have lost it. Dr. Tim's odd failure to recognize Tabitha's basically offensive nature was always a mystery to me, but now they were having lunch?! In an odd way it all made sense: Tabitha's gooey, marrying life was exactly what Dr. Tim was looking for. But I couldn't take the idea of the two of them sitting around a table for two hours eating *salades niçoises* and dissecting my failures as a girlfriend. Theirs would be the kinship poached from a failed relationship, the kind people laughingly describe with lines like "Dating her was a disaster, but I got such a good friend out of it!" It made my stomach turn. I needed to get the hell away from Tabitha and Dr. Tim and their weird nuptial vision quest. Too afraid that I might run into him if I went back, I called Tabitha from my cell phone and told her I couldn't work for her anymore.

I arrived home that night to realize that I hadn't even made plans for the evening. I winced at the stack of bills in the mailbox and realized I'd just been a hotheaded jerk to quit my job with no other option in sight. Exhausted, I didn't even have the energy to go to the video store and nothing good was on cable. I tried to sit down to work at my laptop, but I had an e-mail from my brother saying he'd gotten a weird e-mail from me and that he thought I had a computer virus. Which was just what I needed. I shut the computer down with disgust, vowing to deal with it later. As if it weren't bad enough having no social life, I couldn't even get any work done. I was officially in mourning for my life.

I called Aunt Fran. Weeping.

She had a date.

"Listen up, Niece. Proceed to the corner liquor store. Buy yourself a bottle of scotch. Something decent. And keep in mind that scotch, like men, is at its most useful between the ages of eighteen and twenty-one. Spare no expense; I'll write you a check. Put on something pretty. Call Parakeet. You have yourself an opening cocktail and then you proceed to the nearest respectable gin joint and find yourself a good old-fashioned one-night stand. And stop blubbering, your fairy godmother is on top of everything."

Oh, dear God. This was exactly how I felt when I was seventeen and Aunt Fran made me take a condom to the prom. I knew that that condom wasn't going to come out of my beaded purse and I was right. I wasn't a get-laid-after-prom kinda girl. Obviously, very little has changed.

I contemplated taking her advice and calling Parrot, who would probably invite me to join her wherever she was, but the thought of dealing with her irritatingly durable romance just didn't appeal. Lately, Kirk was everywhere Parrot was, like a whiny, blond reminder of the fact that even my completely bonkers best friend could make a relationship work.

But at least the drinking part seemed worthwhile. I headed for my local Wine and Spirits and brought home a fellow named Glen who promised to deliver a passable evening.

Note to self: when having a tough day, don't drink alone. Past the point of pleasant drunk but not so inebriated that I wanted to sleep, I determined that I could take control of at least one aspect of my disordered existence. It might be a Friday night, I might be high and dry in the sex department, but God Almighty I could still clean. The horrific smell of dead something had grown so pervasive and offensive that I believe I actually considered taking a hammer to the wall and extracting the offending party come hell or high water. Thankfully I was not terribly efficient at this point and managed to forget what I was doing before I located the toolbox.

But I did maintain my cleaning vigor long enough to commit to ripping everything out of my closet. I always seem to have so much clutter and so little to wear. What better opportunity to separate the wardrobe wheat from the chaff? I'm ashamed to say I put "Hey Ya!" on repeat and began to go down the rack, removing anything I hadn't worn in ten months, and trying on old favorites. I was delighted when, during the *"all you Beyoncés, and Lucy Lius"* part, I came upon my full-length red sweater coat. As I twirled it off the hanger and began to toss it over my shoulder, I realized there was a problem. My full-length red sweater coat smelled worse than anything I could ever have imagined. Worse than the cheese I once left forgotten on top of the fridge for three summer weeks. Bad. Noxious. Horrific.

So I very sensibly dropped it into a repulsive heap and went back to the hanger to investigate. There I found what can only be described as the diarrhea of a very small creature. And I noticed that the two hangers to the right of the original had similar smears and a few hairs. That was when I saw it. First it looked like fringe. Then I noticed it had an ear. And another. It was shriveled. It had been dead for quite some time. And it stank.

I might be the only person in the history of the world who's had a mouse, doubtless demented from the effects of some hideous poison, crawl up a full-length red sweater coat, shit violently over an eight-hanger span and die, morosely clinging to the shoulder of a corduroy blazer.

I was admirably calm, considering the situation. I spent just two or three minutes jumping up and down and screaming "Dead mouse!"

My next problem, I soon realized, was removal. I called everyone I knew. No one was home. Only the dead mouse and I saw fit to spend a Friday night in my bedroom. I would have to get rid of this thing myself. I threw out most of the clothes it had touched. There was really no question of salvaging three shit-stained dresses that stank of death. But I couldn't get the actual mouse hanger out of the closet without removing its occupant first. Problem.

I was smart. I put a plastic sandwich bag over each hand and repeated the soothing mantra "ew" over and over. I then attempted to imagine that my right arm was not attached to

my body and pried the rigor mouse off my jacket, quickly
flipping and tucking it safely inside the bag as my father had
taught me to do with dog poo.

I was proud. I wanted to vomit but I was proud.

This was when the doorbell rang.

I don't know why I raced to answer it. But I did. And
standing there looking quite pleased with themselves were
Parrot and Kirk.

And George.

George who hated me but was suddenly standing at my
door.

George.

With his tie loosened and his jacket slung over his shoulder and a couple of buttons on his shirt undone. And his
wavy hair. And his beautiful brown eyes. And his smirk.

It occurred to me then that I was standing there drunk,
with a shit-smeared dress caught around my ankle and a
stinking dead mouse bagged in my right hand.

Who wants to be me? Show of hands.

"I met my first husband after I'd been knocked unconscious. I liked the way he handled the situation and he liked the way I looked prone."

CHAPTER 26

REMEMBER MURPHY'S LAW? They're renaming it for me.

Why? I ask you, why me?

Keep in mind, Parrot is a lovely, highly entertaining young woman. But cool in a crisis, she's not. She never means to make it worse, but damnit if she doesn't always find a way. It took Parrot approximately .03 seconds to take in the sight of me holding a dead mouse in a plastic bag and the smell of shit-stained death.

And then she booted.

It stunned me, in the moments following, to realize that I had been thinking the situation could not possibly worsen. But then there's really nothing like the feeling of being relatively clean one moment and covered in your best friend's vomit the next.

Lucky me, they'd been out for Mexican.

Parrot's retching ushered in a moment of the most epic quiet I have ever experienced, like the whole city was observing a moment of silence in memory of my dignity. Parrot used the combination of her own shock and guilt to create a truly new facial expression. Kirk looked stupider than I've ever seen him, and I suddenly had a vision of what a useless husband he might someday make. I couldn't look at George, whose doubtless irrepressible disgust would be written all over his sharp-jawed face.

But George did the last thing I could ever have expected. He started to laugh. George started to laugh this wonderful uncontrollable gut-wrenching laugh. By the time he began to slump down the wall I heard someone else laughing. It took a moment to realize it was me. There I was, holding a dead mouse, smelling like crap, and sporting a thin film of regurgitated burrito, with tears streaming down my face from laughing so hard.

Sometimes that's all it takes to fall in love.

Kirk and Parrot completely failed to see the humor, which I found totally mystifying. But we all thought it prudent that I advance to the bathroom to clean up (no small task) while George cracked open Jeremy's emergency bottle of Maker's Mark. I do like a man who knows how to take charge and mix drinks.

I showered, and by the time I reemerged my unexpected houseguests had done a fairly comprehensive cleanup. Parrot, who must have felt bad for throwing up on me, had actually put my room back together and separated the salvageable clothes from the mouse-stink clothes, conveniently tying the latter up in a Hefty bag.

Had I been less tipsy at this point I might have put on some real clothing, but for some reason it seemed appropriate, in my drink-addled brain, to don a bathrobe over my cutest bra and underwear. I don't really know where I thought this was going.

George, who burst out laughing once again when he saw me, was sitting in my living room for the first time. And I liked it. It was perhaps for this reason that I failed to refuse the first drink he poured for me. I seem to vaguely remember expressing my thanks for the third, but everything is somewhat blurry after that.

During my shower, Kirk had apparently grown a funny bone, and was now unstoppable.

"Oh, my God, Eliza. That was so hilarious! You're like, standing there with a—" (and here he dissolved into laughter) "—and then Parrot's like—" (dissolved again) "—and I was just like 'SHIT!' You know?"

Parrot herself had rinsed her mouth and regained the ability to speak.

"Liza that was like the most fucked up thing I have ever seen 'member that time we were watching *The Godfather* and the horse head thing happened and my uncle was like yeah that totally happens and I spit out my Twinkie all over the floor this was like way worse than that ohmigod I totally puked all over you I can't believe it thank God you weren't wearing anything good otherwise I would feel way worse and you should prob'ly just buy new clothes to replace the vomit clothes when you're buying new clothes to replace the mouse clothes 'cause I don't think you should ever go near anything that smells like that can I have more Maker's?"

George drank quietly with his usual smirk, occasionally interjecting a comment like "So, has anyone seen Stuart Little? I hear he's been reported missing."

We had a brief flare-up when he asked me if Dr. Tim had dumped me because of the smell of my apartment. I shot Parrot a dirty look for her big fat mouth.

"It's possible," I quipped, "although I think it was this weird idea he had that I was kissing other men."

Why exactly was I bringing this up? Oh, yes, I was riproaring drunk.

"Really? Did you kiss a lot of them?"

"Mostly frogs, as I remember. The occasional serpent offering apples, but I'm familiar with that scene." I get stupid and pretentious when I'm drunk.

"I had no idea you were so popular," he said smugly.

"Yes, you did. You're just too nasty to admit it."

"When was I nasty?"

"You know."

" 'Nasty' escapes my recollection."

" 'Even if you were single, you're more trouble than you're worth'?"

"Wow, you really pay attention when I talk." Smirk, smirk, smirkety-smirk. "And by the way you scored some 'nasty' points yourself."

Even through my tipsy haze I remembered owing George a significant apology for the sharp-tongued harangue I delivered at his Christmas party.

"Um, yeah. I really . . . I took it too far. I'm sorry."

"It's okay."

"No, I mean it, I was completely out of line. Sometimes I get hurtful."

"Apology accepted. Just don't disappear me like you did that poor little rodent."

"You're pushing it, ass-boy."

He cracked up. "I'm sorry, did you just call me 'ass-boy'? Is that an expression?"

"Would you just shut up and drink your drink?" I couldn't help laughing.

This was when I noticed Parrot and Kirk staring uncomfortably as I poured another drink. The last thing I clearly remember was George asking me if I thought I'd ever be allowed into the Magic Kingdom again. If I was still forming words clearly at this point, I couldn't tell you what they were.

Nor could I pinpoint exactly when I passed out.

When I opened my eyes I was staring at a reddish-looking mountain in the distance. It took my brain a minute to place my surroundings. And then I realized it wasn't a distant mountain at all. It was a nipple. And it was about two inches from my face.

Fabulous.

It wasn't the nipple's fault really. Because I was apparently sleeping on the chest to which it belonged. The surprisingly hairy and thankfully masculine chest. This was when I noticed my robe hanging open. Even in my sleep I'm not particularly ladylike. I've never been so glad to be wearing underwear. I was too afraid that moving would wake the person attached to the masculine chest and thought that was a poor idea, at least until I figured out who that person was. And while I hoped upon hope that it was George, somehow the idea that I had had sex with him during an alcoholic blackout and would therefore a) not remember it and b) probably never get to do it again was just too depressingly like my life.

But he was, I noticed, wearing pants, which made unmemorable sex seem less probable. At this point I had to get up, if only to put some more clothes on before he regained consciousness.

Yes, I had spent the night sleeping on George's naked chest, which had a wet spot, where apparently I'd been drooling. I didn't feel like somebody who'd made out with an extremely foxy man the whole evening and I definitely didn't feel like somebody who'd had sex with him all night. But the whereabouts of Parrot and Kirk and George's shirt were a total mystery. I did feel like someone with a serious hangover as the fragile amoeba in my skull sloshed violently when I picked up my head.

George's head was slung back over the arm of the couch, and he emitted the slight piggy snore that becomes inevitable when you sleep with your mouth wide open. I was tempted to stand there and take in the fact that he was actually sleeping in my apartment, but I didn't get the chance.

When the key turned in the lock I assumed it must be Jeremy, completing the walk of shame after a night of academic debauchery. Jeremy and I go way back, and while I would not have been thrilled at the state of affairs, this would not have been nearly the worst scene he'd ever walked in on. (When we were in college there was an unfortunate frat-boy blow job in the living room.) This was why I didn't throw a shoe at George and bolt from the room. Also, if I had tried to move that fast my brain might have spilled out of my ear.

Had I recalled that Aunt Fran had a key to my apartment for emergencies, had I imagined that she would ever use it, had I formed even a hint of an idea that a person could have two horrifying, door-opening embarrassments in the course of twenty-four hours, I might have attempted to do something.

Ah, hindsight. Aunt Fran was not alone.

"Humiliation is good for the soul.
As long as there are no photographers."

CHAPTER 27

EVERYONE DREAMS OF meeting their idols, right? I met one of mine standing hungover in my underwear with a half-naked man on my couch.

By the late '90s, the name Kito Lopez had become synonymous with "groundbreaking theatre." Before turning twenty-eight, Kito had won two Obies, opened six plays off and one on Broadway, been on three *Time Out* covers, and dated most of the men on most of the New York–based soap operas. Certainly, if you had a brilliant voice, the last decade of the 20th century had been a good time to be a Japanese/Jewish/Latino gay playwright, but Kito had played his cards better than most. He was brilliant. He was one of the reasons I had decided to write plays.

He was standing in my foyer looking at me like I was nuts.

When Aunt Fran decides she's going to do something, she does it immediately, if not sooner. Aside from being the only woman I know who can say with authority that a young Hugh Hefner was sloppy with the tongue, she is the only one who could have convinced Kito Lopez to buy brunch for his potential new assistant before he'd even met her. As I was about to discover, that new assistant was supposed to be me. Well, maybe.

After Aunt Fran stopped cackling (the long interlude had given George time to spring up off the couch) she said, "Niece! I can't believe you. Leading me to believe you're not getting any when it seems you've bitten off a nice big hunk. Look out, young man, biting runs in the family. Kito! This is Liza. She's going to make your life a lot easier. And clearly you have similar taste. Liza! Say something, inspire some confidence."

"I forgot you had a key." Oh yeah, that made everything less awkward.

"Apparently." She smiled an evil smile.

Drawing my robe closed with one hand, I somehow managed to extend the other. "Mr. Lopez, I'm tremendously honored, and shocked, to meet you. Like this. Hi. Liza Weiler. Great to meet you. Assistant?"

"Kito needs an assistant. You need a job. Come on, people, it's not rocket science. But on to more interesting matters . . . hello, Shirtless! Have we met? Never mind, I'd remember."

"George Doren. You must be Aunt Fran. I've heard a lot about you."

Untrue. George hadn't had time to hear "a lot" from me about anything. What was he doing? And why was he doing it half-naked and with a great deal more style than I was able to muster?

"Wish I could say the same, darling."

"George was just . . . leaving. As soon as we find his shirt, which, frankly, I don't know why he isn't wearing at the moment. Of course I don't really know what he's doing here. Or why I don't have clothes on. So there we are."

I really know how to make a first impression.

To my great surprise and delight, this apparently earned Kito's respect. Or at least amused him, because he said, "Trust me, I said the same thing to my mother the first time she found me with a shirtless man. At least you're being congratulated."

George was smirking, obviously somehow enjoying this, which really made me want to knock him senseless.

"Why don't you find your shirt now, George, so you can *get going?*"

"Unfortunately, Georgie, my niece is just like me, love 'em and kick 'em the hell out when you're done. But since I haven't loved you yet, I'm still willing to take you to brunch. Why don't you join us? And I'm no stickler for the no shirt, no shoes rule."

Yes, George was definitely enjoying this. I, on the other hand, was willing myself to actually sink through the floor and into the apartment below. Facing the shock and dismay of the couple downstairs as I dropped through their ceiling would have been far preferable to this humiliation.

"Liza," George said with the most irritating grin, "my shirt's in the sink, honey. Don't you remember spilling your drink on me?"

So that was where the shirt had gone. But wait, *honey?* Even George wouldn't, simply couldn't, be low enough to try to masquerade as my . . . my . . . my what? Boyfriend?

"You see that, Liza? A man who doesn't mind getting wet. I like that." Aunt Fran was really useless in this particular situation. Here I was trying to scrape my splattered dignity off the wall of my apartment and she was practically emceeing a bachelor auction.

Before I knew it George was shaking hands with Kito Lopez and Aunt Fran was staring lasciviously at his chest and they were all suggesting that I snag one of Jeremy's T-shirts for George and hurry up and get dressed myself because Kito wanted to buy us all a round of mimosas.

Aunt Fran used to tow me down the street holding her hand when I was little, and every so often I would realize that if my tiny legs ceased churning frantically for even a second,

I would be lifted off the ground and go flying out behind her like a wind sock. She is constantly pushing the bounds of trust.

Trust or no trust, Kito Lopez had a hankering for the warm banana bread at B Bar, and whether it was the glow of Kito's genius or that of George's grin, our table was cozy and bright. Aunt Fran chatted away with George as though they were old friends and Kito seemed totally unfazed by our inauspicious meeting. He kept asking me how George and I had met and whether he was good in bed. Despite my lingering shame, I figured I'd better turn this conversation toward the professional or waste this opportunity altogether.

"So," I broached the uncomfortable subject, "Aunt Fran mentioned you're looking for an assistant . . ."

"Well, I wouldn't say looking," he said. "Your aunt is a little . . ."

"In your face?" I offered.

"Up my nose, doll. I gotta be honest, I don't need an assistant. Assistants are so . . . I don't know. I would feel like Elton John or something. I write plays. They're exceptional, yeah, but it's not like I need somebody following me around and making lattes. You don't make lattes, do you?"

"No lattes," I admitted.

"Too bad. I might actually have gotten over the Elton John thing."

I understood Kito's position, but I also knew that Aunt Fran has tremendous intuition and she never would have brought him over if she didn't think there was possibility here. I decided to push, gently.

"So, tell me," I asked, "the daily life of a Tony winner? You probably have a couple commissions at once. How do you keep up with it all? The readings? The openings? The phone calls alone?"

"Honestly, it's a huge bitch. There are days, I'm like, leave me the hell alone, everyone, or you're not getting your damned masterpiece! Plus, you know, I'm curating this development series at the New Manhattan Playhouse, I do lectures, I am getting crow's-feet and it's terrifying."

"Sounds it," I concurred. "But I don't see them." I can suck up when I need to, and I couldn't help but remember that my play was sitting in a pile somewhere at the New Manhattan Playhouse, waiting to be selected or discarded. The more I talked to Kito, the more I understood I needed in.

"So you, you're a writer, yes?" he asked me.

"Trying to be," I confessed. "Currently I'm a writer who temps, or a temp who writes or something."

"God, so where do you do that?"

"The temping? Actually I'm a little out of favor with my agency right now. I've been trying to figure out a better situation. Attacking my laptop for the first time at eight or nine o'clock at night doesn't always usher in the big inspiration, you know?"

"Oh, sing it, child," Kito agreed. "In my next life I'm gonna be independently wealthy."

"Look." I took a risk. "I'm just going to come out and say something I have absolutely no right to say, but my mother is always telling me I have a big mouth, so ... I know you don't think you need an assistant, but I'm incredibly smart and efficient and I'm pretty sure that I could pay your bills and make your calls and arrange your travel and make your life generally much easier. And you wouldn't have to pay me that much. But you'd be doing a really great thing for somebody who frankly wants to be you when she grows up."

Kito looked uncomfortable and glanced over at Aunt Fran for help, but she was touching George's arm and ignoring us.

"Liza, you're really sweet, okay? And I get it. I've been there. But this is just not meant to be. You know what I'm saying?"

I knew.

"I tell you what, though," he continued. "If you ever want me to read something I could give you some feedback."

I took a deep breath before saying, "Um, actually, I submitted a play to that reading series you're curating."

I waited for him to tell me this was a totally inappropriate conversation and that I was way out of line for bringing it up.

But he said, "Really? Hmm, okay, I'll take a look. I can't make any promises, but I can read it and I can tell you what I think."

My stomach flipped with joy and knotted in fear at the same time.

"That would be amazing," I told him.

"I'm harsh, doll! If it sucks, I'm gonna tell you it sucks. Are you ready for that? I will rip you a new one, I'm not kidding."

"Rip away," I said. And then prayed that I wasn't making a terrible mistake.

On the other side of the table, Aunt Fran and George appeared to be feeling no pain whatsoever. I didn't catch as much of their conversation as I might have liked (certainly I should have been doing some manner of damage control), but I did hear George complimenting Aunt Fran's performance in an old World War II drama with Gregory Peck that just happened to be her least known personal favorite. Of course those two got along. What Mary Kate and Ashley are to underage empire-building, Aunt Fran and George could be to flirting. They were old chums by the time we were through with our eggs, and I was shaken by how naturally our odd foursome hung together. George is the sort of man you could drop out of a plane anywhere in the world and he'd still look as if he belonged. Perhaps I flattered myself, but he seemed particularly to belong at my brunch table. He excused himself to head for the men's room and managed to put our entire brunch on his credit card before any of us could protest. And he didn't even smirk when we thanked him.

Kito leaned over and asked me if there was "room on that chest for two?" I blushed scarlet.

I'm pretty sure any of the three of us would have gone home with George if he'd asked.

Aunt Fran pulled me aside while we were waiting for taxis and whispered something like "Hang on to this one, Liza. With both hands."

Kito hugged me and said he was so thrilled to meet me, shoved a card into my hand with his studio address and said he'd talk to me soon, probably. "I will read! I promise!"

And then they were speeding away in a cab and I was standing alone with George, who was so pleased with himself I could have spat.

"Good news. I think the family likes me."

"I can't believe you did that. I can't believe you acted like there was something going on here...." And then I trailed off because I suddenly remembered that I couldn't. Remember. Whether anything was going on here.

George must have seen the look in my eyes because he got quieter and said, "Liza? You spilled whiskey on me so I put the shirt in the sink. And you were so drunk that I decided to stay and put you to bed when Parrot and Kirk left. But you passed out on me and after a while I fell asleep."

Oh.

Oh, nothing happened.

Nothing at all.

"I'm not that much of a shit, Liza."

"Sorry," I said softly. "I shouldn't drink like that."

"I don't know. I found it pretty amusing. You're meaner sober . . . , cupcake."

I smacked him on the arm. But I could barely keep from laughing with him.

"You suck, do you know that? My whole family's gonna think I have some mysterious boyfriend now. And I'll have to explain a missing T-shirt to my roommate."

"Nah, take it back. It's too tight on me anyway." With that he peeled the shirt off right in the middle of freezing-cold Fourth Street and threw it at me with that freakin' grin.

And then he just walked away. Shirtless, with his coat slung over his shoulder. I stood there, frozen, watching him go.

Halfway down the block he turned and shouted, "Hey, Liza! I'll be coming by to get my shirt back soon! Get ready!"

He grinned, turned the corner and he was gone.

*"We got kicked out of more hotels than you could
stay in in three weeks. He was an astronaut.
He'd been in orbit a long time."*

CHAPTER 28

THERE IS NOTHING quite so exquisite as the
period of flirting that falls between the mutual con-
firmation of affections and the consummation. If there
were an Olympics of flirting, George and I would have en-
sured that the Americans swept. We were good. God, were
we good.

I was as completely enamored as one can be with the
most intensely aggravating, sexy, young suit since Alex P.
Keaton (George is much bigger). Only three days after our
blissfully humiliating evening of whiskey and drool, he
e-mailed me.

From: g-doren@turnbullprince.com
To: lizalikearug@shinygun.com
Subject: If you've been sleeping . . .
. . . in my shirt, you might as well keep it up. Turnbull's sending me
to Tokyo on Friday for at least ten days. When I get back I'll teach
you about sake.

I replied promptly, but not too promptly.

From: lizalikearug@shinygun.com
To: g-doren@turnbullprince.com
Subject: Re: If you've been sleeping . . .
Have a nice trip. If you're lucky, the language barrier will work in
your favor. I'm familiar with sake.

Back at the homestead, I launched immediately into a considerable rant about how just when you find the man of your dreams he gets sent to Japan and really a relationship at this point of germination can't afford a ten-day stall and he'd probably find some absolutely gorgeous Japanese business whiz and be engaged by the time he got back and I would have to die without kissing him again but what difference did it make because I'd have eaten so much ice cream by then that I'd be immense and he wouldn't want me anyway and where was the justice in the world? This was when Jeremy emerged from his room to ask me if I had stolen Parrot's brain and would I please give it back immediately. The Once-and-Future Dissertation had hit a recent snag when unfortunate Jeremy's advisor had a nervous breakdown, and my roommate had been somewhat unforgiving of my idiosyncrasies as a result.

Although George and I very well might have maintained e-mail correspondence during his grand tour, we didn't. He was busy, according to Kirk, who claimed he wasn't getting a social word from George. The Tokyo merger was apparently so overwhelming that it was all George could do to get his DRs in on time. I nodded as if I knew exactly what the hell this meant, although my information was all filtered through Parrot, who could have been getting it all wrong anyway. I spent my free moments concocting terrible scenarios in which George attended orgies, met beautiful industrious women to whom I could never compare, was offered extraordinary positions that would require him to move to Tokyo permanently and then died in fiery plane crashes.

I finally cracked and sent a pitiful missive a couple of days before he was supposed to come back.

> To: g-doren@turnbullprince.com
> From: lizalikearug@shinygun.com
> Subject: hey
> You alive?

He answered the day after he was supposed to have arrived in New York, which was two days after I'd decided he hated me.

> To: lizalikearug@shinygun.com
> From: g-doren@turnbullprince.com
> Subject: Re: hey
> Tokyo is hell. No idea when they're sending me home. Hope you're well.
> George

"Hope you're well"? Oh, definitely the words of a red-hot lover. Hope you're well. Sure. Crazy about me. No question. Hope you're well. Fabulous.

I stewed. At length. I was certainly in no position to contact him further, which was infuriating, and all I could do was wait. And obsess.

Luckily, I had a whole other can of worms to fret about. I was unemployed, yet again. And solely to blame, yet again. It wasn't so cute to be without prospects for the second time in a year. I scanned the want ads for any job that looked even remotely appropriate, but so far it looked like I was qualified for either phone sex or unskilled manual labor. I was pretty sure I wouldn't be too good at either.

Kito Lopez called me the following Friday afternoon.

"I have read it," he said, without even helloing first. "I have read your piece. You have got something here, my love. I am excited. What are you doing right now?"

This was like having a bird tell you you'd done a nice job building your aircraft. I wanted to sing. I explained that I was picking up a barista application at Starbucks.

"Sit down and talk to me."

I did.

"You think it's okay?"

"Okay? Doll, are you listening to me? It's not perfect. You need to work with someone and do some rewrites. But you can do this. You've written a beautiful piece, and you've written a practical piece. Small cast, unit set, producers will love this!"

"It's not ... it doesn't have the weight that your work has."

"Liza, you're a white girl from the Gold Coast. A person can't manufacture a burning sense of injustice. You wrote a terrific, mature, fully realized, very moving piece about compelling people in a real dramatic situation. I am proud of you. Even though I barely know you."

"I don't know what to say."

"Say thank you."

"Thank you," I said.

"Alright, look," he went on, "I am going to do something for you. Because I wish someone had done it for me. I am going to risk everyone in New York thinking that I am a raving, pretentious queen, and I am going to get an assistant."

I was too excited to speak.

"You, doll, I'm talking about you."

"No, I know! I get it! I mean, thank you, Kito!"

"Call me Elton," he said. "I'll pay you twenty dollars an hour. We'll say twenty to thirty hours a week, provided HBO buys another screenplay this year. Can you live on that?"

I would find a way.

"It's just basics, alright? Filing, phone calls, booking my

appearances, paying the bills, keeping Lizzie Grubman out of my hair."

"You know Lizzie Grubman?" I asked.

"Oh please, I know everybody. This will be fun. I'll be writing, you'll be working. It'll be like *Will & Grace* except I'm really gay and you're not so annoying. So Monday? Ten or elevenish. My Pilates instructor comes in early so don't rush."

"I don't know how to thank you," I said.

"Don't thank me yet. I might hate this and then you're back out on the street."

"Deal," I said. With enormous relief, I tore up my application. I could never say *dopio* with a straight face.

"Face your fears like you've got vodka running through your veins. Here, I'll show you what that's like."

CHAPTER 29

THERE ARE TWO KINDS of people in the world: people who try new things, and people who watch other people try new things first so they can decide how they're going to approach the new things when they are eventually compelled to try them. For example, during after-school gymnastics in the seventh grade, Beth Flavin would always vault herself up onto the beam before the instructor could so much as ask for a volunteer to do a reverse triple death flip. I, on the other hand, would cower near the back of the group, watching all the other little girls and imagining myself in a wheelchair, speaking to school groups about the dangers of athletic showboating. This attitude is nearly useless in gymnastics, but is frequently an asset in other areas of life.

The downside is that firsts can be nail-bitingly trying. Starting a new job gives me conniptions.

Temping was a wonderful exercise for this particular peccadillo. After a while it dawned on me that there was no point in getting wrapped around the axle about a position I was only going to hold for four days max. You can stoke the fiery furnaces of hell for a few days as long as you know you're getting out by the end of the week.

But starting my brand-new life as Kito Lopez's assistant defined the complete unknown. After getting over the initial shock that Aunt Fran had mysteriously, *finally* deigned to grant me some professional help, I began to grow anxious. I could barely sleep Sunday night. Too nervous to be excited, I could only lie in bed and come up with reasons it would never work out. He would find me incompetent. I would think he was a diva. He would be allergic to my perfume. I would think he was a diva. He would—oh, screw it. I was afraid he was going to be a diva.

Kito's reputation for brilliance was solidly rivaled by his reputation for being, shall we say, difficult? There were rumors about directors he'd slapped, millionaire producers he'd reduced to tears and even an actor he'd once tied to a chair in order to shave the resistant scamp's head. Excited as I was to spend my days in the presence of greatness, I was more than a little terrified to end up on the receiving end of Kito's wrath. I've always been very attached to my hair.

Kito's studio occupied an enormous loft space on Crosby Street in SoHo. From the outside the building looked like the perfect spot to be beaten, robbed and left for dead. But once I'd been scanned by the tastefully modest battery of security cameras and admitted into the brushed steel vestibule, I began to get a sense of the relative luxury in which Kito lived and worked. Selling a few movie rights goes a long way. I heard an invisible latch on the handleless security door clicking open, and as the door began to swing, apparently of its own accord, I heard a familiar voice calling, "In here, doll!"

Before I could step inside, however, I was arrested by a forbidding hissing, followed directly by two yellow eyes peering around the half-open door. It would have been a cat—at about half the size it would certainly have been a cat. But as it slunk through the door toward me and revealed the entirety of its easily four-foot length, I began to rethink the cat theory. Also, it looked like a leopard. Which is to say it looked like my grandmother's tacky leopard lampshade. (She lives in Boca. What do you want?) It looked like a giant cat wearing a costume made of my grandmother's tacky lampshade. And it hissed at me again. The enormous lampshade-cat was not pleased to see me.

"Nice … great big … scary … kitty," I cooed, attempting the nonthreatening underhand gesture you're supposed to use when approaching strange dogs.

This was greeted with a guttural, spitting hiss and the immense creature recoiled into what I was very sure was a pre-attack stance.

"Doll?" Kito called. "Are you coming in?"

By this point the big scary cat seemed to be growling, something I didn't know cats could even do. It seemed ironic and not a little depressing that being eaten by a wild beast had not even figured on my list of new job disaster scenarios.

"I would like to …," I responded. "I would like to but your, um … puma … is not so into that idea, I think."

"Oh, Cloris? Oh, my God, she's so harmless. CLORIS!! Let Liza in, you bitch!"

Cloris seemed put off by the request, but slowly backed her giant cat behind through the door, watching me throughout. I inched in after her.

When I got inside, the enormous feline was standing with two paws on Kito's waist and purring while he scratched behind her ears.

"She's terrifying, right?" he asked me. "She's an ocelot. Très chic. Very expensive. She was a gift from an ex. I didn't have the heart to tell him it was a little too Siegfried and Roy."

"That's a hard one to phrase," I agreed.

"So," he continued, giving Cloris an affectionate shove

down, "coffee, tea, chai? I don't have biscotti but there are these disgusting energy bars I'm trying to get rid of. Help yourself, as a general rule."

"Thanks."

"I hope you're feeling pumped, because I have a doozy for you to get started on. I have been thinking and this assistant thing has its advantages. Are you very opposed to picking up my dry cleaning?"

The doozy involved an entire three-hour morning on the phone trying to find Kito a health insurance carrier that covered the fairly extensive range of holistic and non-Western practitioners he saw on a semi-regular basis. May I never again have to ask an insurance representative whether they cover reiki, regression therapy and ear candling.

The loft was beautiful, and while Kito pecked away at his iBook I tried to imagine myself so successful that I could work in a similarly luxe environment. I had a little trouble. I'm really better with the negative.

We ordered lunch from Dean & Deluca and ate at the huge kitchen island. Kito filled me in on his new project and asked me lots of questions about my sex life. And especially George.

No more mention of my writing, but I was afraid to push it.

The first huge perk of my new gig became evident in the afternoon. I was petting Cloris (who had warmed up to me almost instantaneously when I dropped a dollop of tuna salad on the floor during lunch) and setting up Kito's bills for on-line payment.

"Liza, my love," Kito whined from across the loft, "could you do me a big favor?"

"Sure," I said.

"Read this speech for me and try to think of a better word than 'breadth' for this guy. I'm blocking."

I couldn't quite believe it. Not only were mine the very

first pair of eyes to scan what Kito had just written, but he actually wanted my advice. It was all I could do not to gush, but since it was only my first day I thought I'd contain.

" 'Scope,' " I offered, when I'd finished. "I feel like you're trying to imply something bigger than 'breadth.' Something with more dimension."

"Scope! Yes, perfect, you're a genius. That's completely what I was trying to think of—OH! I have been forgetting all this time! Doll! Exciting news for you. I'm suggesting your play for the New Manhattan Playhouse development series this summer. What do you think of that?"

I think the tuna sat out too long and I'm hallucinating.

"But I thought there would be … rewrites! I'm sure it needs work!"

"It does need work," he said, "but first of all never lowball yourself when someone is saying something nice about you and second of all how are you supposed to work without feedback? If they do your reading, you'll get feedback. And then you'll rewrite. And then you'll name your first child after me."

The New Manhattan Playhouse was one of the most venerated and exciting off-Broadway houses in the city. They would be gathering the most impressive directors and incredibly talented actors to do concert readings of new plays by up-and-comers. The idea that I could be a part of that …

"They'll never read it," I said.

"Doll, do you know who I am? They'll read it because I asked them to."

"They'll never take it. They wouldn't want to do my little, tiny, insignificant, fledgling play."

"You're right. It's not really that good. Thank you for bringing me to my senses before I stuck my neck out for this piece of crap you've created. Why don't you just hang yourself from the nearest rafter?" He looked at me sternly. "They will take it because it is *fantastic* and because I am curating the series."

Foolishly, I opened my mouth to protest. Kito threw a hand up to stop me. "Not another word. Who are you to argue with Kito Lopez?"

I threw my arms around him. "You have no idea what this means to me."

"Well, I tell you what," he said, "you wanna make it up to me?"

"Of course," I panted. "Anything!"

"Great. You get to walk Cloris."

So it wasn't the perfect job.

"And take little baggies to pick up the doody, 'kay?"

I took a deep breath. As Aunt Fran always says, anyone who wouldn't reach into a pile of shit to pick up a diamond isn't my kind of people.

*"There is nothing more wonderful or frightening
in the world than a kiss that makes you forget
your own name."*

CHAPTER 30

IN THE MEANTIME, Parrot had been hard at work
with preparations for her ides of March birthday. Parrot is
famous for her annual celebrations, which invariably involve
huge efforts on the guests' parts and huge rewards for Parrot.
This year's theme was "Treat Your Bird Like a Queen," and
we were all compelled to arrive costumed as some form of
royalty. Except for Parrot, who came as J-Lo. Why this was
acceptable, I have no idea, but Parrot seems to regard J-to-
the-Lo as a pop princess at the very least. ("So few people
really appreciate that when she was a Flygirl she was totally
busting a move but I was thinking how I need new foundation.") As this was to be Parrot's big night, I was even willing
to put up with her omnipresent arm-candy, Kirk, who I tried
not to judge for going as Affleck, because no one would buy
him as Marc Anthony. I really hate couples' costumes. Come
up with your own damned idea. Be a freestanding human
being.

But truthfully, for perhaps the first time since they'd started
mating, I had begun to crave Kirk's company. Whether he
was aware of it or not—and it's Kirk, so probably not—Kirk

was a tremendous source of George data. His likes, his dislikes, his ex-girlfriends.

Preparing for a masquerade party is to a brainy overachiever like studying for the SATs. I could spend years dreaming up the perfect costume. My Teresa Heinz Kerry was a hit during election year. My Patty Hearst won me a prize in college. But to spend an evening with George, I needed to up the sex appeal. I settled on an old classic, the Wife-of-an-Assassinated-Dictator-in-Hiding. If he didn't want me in a pageboy wig and a brocade cheongsam and sunglasses, he was never going to want me. And if he didn't, well, I could get hysterical behind the sunglasses.

I got an e-mail only two days before Parrot's fete.

From: g-doren@turnbullprince.com

To: lizalikearug@shinygun.com

Subject: (no subject)

So I'm back. Tokyo is a great town. Actually I don't know, I never saw the outside of an office. I'll see you at the Parrotstravaganza. Going to be very thirsty when I get there. You should buy me a drink.

George

Okay, fine, maybe I did a little dance of joy. I was alone in my apartment. Who are you to judge me?

Kirk confirmed that George would be making an appearance at the party, and though it pained me I didn't respond to his e-mail. I hoped it would keep him guessing.

Finally, after months of secret, sweaty fantasies, Parrot's shindig was going to be it: the first time that George and I actually, on purpose, spent an evening together. It's possible that I have never spent more time willing each of my individual eyelashes to curl or focusing Vulcan mind-power to perk up my breasts.

Parrot, whose indulgent father had reanimated her checking

account as a birthday present, had managed to close Ike for an
evening, which I confess made me feel slightly less nervous.
In addition to being fairly unpretentious, Ike served pigs-in-
blankets, which bring me comfort. Having failed, for several
weeks, to make actual visual contact with George, I was feeling prepared to vomit at any moment. I kept half-wishing
he'd show up ugly or suddenly boring so that I could reclaim
my mind and just go on with my life.

I arrived early with the birthday girl and was thankfully
able to commandeer a table with a view of the door. Parrot
and "Affleck" immediately flounced off to the bar to hook up
their vodka drips for the evening. Unfortunately, Parrot's cell
phone had chosen the instant of George's arrival to vibrate itself off the table and I went after it. So I wasn't exactly upright.

I saw the shoes first.

"Under the table so early in the evening?"

I looked up, and if my jaw didn't hit the floor it was only
because my muscles wouldn't stretch that far. He wasn't ugly.
I was sure he wasn't boring. The man behind the tailored
pinstripes was still George. George from my couch. Shirtless-
on-the-street George. The George I'd spent every night for
the last three (at least) months with in my dirty, dirty dreams.
Oh, my God, here was George.

"I was hiding from you actually. Guess it didn't work."

"Are we ready to get some party on?"

"You see, I pictured this being your sort of event. Being
something of a poseur yourself."

"I am a fan of costume parties. It's just the right mix of
style and substance abuse."

He scanned my dress, dark glasses and kerchief, lingered
on the wig for a sec, and went back to the dress.

"That's quite an ensemble you have there. Imelda Marcos?"

"Close. And who are you supposed to be?"

"Prince Rainier. He bagged the hottest woman in history."

"Clever."

"Thank you."

"Not that clever."

"This from the Wife-of-an-Assassinated-Dictator-in-Hiding."

I was stunned.

"Parrot told me."

"I was afraid you were inside my head."

"Not yet. I'm not going in there unarmed."

If he'd asked, I really would've had sex with him right there. In the bar.

"You're very presumptuous," I said.

"You're very sexy in that wig."

Outright compliment! Outright compliment! Sleep with me right now!

"And not bad out of it," he added.

For the rest of my life!!

He slid into the booth beside me so that his hip was touching mine. And he just stared at me. It was so hard not to look away, but I couldn't have if I'd tried. And that was it for me. George.

George was it for me.

I know that the party filled up and other people talked to me. But George stayed beside me the whole night and I couldn't tell you a single thing about the rest of the evening. Except that at some point we excused ourselves. For once I was the one leaving Parrot with a whisper and a knowing look. We took a cab uptown and got out near George's apartment. We walked toward the Time Warner Center.

"I want to show you something," he said. "Lose the wig."

I did.

He took my hand and led me into the lobby of the Mandarin Oriental, and straight to the elevators. "Ever notice," he whispered, "that you can go anywhere in New York if you act like you belong?"

I hadn't, but I would in the future.

George pressed "Ballroom." "One of the few useful things my father ever taught me had to do with expensive hotels. They generally have the best views."

We exited the elevator into the most beautiful and empty room. The park sprawled beneath our wall of windows and the skyline was a forest of twinkling high-rises. The tables were set perfectly, as if the grand ball might begin at any moment. "How did you know it would be empty?" I asked.

"I didn't," he said. "Worth a shot though, wasn't it?"

Yes, yes, yes. Anything you say. Yes.

"Do you always pull out all the stops like this?" I asked.

He paused. "I think I'd like to be different with you. Than I usually am," he said.

For the first time I realized it was possible that I made George nervous. It seemed unthinkable. But he held on to my hand as though I might slip away if he let go.

I wasn't letting go.

If you're very lucky, you get kissed once in your life so well that it hurts deep in your bones, and you can feel the tiny universe inside you tearing open for the first time to admit another human being. If you're very lucky that kiss goes on for a million years and you forget where you are and who you are and what you did before.

I am very, very lucky.

*"Love is like walking a tightrope thirty feet above
a pit of hungry tigers. Think how good it feels
every minute that you don't fall."*

CHAPTER 31

"DIFFERENT," as it turned out, meant that although
we had dinner almost every night that week, and he insisted on paying until I threatened to throw a public fit and
he let me buy a single meal, we didn't sleep together. For a
week. In the wake of Dr. Tim's abstinence campaign, I was
slightly nervous. Until I realized this wasn't likely to drag on
for several dry months and that actually it was a sign that
George was kind of a gentleman.

Unable to keep my boundless elation to myself, I had
pretty much called, e-mailed or telegrammed everyone I
knew with news of my bliss. I felt none of my usual com-
punctions about declaring my romance to the world. No
one was happier than Aunt Fran, who, despite George's and
my protests, insisted on calling the Four Seasons, request-
ing her usual table and instructing that our bill be put on
her tab.

We sat, soaking up the ambiance and the Petit Verdot, and
I couldn't help grabbing George's knee under the table.
Repeatedly. Normally I can't stand those obnoxious couples
who consider their entrees a distraction from three courses

of canoodling, but it was really all I could do to keep my clothes on through dessert. It wasn't my fault. Everything George did was unbearably, achingly sexy. I think it was his chest. And his hands. And his hair. And his voice. I think it was him.

During appetizers, he looked up from his bison carpaccio and said, "You know what I like about you? You're one of the only women I know who's as smart as me."

"Correction," I responded, "I'm one of the only women you know who's as smart as you and actually willing to be around you."

George seemed to wince for a split second and I realized I might just have stepped on his idea of a tender moment. But he moved on.

"You think you're pretty special, don't you?"

"I know it," I replied.

"Well, then I guess you are pretty smart."

"I guess I am."

"You also have an incredibly lovely pair of breasts."

The waiter took this opportunity to materialize with George's ahi tuna and my swordfish paillard, and overhearing us, could not have turned more red if he'd been slapped.

Funny how when you're the one being inappropriate in public, you decide everyone must just find it endearing.

My shoe came off when the chocolate soufflé arrived, and George was reluctant to relinquish his napkin by the time we'd settled the bill.

I am still amazed, as I think back on it, that our cab didn't crash on the way back to his place, as I'm fairly certain our driver was fixedly watching us playing grabass in the rearview mirror.

Certainly I was a bit south of tipsy by the time we got into George's apartment, and I finally got to live out that fantasy about falling into someone's door while ripping their clothes off that I've had since *Working Girl*. I was ever so glad that George lived alone, although I don't think we would have been deterred in any case.

I had had good sex. I had had what I thought of as good sex. But being mind-bendingly laid for the very first time makes you feel re-virginized and deflowered all over. It's as if the awkward naked dance you've been doing for years bears no actual resemblance to what sex really is.

We did it really fast. We did that hot, I-can't-believe-I'm-actually-getting-to-screw-you-so-let's-do-it-before-this-all-turns-out-to-be-a-dream kind of sex. And then we did it really, really slowly for like three hours and I thought my head was going to explode. And then we did it again for good measure.

This sort of sex was the stuff of myth. Or so I thought.

Suddenly Parrot made so much more sense to me.

One day I was a fairly well-adjusted, balanced sort of person with interests and activities and many, many thoughts. And then poof, all I could think about was sleeping with George. I relived it. I visualized it. Everywhere I went, everything I looked at, became a potential location or prop. I walked around thinking things like "You'd have to have a really good grip on that pole while the train was moving," or, "We'd have to put Cloris in the bathroom." I sat at Kito's computer feeling George's hands all over me every afternoon and trying desperately not to slip and insert inappropriate words into e-mails to *American Theatre* magazine and Con Edison.

George just fascinated me. Talking about Bob Woodward or the Dow Jones or his childhood in D.C. And he listened to me for hours. Chicago and Yale and Caryl Churchill and French cinema. Suddenly he was reading my dog-eared copy of *Five Plays by Anton Chekhov* and I was watching *All the President's Men* on DVD.

As Jeremy's lovely new girlfriend Natasha was becoming a

fixture in our apartment, I had a great excuse to spend all my time at George's place. Suddenly I wasn't seeing as much of my roomie, but he still managed to leave biweekly messages on my cell along the lines of "Hooch, where you been? Do you still live here? I saw a roach. Don't forget your half of the rent."

Aunt Fran called and just cackled into my voice mail, occasionally tossing in something like "Grab it all, Niece, every last drop."

Parrot was less pleased with my absence, and more insistent:

> To: lizalikearug@shinygun.com
> From: principessa@magmail.com
> Subject: What the?
> Okay I know you're really in love and everything but I totally have things going on too and last week you missed a sale at barneys I went anyway don't worry but it's so not the same without you and I think kirk is missing george because kirk doesn't really have that many friends don't tell him I said that but when are we going to hang out again or are you just having too much sex for your old friends to still be even in your life what the hell liza are you going to tabitha's for cinco de mayo?

I felt slightly guilty as I knew that Parrot had a point, and it wasn't just the prospect of another Tabitha party that caused a three-day delay in my response to her e-mail. (George was insisting that we go, as he knew Tabitha found him slightly distasteful and thought it would be fun to irritate her. Though I hadn't spoken to her much since my awkward resignation as her wedding lieutenant, I couldn't resist a triumphant return to her social sphere.) But for those of us to whom this sort of whirlwind romance doesn't happen often, it can be overwhelmingly all-consuming.

Looking at me from the outside I'm sure I would have been disgusted, but I just felt like the world was my Cadbury Egg. For a while.

George got a call early one Saturday morning as we lay in his bed, unwilling to get up, and I listened to him having one end of what appeared to be a slightly awkward conversation.

"You're in town already?" he asked, rolling over and turning his back to me. I tried to listen to the muffled voice coming from his cell phone, but I couldn't get a thing. "Tonight? Ah ... not the best." We were supposed to grab dinner and stop by the birthday party of one of his work friends. I wondered who was so important that George would consider preempting our plans. "Yeah. Yeah, okay. I'll do some rearranging. Nine-thirty. Yeah, I'll be there." He hung up and seemed stiff and perplexed.

"Who was that?" I asked.

"Harry," he said.

"Harry?"

"My father."

"You call your father Harry?" I asked.

"On a good day."

George had spoken very little of his tricky relationship with his dad. I knew that his mother had died in an accident when George was little, and that he had been raised inside Washington's Beltway in the lap of luxury. I'd attempted a gentle prying and encouraged sharing by explaining my mother's constant warnings about all the things that could kill you and my father's secretly teaching me and Jack to drive long before we were of age. But George never seemed to want to tell me about growing up, and I chose not to push it.

"So what did he want?" I asked.

"He's in town. He wants to have dinner tonight."

I waited. He said nothing, just lay back against the pillows with an irritated sigh.

"So . . . you're going?" I asked.

"I guess I have to," he said.

I tried to negotiate the best approach. It seemed shrewish to remind him that we had plans and downright obvious to suggest I'd like to meet his dad.

"Well, that'll be nice," I settled on, "just some father-son time."

"Yeah, whatever."

This was not going well. I tried to scurry around and creep in a side door. "What's your dad like?" I asked. "I sort of picture him as this very distinguished, witty politico."

"He's a politician. Picture a politician. That's it."

He threw back the covers just as I was about to reach for him and he started to throw on a pair of jeans.

"Taking you to some terrific restaurant, I bet?"

"Think so." He had a T-shirt on and headed toward the living room. Reluctantly I rolled out of bed, slipped into the button-down George had left thrown over a chair and followed.

This was simply not fair. Why was I not getting an invitation? If my parents had been in town I would have been only too happy to introduce them to George (shocking, I know), and he'd already met my brother, so technically he sort of owed me one family intro to keep things even. But not a word.

"So I guess I should cancel our reservations at O.G.?" I questioned.

"I guess." My boyfriend had gone to bed a genius and awakened an evasive Neanderthal. I waited hopefully for a word with more than one syllable.

"Okay." I finally took the plunge, deciding he probably just didn't realize he wasn't inviting me. "This is really kind of forward of me and probably rude, but I'd really like to meet your father."

He paused in his coffee-making for a moment and looked at me. I watched him register the fact that I'd just invited myself and I smiled slightly at my own bravery.

"I don't think so," he said, and resumed pouring water into the coffeemaker.

What? Wait. WHAT? Not possible. I had no earthly idea what the proper response to that was.

"Oh," I said. "Okay." And then I did that thing that women do when we try not to look like a man just drove a trident into our chests. George must have been aware either of his rudeness or my injured but brave look, because he said, "It's just . . . you wouldn't have a good time, Liza."

"That's silly. Of course I would!" I tried to pry open the tiny window of hope.

George shot me a "back off" look and said, "You don't know what you're talking about on this one, so how about you don't give me any commentary."

I could feel the tears welling up behind my eyes, but I was determined not to let him know. I'd never seen him like this, so closed.

"I don't believe I was offering any 'commentary,'" I sniffed, with as much dignity as I could muster as I turned and strode into the bedroom to get dressed.

"Jesus, Liza, don't do that," he called after me, but he didn't follow.

"What?" I called from the bedroom, pulling on my clothes.

"Don't get all wounded about it. It's not that big a deal."

Not that big a deal? Sure, not that big a deal. My amazing, new, perfect relationship had just been shattered by the realization that although I was good enough to have sex with thirty-seven times a day, I was not good enough to meet George's father. Not pretty enough, probably, not tall enough, not smart enough, not funny enough, maybe not anything enough. An embarrassment, in any case. Tears streamed silently down my cheeks as I buttoned my sweater and strode past George to get my coat.

"Wait," he said, "don't run off."

"I'm not running," I said. "I've got stuff to do today. I don't want to waste an entire Saturday just sitting around here." I wouldn't let him see my face.

"Just . . . take my word on this, Liza," he said, and I thought maybe I heard something sorry in his voice, but I didn't turn around and he didn't come near me.

"Word taken," I said, and I took care not to slam his front door on my way to the elevator.

Into every relationship, a little fight must fall. But for some reason, the first one always seems world-ending. George was being a jerk, but for once I couldn't even open my mouth to tell him. I wanted to live in his shirt pocket, and he didn't even want his only living parent to lay eyes on me. I could think of few things more hurtful. I was mortified and only felt worse when I realized that I must have looked terribly clingy wanting to do something he thought was obviously inappropriate. There it went. The start of something good and it was going to end so soon and so foolishly. Why hadn't I kept my mouth shut?

I wanted to throw myself on my bed and cry, but I was determined not to give in. I had plenty to do and I wasn't going to waste the day pining. I spent the better part of the gray afternoon sitting in my favorite coffee shop in the East Village, trying to sort through Kito's itemized write-offs so his accountant could file on time, but mostly staring over my laptop and out the window. What if I wasn't the sort of girl George wanted to bring home? This was exactly what I'd been afraid of, falling into a relationship in which I was so much more smitten than he was, in which he held all the cards.

After a couple of hours of failed concentration, I cracked and called Parrot. I was afraid to be alone anymore, as I might have started to Google George's father in an attempt to virtually meet him. Plus I was getting tired of checking my phone every six minutes to see if George had called. Clearly he wasn't going to.

"Ohmigod it's amazing that you called right now I'm buying shoes." I said a silent thank-you that Parrot had picked up.

"Hi," I said, and I knew I was about to bawl.

"What's wrong you sound like shit what happened?" she asked, and I heard the sound of an expensive boot dropping on the marbled floor at Neiman Marcus.

"We had a fight," I told her tremblingly, "and I found out that George is ashamed of me and I think we're probably breaking up."

"HOLD THESE FOR ME," I heard Parrot shouting at a salesperson. "I'm on my way sweetie where are you?"

Parrot came all the way down to the East Village to pick up my quivering heap of self and take it for cream puffs. Unfortunately I was too upset to enjoy them.

I explained my misfortune to her, and Parrot immediately phoned Kirk and cancelled their date for that evening. I told her not to, but I was glad she didn't listen.

"Seriously he's getting on my nerves anyway it's like he's everywhere I go and sometimes I'm like go home I have a vibrator I don't need you every second but whatever he listens so it's fine now what are we going to do about this it sounds like George is being an asswipe."

"I know," I sniffled, "I know he is and I'm so pissed off but I don't know what to do about it. I wish I could just confront him on it, which I should have done this morning."

"You know what I would do I would freaking get all hotted up and then show up anyway because who the hell is he and frankly if he's dumping you anyway then who cares if you piss him off it would be so amazing if you just paraded into that restaurant and his dad would be like wow she's hot and George would be like that's my girlfriend and you'd be like not anymore asshole so where are they eating?"

"I don't even know," I told her. "Somewhere I'm not good enough to go."

Parrot froze. "Alright that is not okay I would beat the crap out of anyone who talked that way about my best friend and I really don't wanna beat the crap out of you Liza."

"Thanks, P," I sniffed. "You wanna come home and rent a movie with me and eat ice cream?"

"No we're not gonna be pathetic tonight you're going out with your fabulous friend to a fabulous dinner and right now we have to go find something to wear!"

"Oh, I don't think so, P, I'm really not in the mood."

"Okay you are really in no condition to be making decisions about something as important as what we're doing with our Saturday night."

I had to agree with her.

"You just leave everything to me," she insisted, with a sly smile.

This thing sometimes happens when Parrot is scheming on my behalf: she comes up with ideas that are so far-fetched I would blush to think them up myself, but somehow, because I didn't, I don't see them coming. Parrot sent me home to change while she made some calls. She phoned to say we had a ten o'clock reservation at Vong in midtown and that I'd better put on something half decent. Within an hour she was at my door in a taxi.

"I don't know if I have it in me to be in public," I said, as we rode uptown.

"Don't think about it it's just dinner." I tried not to, but as I stepped out of the cab a renewed sense of desperation fell over me. "I'm serious, P, I'm not going to be any fun tonight—" I tried to warn her.

"Liza!" She slapped me a little on the cheek, not hard, but enough to get my attention. "Strap on a sac we're going in."

We did.

If I had known what Parrot had done, I would never have left the house. The restaurant was all abuzz with carefree people enjoying their Thai fusion, but I would rather have been weeping in a hole somewhere. Left no choice, I followed Parrot as the hostess led us to our table.

And then I stopped dead.

Sitting directly in front of me, gently illuminated by the intimate light of their private booth sat George and his father.

And a girl.

A blonde, beautiful girl. A girl about my age. A girl with very nice jewelry and very expensive breasts, but lovely nonetheless. She made a joke I couldn't hear and Harry threw his head back and laughed and she looked at George for his reaction. Then she looked at me because I was staring directly at her and probably she thought I was an insane person.

Parrot had proceeded to our table and was almost seated when she realized I wasn't with her. I saw her turn back, out of the corner of my eye, and she began to head toward me. But it was too late. George had seen me, standing there like I'd been flash-frozen. He looked stunned, panicked. His father caught the look on George's face and he turned toward me too. Harry Doren was just as I'd imagined him, handsome and distinguished, like Robert Culp in Thomas Pink. With George's brown eyes.

In only a moment, I understood.

George hadn't invited me because there just wasn't room at the table. He already had a date. Someone who surely wouldn't embarrass him like I would have.

I wanted to run. I wanted to turn and bolt for the door and get far away as fast as I could. But my legs wouldn't work. Waiters and busboys careened around me, I knew people were staring, but I was rooted to the spot, maybe four feet in front of George's table.

Finally, he spoke.

"Liza?" he asked, as if I was an apparition and not the girl he was clearly forsaking for the gorgeous blonde. "What are you doing here?" I registered that he was appropriately mortified.

"What am I doing here?" I repeated. I looked at Parrot, who had so clearly set me up. "I don't know."

"Son," Harry turned from appraising me and asked George, "would you like to introduce your friend?"

"No," I said. "He wouldn't." Suddenly I could move again and I did, spinning around and heading for the exit before a scene could be made, before I could say anything I wanted to say.

Parrot was hot on my heels and I knew she'd be ready to apologize, to make some excuse about being sure if I just showed up everything would be great, except she hadn't counted on this. I was so angry and humiliated I could feel myself shaking.

I pushed through the heavy front door and headed toward the street, but somebody grabbed my arm and I turned back. George had followed me outside.

"What are you doing here?" he asked, still looking as though he didn't really believe it was me.

"I'm embarrassing myself, apparently. Why didn't you tell me?"

"Look, it's not the kind of thing you just bring up in conversation, and frankly it's not something I was dying for you to know about."

"Are you kidding me?" I practically shouted. "That's your

response?! Not something you were dying for me to know about! Yeah, I can see why!" Parrot was standing a few feet away, waiting for us to be finished so she could begin her atonement.

I knew George would be furious that I had shown up like this, but I prepared to fire back with a fury of my own. Instead he just scuffed at the ground with his hands in his pockets.

"Yeah, well," he said, "now you know. Harry Doren, ladies and gentlemen. Lock up your daughters."

Wait, wait, wait, something was wrong here. Why was George not making excuses? Why were we not talking about his other girlfriend, the one who was good enough to meet his dad? Why was there no shouting?

"Wait," I said, "your . . ." All of a sudden it was coming together. "*She's* with your *father*?"

"Ohmigod!" Parrot hooted from a few feet away. I shot her a shut-up look in no uncertain terms.

George reddened. "Yeah, what'd you think, she was with me?" He looked at me quizzically.

"Oh, Jesus," I said. "I'm an idiot."

"Did you seriously think she was with me?" he asked, and now I could see him getting angry.

"What do you think it looked like, George? You won't let me meet your father, you won't tell me why and then here you are and I see this hot blonde next to you. What would you think?"

"Yeah, well, maybe now you can see why I didn't want you here! Why couldn't you just listen to me?"

"Why couldn't you just tell me what the problem was?" I demanded.

"Because it was none of your business! My father dates women younger than me, okay? You happy? It's a fucking embarrassment! It's disgusting to watch! Why the hell would I want to bring you to see that?"

"Because," I cried, "I don't care who your father is or what he does! I care about you! And I know you're wonderful so nothing else matters!"

"Really? You know I'm wonderful? You know I'm so wonderful that you were sure I must have some ulterior motive for not bringing you tonight and you know I'm so wonderful that you saw that girl and you were sure she must be with me. That's how wonderful you *know* I am."

"First of all," I said, "I got conned into showing up here tonight. I didn't even know you were going to be here." I looked pointedly at Parrot and George followed my gaze. She waved, but looked somewhat ashamed.

"Yeah," he said, "I can believe that."

"And second of all," I continued, "you've never exactly been shy about enjoying the ladies."

"Yeah, and I've been even less shy about enjoying you. But you don't trust me."

That stopped me dead. He was right. This didn't look like trust. This looked like I was waiting for him to be just as slimy as he'd always pretended to be. I'd mistaken the playboy act for the real guy. And I was the one who was supposed to know the difference.

"You're right," I said. "You're right, I didn't trust you. I'm sorry." He didn't say anything so I went on. "But, George, you didn't trust me either. It would have taken a couple of sentences to explain what was going on, but you wouldn't even give me that. You just shut me down."

"Some things are private," he said stubbornly.

"Yeah, and sometimes they don't have to be."

He looked at me, hard, and I began to wonder if I really had pushed it past the point of no return. You don't generally want to create a scene like this within the first couple of months of dating someone.

"Look," George said, calmer now, "I didn't handle this

well. But you don't get to know everything you want to know every minute that you want to know it."

"I know," I replied. "I get it." I paused. "Shit, I ruined your dinner."

"No, you didn't; it wasn't that great to begin with."

"Did you explain?" I asked.

"No," he admitted, "I just said I'd be right back."

"I'll make you a deal," I said. "You go back inside, I'll go home and you come over when you're done. I'll find a way to make it up to you." I smiled coyly and hoped he'd go for it.

"Yeah?" He smiled back.

"Yeah."

He grabbed me and pulled me in and held on tight and I buried my head in his shoulder. "You're right, I'm sorry. I should have explained ... something," he said.

I heard Parrot cooing her approval in the background.

I pulled away and told him, "On the upside, I truly think this was one of the most embarrassing moments of my entire life."

"Ditto," he said, "although I still have to finish dinner so I say you got off easy."

"I say your dad's getting off easy, from the looks of her!" I teased. I saw him tense slightly. "Too soon?" I asked.

"Just a little." He smiled. "Go home, crazy person. And take your crazy friend. Don't think I don't know whose idea this was," he chided, and waved a teasing fist at Parrot as he headed inside.

She came over and put an arm around me. "I'm an asshole," I told her, "and you helped me get that way."

"Hey you just needed some information and I got it for you and you made up right?"

"Not because of you! I almost made a scene in front of an entire restaurant!"

"Okay the foundation was good though it's not my fault where you take it from there," she said.

"Beer? My place?" I smiled.

"Please immediately I hate drama," she whined.

I suppressed the urge to argue.

"If looks could kill I would know by now. I've spent years trying."

CHAPTER 32

THE PLAYWRIGHT CHARLES L. MEE once wrote, "Another person is a foreign country." I should embroider it on a pillow.

In the days that followed my wretched misstep over George's father, I worked hard to...well, to cool it a little. Why do human beings do this? We wait forever to meet someone who fits us and then when we finally do we immediately begin searching for the place it's going to start unraveling. I was not a little disgusted with myself.

George and I talked in rather constructive terms about our mutual mistakes, and then we moved on. I didn't feel like I was on probation and I even relaxed a little. Good Lord, if he was going to stick with me after that ...

It was almost Cinco de Mayo, the day of what was to be my first EVER blissful Tabitha celebration. I suspected it was only Tod-with-one-D's insistence that garnered George's and my invitations to this shindig. When I called to RSVP, Tabitha explained quite coldly that Dr. Tim would be sitting this party out; apparently he was happy for my happiness, but didn't need to see it up close. Admittedly, I was relieved. The last thing a new relationship needs is a living reminder of mistakes and failures past.

Granted, I looked forward to finally approaching Tabitha with the confidence my recent good fortunes had built, but mostly I was excited to revisit the scene of my first kiss with George.

As we were dressing to leave, I asked him, "Do you happen to remember what happened on the very site of tonight's festivities some five months ago?"

"I think I thought about you and had a little, ah ... private moment ... before going to Tod's party."

"You did not!"

"I think I may have."

"That's disgusting."

"You don't find it disgusting."

"Don't talk like that or we'll be late for the party."

We were late for the party.

So late, in fact, that I think Tabitha thought us rude, and I knew Parrot would be in a snit.

Our hostess, hard at work giving long engagements a bad name, was standing in the doorway waiting to pounce when we got off the elevator.

"Well, I guess it's true, then, about you two."

"Happy May," I chirped.

"Don't you look interesting, Liza! Is that one of those vintage dresses?" For a woman sporting a sombrero and a peasant skirt, she had a good case.

"Tabitha, you're turning into an old married lady already," George replied for me. "That's a Zac Posen. I bought it for her. Doesn't Tod buy you anything nice?" George gave Tabitha a sarcastic punch on the arm and we breezed past her.

George made small talk with Tod-with-one-D briefly, while I disappeared to get a couple of drinks from the cater waiters. The apartment I had once so admired was now festooned with tacky streamers and every drink that passed me had a little cactus cocktail stirrer, which I was fairly sure had nothing to do with Cinco de Mayo. Nonetheless, it was truly amazing how much less offensive Tabitha's guests all seemed this time around, knowing I had an ally in the room. I located Parrot smoking on the balcony and she gave me a solid and well-deserved dressing-down.

"Do you have any idea how fucking boring this thing has been and Kirk is totally just off talking about money with work people and there is no one cool here and the food sort of sucks and everyone is looking at my dress like it's fucked up or something where have you been?!"

"Your dress is fantastic but these people have never seen this much flesh on a clothed person. I have been banging my boyfriend in the filthiest, most wonderful way possible and I know that you are far too happy for me and far too into that sort of thing to really be pissed."

She got the sort of sweet, head-tilted, crinkly-eyed look she gets when we find My Little Pony figures at flea markets. "Lizaaaaaaaa you totally love him ohmigod you're like in love you love him ohmigod it's so sweeeeet!"

"Ummm, P, we do not say the word. We are not ready to say the word. We do the sex thing instead."

"THAT IS SO GREAT!" She hugged me and I knew I was forgiven.

"Is it like so amazing?" she asked, head still at an angle.

"It is like . . . I had no idea. I just had no idea."

"You lurve him!"

"Parrot!" I reprimanded her.

"Right right right right not saying the word."

But the truth was I was thinking it. I was thinking it all the time. I knew it was too early and weird and obsessive to think it, but I did. I couldn't look at him without knowing I loved him.

I glanced inside and saw George standing by Tabitha's makeshift bar, handing a margarita to a pretty brunette. He said something and she tossed her hair over her shoulder and laughed. In about two seconds, the warm, fuzzy feeling I'd been nursing turned to an insistent, gnawing envy.

Parrot followed my gaze. "Who's she?"

"I don't know," I said. "Not important." I turned away. But it was getting to me. The fact that women noticed him everywhere we went was getting to me. I'd never been a jealous girl, but then I'd never dated *that guy* before, the guy everyone wants to be with. I guess maybe I just couldn't understand what he was doing with me.

"So," I said to Parrot, determined not to care that George was inside talking to another girl, "what's up? What's going on with you? I feel like I haven't seen you at all lately."

But Parrot was intent on watching my boyfriend even if I wasn't.

"Ooh she put her hand on his arm I think they know each other who is she?" Parrot was like a bulldog.

I turned to look. It was true, they seemed familiar. But I was doing it again, damnit! We had just had this whole big discussion about trust. And what exactly did I think was going on here? He was talking to a girl at a party and I was working myself into a lather over nothing. Nothing!

"You should go in there," Parrot nudged me, "you should never let your boyfriend talk to an attractive woman if you can possibly avoid it because otherwise you never know what's going to happen and then suddenly you'll wake up one morning and find Rebecca De Mornay standing over you with a knife and you'll know you could have stopped it but you didn't."

"That didn't make any sense, P," I replied. "And if you can't trust the man you're with there's no point in being with him at all. Besides, George has never given me an ounce of reason not to trust him. I don't want to be one of those shitty women who tracks her boyfriend like a hawk. It's sick. It's not appealing and I don't want to do it. I don't *need* to do it."

I tried to mean it. George was who he was. Women liked him and he knew it. I couldn't freak out every time someone chatted him up at a party. Especially not again, so soon. At some pains I distracted Parrot from her vigil and we hung out on the balcony and tried to talk about other things.

"Ooh," I told her, "the people from the Applause Channel called to say Will's *High Hopes!* episode will be on in a couple of weeks. I was thinking of having some people over to share my horror."

"Oh totally I can't wait they're gonna crucify that guy!" she gushed, but I caught her looking over my shoulder again.

"Hey, Eliza!" Kirk materialized with a small plate of food for Parrot. She had trained him well. "You look really nice," he said to me.

"Thanks, Kirk. How've you been?"

"He's great," Parrot answered for him. "Do you like his shirt I bought it for him and he wanted to get the blue but I thought the pink was way better don't you think I was totally right because of his hair and how tall he is?"

"She made a good call," I told Kirk sheepishly. Parrot does know how to dress a man and Kirk certainly stood to improve in a few areas. Apparently, he owned white jeans.

"Where's George?" Parrot asked him, peering inside again.

"Oh, I feel really bad for him, actually," Kirk replied. "His ex-girlfriend is here and she kind of trapped him by the bar."

Parrot and I looked at each other and simultaneously snapped our attention toward the living room. I couldn't see George.

"Who is she what's the story is she hot?" Parrot fired at Kirk.

"Um, I don't know," he said. "Her name is Maria. She was in our analyst class."

"So you work with her?" I said.

"Yeah, well, different department," he said, "so I don't really see her."

"How long did they date what broke them up does she still have feelings for him?" Parrot was interrogating Kirk with a fury and efficiency she only attains when she's being protective. I think he was a little scared but Parrot was no longer foreign territory for Kirk.

"Um, I think like two years and I don't know why they broke up. I don't really talk to her." Kirk did the best he could. "Eliza, what do you know?" Kirk was looking to me for answers, but I had none to offer.

"I ... nothing," I said, trying to appear calm. "This is the first I've heard of her." It sounded even worse saying it out loud. That George had an ex-girlfriend, a two-year relationship, with a girl who was at the party with us was hard enough. But that he saw her, possibly every single day at work, and never said anything was a lot worse. I felt my ears turning red.

"Hey, no fair abandoning me, people." We all turned suddenly as George slipped through the glass doors, holding a Corona, which he handed to me. We all must have looked suspicious because he said, "Did I interrupt something?"

"Maria?" Parrot spat with disgust. I would have muzzled her if I could have.

George looked at Kirk and I could see he was peeved. "Thanks, buddy," he said, annoyed.

"Yeah ... sorry," Kirk said, as though he knew he should apologize but wasn't sure what for.

"You dated for two years you work together what's the story?" Parrot had only been warming up on Kirk, and she now turned her interrogation techniques on the prime suspect. I was not about to allow this.

"Parrot!" I snapped. "Completely inappropriate." George looked grateful but embarrassed.

"I'm looking out for you," she insisted, "sometimes you have to ask the right questions." I sensed Parrot getting into her *Matlock* mode and she's almost impossible to derail once she gets going.

"P," I said firmly, "you need another drink." I gave her a look that meant business and she pulled her head out of the strange bloodhound posture she'd adopted.

"Fine," she sniffed, "but De Mornay!" She took Kirk by the hand and dragged him inside.

George and I shared a brief but uncomfortable silence. But the cat was out of the bag and her name was Maria.

"Okay," I said, "you have an ex here. It's fine." It wasn't, but I knew I was doing the right thing.

"There was just no reason to mention her," he said.

Right. No reason. Except that you work with her. No reason.

"Of course not," I said. "So . . . you work with her?"

"Yes." He sighed. "I work with her. We broke up two years ago. We're not even in the same department. I rarely see her. There's nothing to tell."

"I'm not saying there is!" I was not about to give up credit for the grudgingly mature way I was handling the situation. "Like I said, it's fine." I was going to make it fine. "You could tell me, you know. Stuff like this. People have pasts, I have one. It got you here; it's all okay with me."

Having successfully navigated our first fight, George and I were now negotiating our first tense conversation. I could tell that he was carefully considering sharing something with me, and I was afraid to say anything that might shove him in the wrong direction. I kissed him on the cheek and walked with my beer to the other end of the balcony. I waited.

After a moment I felt him standing behind me. "Okay, look, the short version," he said quietly. "Four years ago we started dating. Because she was there. On and off for a couple of years and then I ended it because I wasn't that into it. And maybe I was kind of a dick about it."

That wasn't so bad.

"Since then," he continued, "every now and then she calls me ... yeah, I've ... hung out with her ... a couple of times. Not for months."

I knew what "hung out with her" meant. But he was telling me something, he was opening up. I didn't love it but I'd asked for it and now I was getting it.

I flashed a brave grin over my shoulder at him and said, "See? That didn't hurt a bit, did it?" There was nothing else to say. I had to be gracious, if not grateful, since he'd opened up.

George slipped his arms around my waist and we stared at the skyline.

"Déjà vu all over again, huh?" I said. I was determined to bring us back to the happy, sexy place we'd started from that evening.

"Tell me you don't have any saintly doctors you need to be loyal to," he said.

"Not a one."

I turned and he pressed his lips to my forehead. Inside I could see Tabitha marshalling her guests for yet another supercilious toast, and all I could think was that nobody inside was as much in love as we were, looking in from the balcony. I was going to enjoy my kiss this time, no guilt, no ghosts.

"Can I tell you something?" he asked.

"Mm-hmm."

"You're one of the only people I know who doesn't think I'm an asshole."

I laughed.

"I do think you're an asshole. I just find it amusing. Like father, like son." I grinned up at him. I didn't even mean to say it. I was just smarting from the whole ... Maria.

The cloud that passed over his face blocked out the cheering that was happening inside. I knew what I'd done. George looked like he wanted to say something, but he just stared at me like I'd punched him.

Somebody inside ripped open the glass doors and gurgled something inane about how we were missing the margaritas. And before I could say that I was kidding or ask how he could possibly take me seriously when I said something like that, George turned and went inside.

I felt like I'd stepped off a cliff. Enormous knots had formed in my stomach in seconds. Knowing that you've done something very bad to someone you'd throw yourself in front of a train for is a terrible feeling. And it was that same thing, that same lethal tongue firing indiscriminately every time I felt a little insecure. This time I'd fired in the wrong direction.

I chased after him, but George had quickly entrenched himself in some work conversation, laughing in that sort of weird, phony way guys seem to have when they're trying to ignore something. He knew I was there but he didn't look at me. If Tabitha hadn't cornered me and started to vomit up her wedding plans, as though I'd be interested, I might have gone to cry in the bathroom.

Some forty-five minutes later I mustered the courage to sidle up to George and slip my arm through his. He might have stiffened for a second or I might have imagined it.

He was a little drunk.

"Hey, do you guys know my girlfriend, Liza? She thinks I'm an asshole. Liza, have you met Steve and Daneesh? They're fellow grunts at Turnbull."

He put his arm around me and I barely said a word until he muttered something about getting our coats, and we were in a cab before I knew it, staring in silence out opposite windows.

There was a lump in my throat, but I squeezed out, "George, you know I was kidding, don't you?"

He didn't turn to say, "What?"

"Before, on the balcony, you know I didn't mean that? You know I think . . . I think you're the most amazing—"

"I don't think I know what you're talking about."

"Look, I had no idea you would take—"

"Liza, you're ridiculous. Of course I knew you were kidding."

The look he shot me and the way he said it made me drop the subject. I couldn't believe I had done this, opened my big mouth and ruined a beautiful moment, a wonderful evening. I felt nauseous thinking about how deep the damage might have gone. I was joking! I meant to be joking. He had to know that. And after the other night ... how could he not know? But I knew I'd pushed it a little too far, poked at a sore spot. I'd meant it too much. We looked out our windows and didn't say anything.

It wasn't until George was snoring next to me not long after we got home that I realized we hadn't gotten to re-create our New Year's kiss.

*"What could be more embarrassing than running
down the street naked, with your hair on fire,
in front of the White House Press Corps?"*

CHAPTER 33

OKAY, SO THINGS were not perfect, but George
and I moved forward. Even if there was a little gnawing something underneath, we still laughed and joked and
rolled around as usual.

A few short weeks later, however, I was facing a major distraction from all things relationship: *High Hopes!* would be
airing at last. Jeremy's girlfriend, Natasha, who had not yet
entered our lives during my theatrical debacle, thought it
sounded like the perfect occasion to gather and celebrate, so
Jeremy got on board and offered to bring in pizza and beer.
Though I was loath to watch my play massacred all over
again, I couldn't help salivating at the idea that Will Atherton
would soon be crucified on national television. Finally everyone would see what a fucking terror he was and I would be
avenged. I didn't relish the idea, but I even called to alert my
parents that I might appear on TV, for fear of their reaction if
I kept my mouth shut and they happened upon it anyway.

On a Tuesday night, over several six-packs and a few extra-
cheeses with pepperoni, we all gathered in our modest living
room. I had cleaned thoroughly and Parrot had forced Kirk

to get a haircut in honor of the occasion. Aunt Fran arrived with a nice bottle of gin and Kito even came, promising to share stories of his own horrific theatrical implosions. George brought me a pair of sunglasses so I could go out the next day without being recognized.

I was nervous, but mostly that I'd look ten pounds heavier on camera. We dimmed the lights and crowded around the coffee table and Jeremy turned up the volume as the narration began.

The show began with a cheesy montage of close-ups of various young artsy types saying things like "I wanna be on Broadway" or "I'm gonna make it! I have to!" I had been right all along—this show was embarrassing and I didn't need to lose any sleep over the fact that my talent was not being adequately showcased. The opening credits faded and there was a tracking shot of Will, walking through Times Square at night, looking pensively at all the marquees. A booming male voice said, "Will Atherton is a twenty-six-year-old theatre director, trying to make it in a tough business." They cut to a close-up of Will, wearing his signature black and clutching a deli coffee cup, saying, "I just want to tell stories. I've always wanted that. I believe in the theatre, in the magic of what it can do. It's my passion, my love."

"Bullshit!" Kito piped up. "Lose the turtleneck, kid!"

We all laughed. The booming voice-over continued.

"During the next month, Will will have to tackle a new play. He'll be responsible for the casting, the rehearsals, the production. It's a big challenge for a young director." Shots of Will sitting on a park bench, going through headshots, watching a drama class from the back of a rehearsal studio. It was all so clearly staged for the camera.

They cut to Will, sitting in a dim theatre, talking to the camera. "It's tough: I'm working with young actors, an inexperienced playwright—"

Several of us, myself included, vocally bristled at his statement, and Aunt Fran squawked, "Shut up and show us your tits!" She brings a little flavor of New Orleans wherever she goes.

Will continued. "This play is called *Georgia Allen's Window,* and it's by a young playwright named Liza Weiler. The play has got problems, it really does. I see good raw material here, but we're going to need to cover a lot of ground to get this piece ready for performance. It's a little bland, a little, um . . . I don't know how to say this . . . boring?"

"He fucking sucks!" Parrot shouted. I reddened.

The camera followed Will as he futzed around in auditions, and all of a sudden there I was, at the first rehearsal. I looked . . . scared. Standoffish. But not fat. That was good.

Then there was that first angry conversation in the hallway, the one where I'd first told Will I was worried. They'd done all this strange editing, washing the whole screen in flashes of red while I was talking. I looked bitchy. I squeezed George's hand. He whispered in my ear that I shouldn't worry, that all of these reality shows had to create conflict.

I slammed most of my beer during the next commercial, and everyone told me that I looked great and oohed and aahed over how cool it was to watch me on TV. But when we came back from the break it only got worse.

The narration started with "Will has encountered a serious problem with his playwright." And they cut to Will telling the camera, "She's tough. She's defensive and pretty unsupportive and frankly it gets me nervous having her around the cast. They need to feel safe. They need to feel like they can explore and her presence is very negative, very judgmental."

There was another shot of me watching rehearsal, looking deeply displeased. I couldn't believe I'd really looked like that. Aunt Fran shot me a disappointed look. Every other shot seemed to be of me snapping at Will or furiously handing him a note. The producers hadn't just created conflict—they'd created a villain. Brave young director takes on mean, diva playwright. And I'd given them way too much help.

I could feel the little crowd in the living room getting more and more uncomfortable. I couldn't blame them. I hadn't even realized what a raving terror I'd been. I swallowed hard.

It was all coming to a climax. I saw myself yelling: "IT WILL BE A PIECE OF *bleep*! IT'LL BE NONSENSE, WILL, which frankly it's dangerously close to being right now." A shot of Will looking shocked and wounded, the actors uncomfortable behind him. "I HAVE HAD IT! I'm done! Do whatever the hell you want with the play. Cut it in half if you want. But put it in the *bleep*ing program that it was your doing and not mine! I'm outta here."

They had bleeped me. Twice! I was mortified. I was despicable.

No one in the living room made a sound. We watched, in dead silence, as Will broke down and cried, right there in the theatre, seconds after I'd walked out.

I couldn't believe what I was seeing. It seemed endless. I had to sit there and watch Will conceiving the giant vagina and all the nakedness. And they showed me scowling again at the performance before the closing interview with Will.

"It was a tough road," he said, out of breath and euphoric, "but I'm so proud. I know I've done great work. I think it's going to get a great response." And then he whooped, as if he were at a football game, as the credits began to roll.

Nobody moved. Nobody spoke. Even George was frozen at my side. When the credits wrapped and a commercial came on, Kirk finally said, "I think it's over. You were great."

Parrot slapped him on the arm. "They were fucking out to get you I am so writing a letter I might even go down there and beat the crap out of someone."

I could feel everyone searching for the right thing to say, but there was really nothing.

Kito said, "You can't win in this business, doll. Damned if you do, damned if you don't." Within minutes he'd made an excuse about an early Pilates session and exited quickly.

My parents called immediately. My father called me a "tough cookie" and my mother told me to get my hair out of my face, that it had been distracting her the entire episode. Natasha said this was a perfect example of how you couldn't trust reality television and you never knew what was really going on in these shows. It didn't matter what anyone said. They were easily as shocked as I was to see me being horrible and malicious and picking on this deeply feeling, if wrong-headed, kid who was trying to do the best he could. I wasn't making points, I was just hitting him over the head with how much smarter I thought I was. Because I was frustrated and felt powerless, I was lashing out, and I was better at it than I'd even realized. Every blow had landed, I now saw. I didn't look smart, I looked mean.

Suddenly it all began to snowball in my head, all of my mother's warnings, the things I'd said to George, the way I'd treated Will. Aunt Fran went for her coat and requested in a not-so-delicate way that I walk her out. I complied.

When we got outside, she took a deep breath and said, "Alright, kid—"

I cut her off. "Please, don't," I begged. "I know. I know everything you're going to say, so please don't say it."

"May I suggest that you keep your mouth shut and listen for a minute?" I could tell that I'd pissed her off even more, but I was simply too beaten at that moment to hear what she thought. "You should never have agreed to that show," she began. "What do I always tell you about a public face? You never put yourself in a position you can't control, Niece! This is Hollywood 101! You're not new to this horseshit, you should know all this!"

"I know—"

"Your career is too damned valuable, your reputation means too much to risk it on some cheap television stunt! What did you think was going to happen? Did you think someone was going to see a three-minute clip of your play and boom! Straight to Broadway? There are no shortcuts, Liza!"

"Certainly not with you around," I muttered.

"Just what in the hell does that mean?" she rasped at me.

I took a deep breath. "I'm sorry," I said. "That was way out of line. When I agreed to that show, I was desperate. I was failing, and I was ready to do anything, *anything,* to get somewhere. I made a mistake. But do you know how it feels to be related to *you* and to know that all you'd have to do is pick up the phone? One phone call, all these years it would have taken one phone call, and my work would be getting read everywhere! Because you're you! Because people listen to you and they would listen to me because of you! But you've never done it! And yes, I'm so grateful to you for Kito, but I have no idea why you picked now to help me! Why am I suddenly good enough now when I never have been before?"

I was ashamed to cry in front of her, to be so naked and exposed, but it was better than faking it and having another word battle.

Aunt Fran's flinty stare was tempered with something I later recognized as sympathy. She didn't speak for a long moment and I dangled there, waiting.

She lit a cigarette, took one long drag and exhaled away from me before speaking. "You've always been good enough," she said. "But you've never been humble enough." She paused, I understood, to let the meaning sink in. "You're smart as a whip, kiddo, and you're gifted. You have been from the word go. But you've got too much to prove, and you don't want to play the same game everybody else plays. You don't want to take the hits, and believe me, Niece, life is all about being able to take a punch, not land one. I called Kito because you were finally getting off your duff and risking yourself. I could have gotten you everywhere as Frances Weiler's niece, but frankly I thought you'd like to see your own name on the Playbill."

I didn't know what to say. I had been blind to all of it.

She stepped into the street and a taxi appeared as if on command. "You're going to have to be willing to be breakable for a while. I have it on good authority you won't shatter." She looked into my face and then she drove away.

I sunk down on the stoop. The front door of our building opened behind me and George stepped out onto the stoop. "I thought maybe you'd gone into witness protection." He sat down beside me.

"They're picking me up in ten minutes," I said. George leaned back on one hand and rubbed my neck with the other.

"This is why I don't do public appearances," he said.

I wanted to laugh, but I couldn't. "Am I really like that?" I asked quietly.

He laughed. "You have your moments." He was kidding, but he wasn't.

"I've done this . . . I've been harsh with you." He started to deny it but I stopped him. "I have, I know I have."

"You've got a tongue on you, Liza. Normally I enjoy it." He flashed a devilish grin but sensed that I didn't see the humor. "And then sometimes I guess I don't."

I suppose somewhere I expected him to deny it, to insist that I was an angel, even though we both knew it wasn't true.

"I don't want to do it. I don't want to be that horrible bitch."

"Would it make a difference if I said I still like you?"

I put my head on his shoulder. "Yeah," I said, "but not enough."

*"Some days, there just isn't sufficient liquor
in the cabinet."*

CHAPTER 34

I TRIED, IN THE DAYS that followed my exposure to
the TV-watching public as a rotten, nasty bitch, to get my
head in order. Clearly, the universe had seen fit to phone in a
review of my recent performances, saying, "Ms. Weiler
would do well to rethink her character, or risk being replaced
in the role of a lifetime." To make matters worse, after the incident with George's father and the Cinco de Mayo party, I
was still carrying a hint of that jittery feeling, the one that re-
minds you every new relationship plays out dangerously
close to the edge of a cliff. Perhaps it was the revelation of a
serious flaw in myself, or perhaps the not-so-gentle reminder
that human beings need, in general, to be treated with care. I
tried to synthesize the whole incident down into a couple of
pithy lessons about myself and my relationships, but it's hard
to do that when the better part of your behavior has been
brought into question. I knew I had to tread more carefully.

I think my string of revelations would actually have
brought me and George closer together, maybe even made
way for us to be more honest, but technology had other
ideas.

On May 18, while doing some work at Kito's loft, I got an
e-mail from George:

To: lizalikearug@shinygun.com
From: g-doren@turnbullprince.com
Subject: oops
Liza,
Don't know if you're aware, but the Bugbear virus extracts old
messages from your sent box, and forwards them randomly to the
folks in your address book. I think you've got it. I'll call you in a few
days.
George

Attached was the following message from early December.

To: principessa@magmail.com
From: lizalikearug@shinygun.com
Subject: fucker
P,
If I could only express to you how fucking distasteful I find
spending any time with George, I doubt you would ever force me
to join you all in your boozy shenanigans again. The man makes
my skin crawl. I don't know if I've ever been more outraged by five
seconds of conversation with anyone. I literally wanted to throw
up. The only reason to EVER date a guy like that is so he can
throw excessive amounts of cash at you until you realize it's not
worth it, and obviously he's experienced a bevy of insubstantial but
willing women who know this. He may be amusing but I think he's
actually a shitty person. Don't make me go out with you guys
anymore.
L.

I tried to call him at work right away, but for the next four
hours all I got was voice mail. Same with home and cell.
There was so much I needed to tell him and I didn't want to

do it in an e-mail. I had sent that message to Parrot months ago, right after George had saved Jack from being pulverized at Cherry Tavern; it had made me so hot for him I think I was actually terrified. And he didn't see the e-mail Parrot wrote back to me that said, *"You want him so bad,"* or the one I sent back to her that said, *"I know. It's a serious problem. But timing is everything...."* But now I couldn't tell him that, because clearly *"I'll call you in a few days"* meant "I'm going to spend the next few days deciding on the best way to never see you again."

I e-mailed him begging him to call me. I called him every hour at every number I could think of.

I phoned Parrot in hysterics. She sat with me all night, and since I had launched into a full-scale panic in front of an extremely kind and understanding Kito, I was given the next day off. I made Parrot call Kirk to see if he could find George and deliver my desperate pleas for forgiveness.

Finally I knew the right things to say and I couldn't get a chance to say them. No one had ever gotten in like George had; I'd never let it happen before and never wanted to. And the further I admitted him into my private and well-protected world, the more afraid I was to wake up one morning and find that I really was just another in a long string of briefly amusing conquests. Even worse, to find that I wasn't amusing any longer. But that didn't matter anymore. I was willing to risk being shattered.

I think befuddled Jeremy went to stay at Natasha's eventually because he didn't know what to do for me. And Parrot could only ramble while I sniffled and contemplated my doom.

"Liza the thing is that he doesn't understand how you are about him and I mean I know because I know you and I've been watching this whole thing and even though George sort of seems really tough and hard and everything maybe he's really sensitive and you just don't know it yet because you haven't been together that long and you haven't seen that side of him like Kirk is really really allergic to mascarpone and I didn't know that and then he didn't want my aunt's tiramisu and we had this huge big fight and didn't have sex for like three days and I'm sure this is just like that and it'll all be fine."

But I didn't think it was fine. When he hadn't called me five days later, I knew I was in really big trouble. Oddly enough, Kirk did call.

"Eliza, this is Kirk, you know, Parrot's man-friend?"

I used to think he was kidding, but now I really think Kirk thinks there's an "E" in front of the Liza.

"Hi, Kirk!" I brightened. I prayed that he would have something good to tell me.

"Um, yeah, Eliza? Um, George's like, in a bad way, I think. He's been really nasty in the office and I think he's getting drunk every night."

Secretly, I confess I was rejoicing at the news that maybe he was hurting half as much as I was.

"Has he said anything?"

"Um, no? He's like, pretty much not talking to anyone."

"Yeah, well, he's definitely not talking to me."

"Um, yeah, Parrot kind of said that? Um, I think you should talk to him, Eliza."

"Well ... I would really like to do that, Kirk, but I don't think he's into that, seeing as he's not, as I said, speaking to me."

Though for a moment I'd hoped he could provide some valuable insight, Kirk was quickly becoming the human salt in my emotional wound.

"Right, but, see, I think, like, from what Parrot told me, that he thinks you don't really think very highly of him?"

"Yeah, I know that, Kirk."

"Right, okay, but, Eliza?"

"Yeah?"

"I think you should just try to tell him anyway...how you, like . . . feel."

Even as it became clear that Kirk was less articulate than I had previously imagined, I realized he had a better bead on the situation than I did. Maybe what George needed was a grand gesture, a risk on my part. Maybe I had to bring the mountain to George.

After thanking Kirk in what turned out to be a ridiculously tender moment, I racked my brain for the best way to express my feelings. It came to me quickly: I'm a writer—I would put it into words. I sat down to compose a painfully honest, beautiful, moving and eloquent e-mail that would over-whelm George and bring him back to me immediately. I needed to be exposed, open, brave, none of which came nat-urally. I needed to say some of the words I was always writing for other people.

> To: g-doren@turnbullprince.com
> From: lizalikearug@shinygun.com
> Subject: (no subject)
> I'm sorry.
> I'm so very sorry for ever making you doubt me. I don't know who I
> thought you were looking for, and I don't know why I couldn't
> believe it was me. I pushed because I was afraid that if I let you in
> too far you'd break me in two. But that isn't you, it's all me.
> And e-mail is the worst possible way to say this, but:
> I'm in love with you. I've never said that to anyone before in my life.
> If you'll ever speak to me again, I'll say it in person.
> Liza

Words can fail you at the most inopportune times. His re-sponse came back immediately.

To: lizalikearug@shinygun.com
From: g-doren@turnbullprince.com
Subject: Out of the Office (autoresponse)
I will be out of the office until June 5. For matters requiring
immediate attention, please contact David Koster at
d-koster@turnbullprince.com.

I felt the bottom fall out of the world.

*"Losing it once in a while is good for you.
Just be sure to find it again later."*

CHAPTER 35

THEY SAY IT'S BETTER to have loved and lost than never to have loved at all. Has anyone weighed in on telling someone you love them, via e-mail, and having them never speak to you again? Or on finally, after twenty-eight years of life, finding someone who you not only can love, but, in fact, cannot help but love, and then realizing that with a few carelessly chosen words, you've essentially eliminated any and all chances for your own happiness? Because if nobody's covered this particularly rocky ground yet, let me be the first to place it somewhere between getting your hand stuck in a combine and being hit in the head by a chunk of frozen sewage falling from a passing 747. It sucks. It's terrible and rotten and bad, bad, bad.

And it hurts. Christ, does it hurt.

George was nowhere to be found, his out-of-office e-mail consistently bouncing back to me every time I tried to contact him. Kirk was no help. Apparently George had flown the coop without telling anybody anything. He could've been using his accrued vacation days for an impromptu jaunt to Maui, or he could've gone underground to live in the subway tunnels and eat rats. This lack of information wasn't exactly comforting, as I was able to convince myself that I hadn't only broken his heart, perhaps I'd driven him insane and ruined his life all in one shot. Granted, this seems a little extreme as I reflect on it now, but I was not at my most rational.

Parrot was a true rock throughout. From the first phone call, she was at my side without question whenever I so much as peeped. Even Kirk had tried to join the vigil, but I think my endless unanswerable questions about George's whereabouts had frightened him away. Kind Jeremy had prepared Natasha for my near-breakdown state, and the two of them spent hours trying to convince me it would all work out. He even held me when I started crying during a *Golden Girls* rerun (Blanche's dead husband was named George).

"This will be a funny story you guys' tell at parties," Natasha promised me.

"It won't," I insisted.

"Liza," she returned, "you messed up. But something you said in an e-mail a hundred years ago is not the sort of thing that makes someone leave you. Unless he's an idiot."

"Maybe it's not the sort of thing that makes someone leave *you*—"

"No! I'm serious. This is not right. And for him to refuse to even speak to you about it . . ."

"You're forgetting, though, about Cinco de Mayo. And dinner with his dad. And the stupid, stupid Christmas party. I've done this before. There was a pattern. I have a pattern of cruelty. Millions of people got to see it on national television! No, I pushed George away. Over and over and over again. It makes sense that eventually he would take the hint and leave!"

"LIZA! You are not cruel!" Jeremy piped up. "Yes, you're a little tough sometimes, but so what? You're also generous and loving and supportive the rest of the time. I'm sorry, I know you're crazy about this guy, but does any of his behavior strike you as a little irrational?"

"What if he's just really sensitive?"

"What if he's selfish and immature?" Natasha asked gently. And she looked at me like someone who'd just told a child there was no Santa Claus.

"What if he is?" I said. "I don't think I care."

Days dragged by and still no word from George. The longer I waited, the more sure I became that he had just disappeared, that I'd never hear from or about him again and that that would be my punishment. I would roam the earth searching for a trace of him. I would be like that sad Kiefer Sutherland character in *The Vanishing* who gets buried alive trying to find out whatever happened to Sandra Bullock.

But on Wednesday the fifth, Kirk reported to Parrot that George was back in the office. No explanations. Just back. And still not attempting to contact me.

Jeremy gave me ample time to bemoan my woes before he finally jumped with both feet on the anti-George bandwagon.

"It's just not cool, Big L. I can totally see where this guy's coming from and I'd be hurt too, but I know you. I mean, I've lived with you a long time and you're somebody that nobody could walk away from that easily. And he's gotta know what you're going through. You deserve better than that.

"Oh, and Natasha sent you her copy of *War and Peace*. She said you should look at Natasha and Andrei. Natasha the character. I mean, Natasha, my Natasha, said you should check out the story of Natasha, the character, and Andrei, the prince. Also a character. She insults him and breaks his heart and he goes off to war and she feels bad and realizes what she missed out on and she goes after him and he forgives her."

He forgives her and then he dies. We've all read the book. Poor Jeremy. He tries.

"We're built to survive certain tragedies.
It just turns out that a lion attack isn't one of them."

CHAPTER 36

PERHAPS THE MOST DANGEROUS thing about falling in love, especially ill-fated love, is the way it can make you forget that you're a person with a life. I have seen far too many capable, healthy people with jobs and families and great apartments simply turn into puddles of self-pity all because of a star-crossed relationship that took a lousy turn. I never pictured myself as the type, but there I was, two weeks after George made his sudden and dramatic exit, barely working and barely getting through the day. It was like I'd just forgotten that I had an identity before George.

Unlike Kito, I was shocked when the literary manager at New Manhattan Playhouse called to tell me that they would indeed be pleased to include *Georgia Allen's Window* in their summer reading series. Orson DeMayo, a young hotshot out of UCSD had expressed an interest in directing the piece. They wanted me to come in and discuss casting. The reading was scheduled for the first of July. The part of me that knew how delighted I should have been expressed my joy and thanks. The rest of me could only think that George wasn't going to be there for my first New York triumph.

Kito was thrilled and proud and couldn't understand why I was still wallowing in misery.

"Sweetie," he asked one afternoon while I was tidying up the loft, "you're having your first big reading, at a big theatre, in the big city. Why are you not dancing?"

"I don't really feel like dancing," I said.

"It's the guy, right?"

"Right," I admitted. I was so pathetic and exposed and I didn't even care anymore.

"Oh, God, honey, what can I tell you? Look, men are a bitch. The important part is to keep in mind that there's always another one incoming. And in the meantime, hello? Career? Anyone? Anyone? Perk up, doll, you're the meanest playwright in New York, remember?"

Unfortunately, I did. By this point, I was so worn out, I was prepared to just sleep through the rest of my life, career and all. Aunt Fran attempted a rescue, as usual.

"Niece!" she barked, when I picked up the phone. "No word?"

"No, Aunt Fran."

"I'm thinking of hiring a detective. He could've been killed, you know. This is New York."

Though I appreciated the sentiment, I assured her that I had it on good authority George was simply avoiding me.

"Liza, you know I don't like to interfere in your life. But when they say youth is wasted on the young, they're talking about you. Now listen up! You remember Kissinger, that schnauzer I used to have? That dog would've taken a bullet for me. He bit Jack Kerouac during a card game, once, but that's not the point. Kissinger once carried a dead squirrel into a dinner party and I screamed bloody murder in front of Natalie Wood and Robert Wagner. That dog didn't come out of the closet for a week. Understand?"

"I think so."

"No, you don't. You've hurt his feelings, Liza, but that's not the damned problem."

"It's not?"

"No, the damned problem is that you've embarrassed him. Men can take bullets, but they can't stand to be humiliated."

"You're saying I should've shot him?"

"I'm saying you need to find a way to give him back the power. He can't come back without a reason or you're still in control. Say your piece and let him go, Niece. If he does not come back . . . I'll think of something more dramatic."

I sat and stared into the middle distance for about an hour after hanging up. I had a feeling Aunt Fran was right. Or more to the point, I had a feeling I was going to have to let go one way or the other. I really didn't want to end up buried alive.

I just needed to give it one more shot. There was only one way I knew of to corner him, and though I was fairly sure I'd make things worse, I couldn't do nothing anymore. I donned my orange cashmere halter, because George always liked it, and my great butt jeans, which never seem to hurt. I went to his office.

I knew he wouldn't be out before six, so I bought a venti skim chai and stationed myself in the window of the Starbucks across the street. The downside of my plan became evident an hour and a half later, when my chai was gone, my bladder was insistently full, and George had still not emerged. The situation was becoming dire.

I considered bribing a barista to watch the entrance to George's building, but realized "the handsomest man you've ever seen" would have been an inadequate description to give to a perfect stranger who might well have his or her own taste.

I had no choice. I had to risk it. I practically backed into the bathroom (and why are Starbucks bathrooms always so filthy when everything else there is frighteningly spic'n'span?), peed as fast as a human being can and scooted back to my post. And there was George.

He was making his way through the revolving door in that blue shirt with the white collar and cuffs that I liked so much. He looked worn, which was gratifying, and preoccupied. And sort of . . . empty. Where, I wondered, was the swagger I so loved?

I'd decided to approach him from behind as he made his way to the subway. I wanted to catch him by the arm and whisper something into his ear, like, "Hey, don't I know you?" Lauren Bacall would have pulled it off.

I, on the other hand, am a slave to the trappings of reality. Pesky things like traffic lights are always getting in my way. Cars began to rush between us and George was about to turn the corner and disappear. I couldn't lose him again.

So I ran out into the street.

People in movies seem to be able to dodge three lanes of speeding uptown traffic all the time. I almost lost the use of my life. Thinking I had an opening after a silver Lexus whizzed by me, I attempted to dash across the center lane when an out-of-control taxi zoomed out from the right lane and almost took me out. The cabbie screeched to a halt and leaned out the window to scream at me, which of course made all the other cars slow down to watch, and the people on the sidewalk craned their necks and suddenly I was the center attraction at Madison and Forty-seventh Street.

He saw me. Of course he saw me. The crazy girl in the middle of the street in the orange sweater was staring straight at him. How could he miss me?

And he started to walk away.

"George!" I shouted. "Wait!"

The light changed and I made it across the third lane. He was only yards away and I ran.

"Wait!" I called.

I caught his shoulder and he had to turn around.

"You were just going to run away and never speak to me again?" I demanded. "It doesn't work that way! You don't get to do that."

"I don't want to do this, Liza."

"What? Me? Us? What is it you don't want to do?"

"I'm not having this discussion in the middle of the street." He barely looked at me. He just looked over my head like maybe I'd vanish if he just wanted it badly enough.

"Then let's go somewhere," I pleaded.

He didn't say anything.

"You can't really think that I meant what that e-mail said. You have to know how I feel about you."

"Liza—"

"No, listen to me! I love you. I'm in love with you. There is no one in the world who I respect or admire or...or bloody *trust* more than you. And the rest of this is bullshit! The things I've said, the mistakes I've made. I was scared, George. I was just scared. Why don't you get that?"

He looked at his shoes for a long time. I willed him to raise his eyes and look at me, but he wouldn't. I was saying it. I was saying everything I'd been unable, too afraid, to say for so long, and for the first time in my entire life I was actually allowing myself to mean it. But he wasn't looking at me. I prayed silently. *Please,* I thought, *please, please, please ...*

"Sometimes," he finally said, "people should go with their instincts."

"George. This is what I've been trying to tell you! My instincts were—"

"Not yours." He paused. "Mine."

He looked me in the eye for the first time. And there was a wall where I'd never seen one before.

"I don't ...," I stuttered, not knowing what to say. "I don't think I understand."

I could tell that all he wanted to do was get away from me, but I wasn't going to let him.

"I'm sorry," he said.

I couldn't breathe.

"George . . ."

"I have to go. Take care of yourself."

I opened my mouth, but I couldn't make a sound. I wanted to evaporate, to lose consciousness, to sprain my ankle so he'd have to take me to the hospital and we could start all over again and this time I wouldn't fuck it up.

But I just stood there.

He turned away.

"George . . ." It came out as an eerie, choked animal sob.

He stopped.

He started to turn back to me.

And then he changed his mind.

I watched him fade away.

"A good friend will take a bullet for you,
but I prefer a friend who won't let it come to that."

CHAPTER 37

WHEN YOU KNOW SOMETHING is over, really over, when all the panic has gone and there's no more pressure because nothing you do will matter, a whole new kind of grief sets in. I fell into bed feeling absolutely hollow and I slept through the night.

Aunt Fran had flowers delivered to my door on Thursday morning with an invitation to "Celebrate your pain at my place tomorrow. Be there at four. Wong will be joining us."

Arthur Wong was a Chinese textile magnate who had captured Aunt Fran's affections some few months before, and what followed was one of the most enviable romances I could imagine. Mr. Wong seemed to understand Aunt Fran's fanciful nature as well as her thorny tongue, and she was actually very sweet to him when she thought no one was looking. Mostly they just seemed to delight each other. Feeling as though my broken heart had been somehow cauterized by the finality of my exchange with George, I decided that a wine-soaked supper with a functional older couple would be about as fine an evening's entertainment as any I might come by.

Besides, it's easy to say yes to invitations when you're dead inside. One place is pretty much like another.

Aunt Fran took one look at me and sized up the whole situation.

"Damn near killed you, didn't he?"

I nodded.

"Never happened before, has it?"

I shook my head.

She clucked. "The big ones are like that. Welcome to the world, kiddo. You couldn't stay in the tower forever."

I was so drained that for once I was unprepared to banter.

I barely touched the exquisite coq au vin that Mr. Wong had prepared for us. Nor did I enjoy the wine with my usual appetite. I sat there and moved food around on my plate while Aunt Fran and Mr. Wong rehashed the details of my sordid tragedy.

"Your friend's honor has been injured," Mr. Wong ventured.

"I don't think it's his honor, Wong," Aunt Fran rebutted, "I think it's his ego. All men want their women to revere them as gods. You know it, I know it, the Pope knows it."

"I am afraid I do not agree with you, Frances. A man desires only respect."

"Men, Wong, and believe me I know, desire one hell of a package. And you know what really flips my nut? I thought she had a good one here. I saw these kids and I thought, this is how it's done! This is—"

"Enough!" I lost it and my fork clattered onto my plate. "It doesn't matter! It's over! I fucked it up and I lost him and I'll never get him back!" Tears streamed down my cheeks. "So it doesn't matter why it happened or who's right or what the hell men want! The point is ... the point is I had ... *it* ... for the first time in my life. I had the thing. And now I don't."

I had never seen Aunt Fran look so sad. Because she didn't know how to fix it either.

I took my leave early in an attempt to keep from ruining their entire evening. It was probably too late.

I walked all the way home, which was a considerable distance, but the air felt good. Moving felt good. It occurred to me that I'd spent nearly as much time in agony over George as I had in ecstasy. As much as every breath and step I took hurt, I felt like a member of the human race in a way I never had before. Like an adult. Battle-scarred. Well, I suppose scars only form as you heal, so maybe I was more wounded at this point. But at least I was moving.

If I'd never had my heart broken before, I'd also never experienced the tremendously complex recovery period that follows. For the first few weeks, all I could do was feel sorry for myself. Many a mint milano was sacrificed to my grief. *Many.*

When I hit the fourteen-day mark, a fed-up Jeremy intervened. He breezed in one afternoon, flushed with his progress on the Once-and-Future Dissertation, took one look at my rumpled pajamas (it was four-thirty in the afternoon) and Pepperidge Farm detritus and sprung into action.

"That's it!" he barked.

"You're blocking the TV," I drawled.

With one well-placed smack, Jeremy wrung a death blip from the cable box.

"Now I'm not blocking anything."

"I was watching that ..." I trailed off. Really I'd been watching my third date with George. In my head. I think *Power Rangers* was actually on the TV.

"Big L, you know I love ya. You know you're the greatest. You know I'd do anything for you."

"I believe I know this."

"Good. Because this is gonna hurt. UP!"

"I'm comfortable."

"I don't care. Now go put some clothes on because we are going outside."

"I don't want to go outside."

"Liza, get off the damned couch or I'll get you off the damned couch."

It is rare that Jeremy gets sufficiently peeved to take this sort of action, and I confess that I'm often tempted to see just how far he'll go.

"Make me." I thought it was funny.

"Fine," he said.

I didn't know that my roommate was capable of throwing me over his shoulder like a sack of potatoes, but the next thing I knew I was standing in front of my closet watching him select clothing items that really didn't go together. He laid them out on the bed.

"You have five minutes," he said. "Five minutes, and then I take you outside in your pajamas."

He shut my door. Left with no other options, I got dressed. Not in what he picked out, because frankly I would never wear navy and black together, but dressed nonetheless.

It was a beautiful afternoon, just at that time of year where June is deciding whether it's a spring or a summer month. The obnoxiously abundant spring rains had made all the trees leafy and the grass green. We bought Italian ices in Union Square and strolled east.

"Isn't this better?" he asked.

"If you say so," I acquiesced.

"I have never seen you even remotely like this, Liza. Honestly, you're scaring the crap out of me. What the hell is going on?"

"I don't know," I said.

"Can I tell you what I think?"

"Can I stop you?"

"I think this guy is not worth all this. I think no guy is worth all this. And if this were Parrot, or me, or anybody else you know, you would say it was ridiculous and pathetic and you wouldn't stand for it. You fell for somebody and you got hurt. You had a breakup. You don't get to just shut down. Nobody died here, Liza. You feel bad. And I'm sorry you feel bad, but sometimes how you feel is just how you feel, you know? You've gotta get the hell over this."

"Don't tell me how to feel, Jeremy."

"I'm not. I would never presume to tell you how to feel. But I will tell you how to act. You're behaving like an infant. Adults get to feel however they want, but they don't get to sit on the couch for two weeks and act like they're not alive. And the girl I've been friends with for ten years would know that. So I'm trying to wake her the hell up."

He was right and I knew it. But I was furious all of a sudden.

"Are you listening to any of this?" he demanded.

I didn't say anything.

"You're getting pissed off at me."

"No, I'm not," I said.

"Yeah, right, sister. I'm not buying it! I know you! You're getting pissed off!"

"Jeremy, I'm not pissed off at you."

"Really? Then you're even more pathetic than I thought."

"EXCUSE ME?" I demanded. I brandished my Italian ice scoop at him. "Who the hell do you think you are to stand there and tell me how I should be handling this?! You have no idea how I feel! And I don't see you putting yourself on the line very often so it's real easy to tell me that I'm not do-ing it right! You know what you can do with your advice, Jeremy? You can roll it up into a neat little ball and you can shove it up your all-knowing ass!"

"Well, good morning, Liza Weiler!" He smiled.

It took me a second to figure out that I'd just been the vic-tim of a successful intervention. "Are you kidding me?" I had to laugh a little.

"I would never kid you," he said.

"You are such a rat!"

"And you almost stuck that little wooden spoon up my nose!" he countered. Which was true.

"Yeah? And what are you gonna do about it?"

"Come with me." He took my arm. "I'll show you exactly what I'm gonna do about it."

"Where are we going?" I asked.

"The park."

"Which park?"

"Which is your favorite park in all of New York except you can't get in because you don't have a key?" he asked.

Gramercy Park was gated on all sides. Only the surrounding residents were graced with the freedom to stroll the manicured paths and sit reading on picturesque benches.

"Gramercy Park." He reached into his pocket and held something shiny in front of my face. "And what does this look like?"

"You did not come up with a key to the park, Jeremy."

"I didn't?"

"What did you do?"

"Natasha's grandmother lives in that building right over there." He pointed to a 19th-century brick job with climbing ivy and gingerbread.

"Now," he continued, "take this key. And take this." He produced a paperback from his back pocket. *The Collected Poetry of Dorothy Parker.* "From Natasha. She said it was the right thing. Go find yourself a bench."

I thought I might cry.

"You know there's nobody like you in the whole entire world, Jeremy Wright?" I hugged him. "Thank you. So, so, so much."

"And thank you. For not actually sticking that spoon up my nose."

Mrs. Parker and I let ourselves into the park as if we'd been born there. The flowers were even prettier from inside the gate. You could almost forget that you were in the middle of Manhattan. I took great care in selecting my bench and took a deep breath. Jeremy was right. I was awake.

I read.

If there was one thing Dorothy Parker did better than anyone it was heartbreak. I sat beneath a tree for hours and cried alone and wallowed for what I knew would have to be the last time. The hurt might stay, but I'd have to try to let it go. I waded through pages and pages of insightful and bitter verse, and slowly I realized my agony wasn't so original. I heard myself laugh out loud for the first time in weeks. And I knew I would be alright.

*"Pick yourself up, keep breathing, and one day
it'll happen all over again."*

CHAPTER 38

IT HAS COME TO MY ATTENTION that most
of life's dramas, no matter how they may seem to pick you
up like a twister, whirl you around by the ankle and bash
your head on a rock, eventually deposit you back on solid
ground. Bruised, perhaps, but standing. Only a few weeks after my "tragic" breakup, I found myself walking upright
again, having pulled myself up by the invaluable bootstraps
of healthy rage.

I was pissed.

Finally it had dawned on me that I couldn't be solely to
blame for what had transpired between me and George; a
tango ain't the only thing that takes two. And since I'd done
my best to remedy the situation and George had done *absolutely nothing* to make either of us feel better, I had finally begun to understand that I was better off without him. He
wasn't the right guy for me. He was worthy of nothing so
much as my disdain.

The fact that I missed him every minute of every day was
something I was going to keep to myself. (Along with the fact
that although I'd changed my sheets I refused to change one

pillowcase that still carried George's faint scent.) Jeremy was right; I'd always been so tough on people who fell apart when they lost someone in a breakup. People who acted as if food didn't taste as good and colors didn't seem as bright just because they'd been left. And though I was one of them now, I was moved to pretend that the old me was still in charge. As a wise roommate once said, you can't help how you feel, but you can help how you act. I was going to act as if there had never been a George.

My friends marveled at my suddenly admirable mental state. Parrot and Jeremy and I sat sipping wine outside of Time Café one evening taking in the delightful early summer scene on Lafayette Street.

"You look great," Jeremy told me.

"He's so right you can't even tell how much ice cream you've eaten and you're like so happy and fine and everything I'm totally going to fix you up as soon as you say the word." To Parrot, one man's exit was another man's VACANCY sign.

"I'll let you know," I promised.

"Do it I'm serious do it!" she insisted.

"I will, P, I really will. Just not quite yet."

"Alone is good," my roommate interjected. "Sometimes there's nothing better than having some time to yourself. And you have so much great stuff coming up! Your reading—"

"That's right what's the date again I'm bringing tons of people you are gonna be so famous!"

"It's just a reading."

"It's not just a reading!" he insisted. "It's a really big deal. You have an amazing cast and a great director and people, big people, are going to see your work. It's a big, huge opportunity that you've worked really hard for. Lean on your own horn for just a second, Liza!"

"We did get Michael Mason," I said. "I just found that out yesterday." Michael Mason was a multiple Emmy winner who played a hard-boiled but loveable detective on network television's longest-running cop show. And now he was going to play my vengeful neighborhood troublemaker. Orson, the director, had assembled three terrific actors to play Georgia Allen and her other neighbors, including Rick Imbruglia, a very handsome up-and-comer on the downtown scene. I couldn't believe how well things were shaping up. We would have two days of rehearsal and then I'd have my first shot at semi-major exposure.

"What are you wearing did you figure it out yet should we go shopping?" Parrot had her usual angle covered.

For once, fashion wasn't my first priority. The audience wouldn't be looking at me. I just hoped they'd be hearing me.

In any case, I didn't have much time to dwell. July 1 rolled around before you could say final rewrite. Our rehearsals had gone swimmingly. The literary manager at the New Manhattan Playhouse assured me that the audience would be filled with representatives from other off-Broadway houses all over the city. Orson did a phenomenal job. I barely had to open my mouth, save for answering the occasional question from diligent actors, and anyway I was pretty focused on learning to be a constructive part of the process. You know, not the sort of playwright who makes a director cry. Fortunately, no one involved in this reading seemed to have caught my diva turn on TV.

Michael Mason was even better than I had hoped and made a point of taking me aside to tell me how much he liked my work. (He also made a point of telling Aunt Fran how much he liked her work when she met me after rehearsal. Apparently they had a thing in the late '70s.)

Rick Imbruglia, who would soon after be cast in a pilot about teenagers who are played by people in their thirties, was gorgeous. Unignorably gorgeous. Six months before I would have been scraping my jaw off the floor. But now I really couldn't bring myself to care much.

Rick, it would seem, could not say the same. He caught up to me as we were leaving our second rehearsal.

"Your play is really special. Really," he said.

"Oh, well, you're doing such a great job," I told him.

"I do so many of these things, you know, and it's so rare to find a script that you really connect with." Rick was one of those actors who took his work very seriously. The kind who likes to talk about his "craft" and his "technique" and his "commitment," even when he only appears in two scenes. He was lucky he was so good-looking.

"That's really kind of you to say. I'm so thrilled to have you guys working on it."

"I can't believe I've never read your work before. You're so dynamic and fresh. That scene I have with Anne is just … I actually felt like I was inside it, you know? Like I could have lost control and really gone for it. I don't usually experience that in just a rehearsal."

I was blushing. I didn't really know what to say and mostly I felt like he was blowing smoke, but then again, the encouragement was nice.

"Hey, ah … would you like to get a drink with me sometime? I would love to talk some more about theatre with you."

"Oh … wow, I would … I mean, I would love to talk more with you …"

He sensed that I was going to try to dance my way out of this.

"No problem. Understood. I didn't mean to overstep."

What was I doing? There was a foxy, talented man standing in front of me thinking I was great and I was going to turn him down? Without even getting to know him. And for what? Because I was carrying around some stupid made-up romance that barely ever existed outside of my mind?

"I would love to have a drink with you, Rick. And talk about theatre. Or whatever …"

"Great!" he said. He kissed me on the cheek. "I'm going to the F train. I'll see you tomorrow." He hoisted his messenger bag over his shoulder and started off. "Don't be nervous!" he called back. "They're gonna love you!"

I allowed myself only the briefest moment to think about how much I should have enjoyed his attention.

"It's good to be the star. The pay is great, the hours are terrific and someone always saves you a seat."

CHAPTER 39

I AWOKE ON JULY 1, elated, but with my stomach tied in knots. It was that morning-of-the-exam feeling. This was always the part I had trouble with—the letting go. You work so hard and then you surrender control and hope for the best. At least this time I knew I had made a contribution and not been a detriment. One lesson learned.

Aunt Fran met me half an hour before the reading for a pep talk.

"This, Liza, is just one step in a long career. Don't give it too much weight."

"Hmph."

"Don't hmph me, Niece, when I'm about to say something sentimental."

"I don't believe it."

"You shut up and listen for a minute. You, my young protégée, have written an extraordinary play. And I am so proud to see it given its due."

"Aunt Fran—"

"I'm not done. You're beautiful, Liza. You're an incredible

woman. And every once in a while some fool will come along who won't acknowledge that. But tonight, you're going to sit in a room full of people who will. And goddamnit, I'm gonna be one of 'em."

I teared up. I couldn't help it. "I owe you an apology," I told her. "You were right. About a lot of things. I'm sorry I've been so . . ."

"Headstrong? Loudmouthed? Just like me?" She smiled. "Apology accepted. You go get 'em, kiddo."

That night, four actors in front of music stands read my play almost exactly as I'd imagined it in my head for two years. They were glorious. I could not have been happier. I was remembering what it felt like to succeed for the first time in longer than I could remember. People actually stood at the end. Parrot (on time for the first time maybe ever), Kirk, Jeremy and Natasha led the ovation.

I was flooded with congratulations. Kito stood beside me and whispered important names and titles into my ear so I could pretend I knew who people were when they approached. Cards were pressed into my hands, compliments offered over and over. VIPs I'd been trying to contact for years suddenly stood in front of me asking for meetings. Having finally been knocked down more than a few pegs, the sudden rush of approval was a shock.

"You're a fucking genius you know that I can't believe I'm even friends with you you little bitch." Parrot was crying as she hugged me, and proudly displayed her family's penchant for cussing at emotional moments.

"Liza, I'm so very glad I was here," Natasha gushed. Overwhelmed, Jeremy actually picked me up in a bear hug.

"Niece!" Aunt Fran swept in. "She's brilliant!" she shouted to no one in particular. "We're going to go across the street for a drink so you can hold court like an old pro. Lord knows you've been watching me long enough to know how." The theatre was emptying out. "And I believe a certain artistic director would like to discuss the possibilities of developing your fine play," she whispered. "Knock 'em dead, kiddo! What did I say? Knock 'em dead!" She swept out.

I ran backstage to get my purse and when I came back through the theatre it was almost empty. Someone I could just make out was standing in the back of the house by the doors. At first I thought he was a mirage, but he didn't disappear.

The first and last person I had wanted to see that evening was actually standing there waiting for me. I knew I had to walk right past him to get out, but for a second I couldn't move. And then without even wanting them to, my legs started to carry me toward him.

I stopped a few yards away. He just stared at me.

"What are you doing here?" I asked.

"I don't know," George said. He looked about as haggard as I'd felt for the past month.

" 'I don't know'?" I questioned.

"I just couldn't miss it," he said. "Kirk told me."

I paused. Seeing his face had knocked the wind out of me. But watching him stand in front of me, saying nothing that I wanted to hear, I began to feel that rage that had gotten me on my feet again.

"You watched?" I asked.

"You're extraordinary," he said. "I mean you're an incredible writer."

"Thank you."

We just stood there.

"I have people waiting for me," I said.

"Liza," he started.

"What?" I demanded. "What, George? What do you want? What are you doing here?"

Say it. Say you miss me. Say you can't get over me. Say you want me back and this has all been a horrible dream but it's over now.

"I just . . . wanted to see your play. Done right."

Run, I thought. *Run. Run. Run. Because you'll only be able to hold on for another minute.*

"I have to go," I said.

"Okay," he said.

"FUCK YOU!" I shouted. I didn't know I was going to say it. "Why the hell would you show up here?! This is my night! I don't want you here!"

"I . . . Fine." He started to go.

"Oh, no. No way do you get to show up and then say two words and walk away. After I tried for weeks to get ahold of you! Unh uh!"

"What do you want me to say?!" He was just as angry as I was, I suddenly realized. "How many times did I have to hear how little you thought of me before I walked away?"

"Are you five years old? Do you not listen?! I could not have tried to tell you more how much I think of you! Yes, okay, I am too harsh sometimes, and lash out when I'm threatened. I know that now, mostly because of you. But you tell someone that! You say it out loud. You don't keep your mouth shut and then make the silent, gradual decision to run away. What happened to our thing, George? We fought! We bickered and we got turned on and then we couldn't keep our hands off each other! I thought we both enjoyed that!"

"This was different," he insisted.

"How?! Tell me how it was different!"

"Because it was! Do you know how it feels to stand in front of someone you love, the *only* person who you think might actually see you, and have them talk to you like—" He broke off.

I don't think he knew what he'd just said. But I did.

"I have never been with anyone the way that I was with you, and you still just thought I was some asshole who was showing you a good time. You never trusted me. You proved that over and over." It was as if he were getting too close to the truth, and I saw that wall go up in his eyes. "I'm looking for a woman who's a little more appreciative."

I ignored the last remark. "Look, I didn't do all of this right. I'll say it again. I fucked up and I am sorrier than I have ever been in my life. But you chose to hear a few words over everything else I was saying and doing, and you never gave me the chance to make it better. You never made room to let me be a little scared too."

I saw him ice over again at the sound of the word *scared*.

"Look, baby, I'm sorry if the presents and the nice dinners dried up, but I'm sure you'll find some other sucker soon enough."

I slapped him. Hard.

He was stunned. And then he laughed.

I was shaking.

"If that's what you think, if you could spend months with me and think that, then for all I care you can go live in your sad little world and turn into your father and hate yourself forever. But it's not my fault. I'm not going to try to be responsible for that anymore. And as for saying things to hurt the person you love, I think we're even now."

I left him standing there. I was too angry to cry and too hurt not to. I walked around the block six times. By the time I had composed myself to join everyone at the bar they'd begun to wonder where I'd gone. But I faked my way through the evening, and with the exception of the occasional inquisitive look from Aunt Fran, no one was the wiser.

I couldn't sleep that night. I lay awake in my overheated room with no air-conditioning, tangled in the sheets and unable to get comfortable. I just kept seeing George's eyes, how much hurt was behind them. For the first time I realized that I wasn't the one who had caused all that hurt, and I couldn't be the one to take it all away. Yes, I'd screwed up, I'd been insensitive, I hadn't perceived the situation right. I'd run from my fears and I'd sacrificed George's dignity to protect my own.

But it was George who chose to walk away. It was George

who decided not to risk being hurt. It was George who ended it all.

I knew I'd been brave that night. Finally, in the end. I had said what needed to be said instead of what would have been easier. But I couldn't be brave for both of us. For the first time, I didn't even want to try.

*"What Bette didn't know is, there are nights
that don't even have seatbelts."*

CHAPTER 40

THE FOLLOWING DAY, I accepted Rick Imbruglia's invitation to a Fourth of July barbecue on the roof of his building in Hell's Kitchen. He promised cold beer and a view of the fireworks. Truth be told, I'd had enough fireworks and enough promises for a while, but I knew that the time had come to move on. I didn't have to have a good time. I just had to pretend until I fooled myself.

And I had plenty to keep me occupied. I'd scheduled three meetings with theatres interested in further workshopping my play, and Michael Mason wanted to bring me in to meet with the writers on *Justice Files*. Kito was taking me to lunch with his agent, Susan Verity, who, after umpteen million phone conversations, had suddenly taken it upon herself to learn my name. In only a few weeks, a giant skylight of hope had opened over my long-gloomy career. I had so many reasons to smile.

Parrot was convinced that I should get right back on the horse. Or on Rick, in this case.

"Ohmigod first of all he's like totally hot how could you not want to sleep with him I wanted to sleep with him but I can't because of stupid Kirk so you totally totally should and also the fact is you're a human being and human beings need sex so what's wrong with just taking care of your own needs and also he thinks you're like a genius which you are ohmigod I'm like totally out of Doritos."

I was honestly more interested in Doritos than I was in Rick, but I convinced myself that I should do some rooftop networking. There would most likely be some interesting theatre folk underfoot. It's a tiny town, New York.

By the Fourth, I'd sufficiently psyched myself up to go out and be social. I decided to go the casual but sassy route—jeans and a white tank top. While I was fastening the clasp on a multi-strand silver necklace, I noticed for the first time in weeks that I was looking pretty cute.

Around four-thirty, I was snatching up my keys and trying to decide between bringing Presidente and Red Stripe to the party when my cell phone began to sputter insistently. I didn't recognize the number, and thinking it might be another exciting meeting, I picked up.

It was Mr. Wong.

In her inimitable style, Aunt Fran had celebrated the Fourth of July with some fireworks of her own. In her heart. She'd gone into full cardiac arrest and been rushed to New York Hospital.

I blurted a panicky explanation to a dazed Jeremy (who was sprawled on the couch poring confusedly over a pile of cookbooks for the dinner he was going to fix for Natasha), bolted out the door and almost got hit trying to hail a cab. I arrived out of breath in time to hear the ICU doctor telling Mr. Wong that Aunt Fran was recovering from surgery. The next few hours would be critical, which was a nice way of saying that by morning she could be dead. And there was nothing we could do.

I called my parents, who arranged to be on the first flight

the next morning. I felt like a very small child and it took everything I had not to cry on the phone. I wished they could get there sooner.

Mr. Wong and I sat on the plastic couch in the waiting room and stared at our feet. Neither of us knew how to console the other, but I think we both felt as though we should try. Aunt Fran has been like the sun in my solar system since I was a little girl. I had never imagined how incredibly dark the world would be without her. And after only a few months of knowing her, Mr. Wong seemed to feel roughly the same way.

We sat and sat. Doctors passed by repeatedly, but they would only tell us that Aunt Fran wouldn't be conscious for a long time. I knew they meant to add "if ever again." Around one-thirty in the morning I finally convinced Mr. Wong to stretch his legs and find a muffin in the hospital cafeteria. I'd tried to ask for an update at the nurses' station, but they just said nothing much had changed. Aunt Fran was still drifting somewhere we couldn't reach her.

I kept thinking about how foolish I'd been to assume, over the past few weeks, that things couldn't get any worse. My self-absorbed tunnel vision had denied me a whole range of tragedies to imagine. I was curled on a plastic couch willing Aunt Fran to wake up and be alright when I fell asleep.

I awoke several hours later to Mr. Wong gently squeezing my shoulder.

"Liza," he whispered. "Liza?"

I jerked my head up. "What did they say?"

"No, no. There is nothing new. But your friend is here. I thought you'd want to see."

I sat up, hazy and thinking how considerate Jeremy was, how he was probably the best roommate a girl could ever have, to come to the hospital in the middle of the night after his big dinner.

Except the man standing in front of me wasn't Jeremy and I had to take a second to make sure I was awake. It was George. He dropped down in front of me.

"I went to your house and Jeremy told me."

"You did?" I squeaked.

"Is she okay?" he asked.

"We don't know."

He reached out to brush a chunk of hair out of my eyes.

I heard Mr. Wong raising his voice and saw him over George's shoulder, trying to wring some answers out of the attending physician. The doctor seemed annoyed and brushed past him.

"What did they say?" I asked.

"They will not tell me anything for hours. They say we cannot see her. No one will tell me . . ." I thought he might burst into tears. It crossed my mind that for the first time in recent history Aunt Fran had found someone who really deserved her.

George stood and put his hand on Mr. Wong's shoulder. He sat the older man down next to me.

"Let me see what I can do," he said.

"What can you do?" I asked. "They don't know anything."

"Just let me see." He squeezed my knee and started toward the nurses' station. He stopped and turned. "What can I bring you? Coffee? Water? Are you hungry?"

We both just shook our heads.

"Back in a few," he said. I watched him approach the duty nurse.

"I'll be right back," I told Mr. Wong, and I followed George.

He had his back to me and the nurse at the station was handing him a phone. "Do you happen to have a hospital directory?" he asked. "One that would list board members."

The nurse looked wary, but she found the paper he was looking for. George consulted the list for a moment and dialed a number. He still hadn't seen me behind him and I just stood and watched.

The phone must have rung five or six times before he said, "Mr. Carlisle, this is George Doren."

From five feet away I could hear the angry voice on the other end of the line.

"No, sir, I'm not drunk. I'm sorry to call at this hour but it's an emergency." There was a pause. "No, I certainly wouldn't. I don't know if you've heard, sir, but Frances Weiler was admitted to your hospital this afternoon. She's had a very serious heart attack and a triple bypass." Another pause. "I knew you would, sir." Pause. "That's actually why I've called. Her family's been here for hours and hours and they're not getting any answers. I know how busy the doctors are here, but I think it's important that the family be kept better informed. Especially since I'm sure the press will get wind of this by early morning." He waited. "That's right, sir. I appreciate it very much." He listened and turned as he said, "Me?" He saw me. "I'm a friend of the family. Thank you, Mr. Carlisle. Goodnight, sir."

We looked at each other. He thanked the nurse, who clearly wasn't sure whether to be impressed or annoyed, and returned the phone while I waited. We headed toward the vending machines in silence.

"Who was that?" I asked.

"Peter Humphrey Carlisle went to Princeton with my father. And he's on the hospital board. Aunt Fran is a big deal to a lot of people."

I didn't know what to say.

"I didn't know what you needed. I just figured maybe . . ." He trailed off, distracted by something over my shoulder. "You might want to head back."

I turned to see Mr. Wong springing up to greet an approaching doctor who looked both annoyed and humbled. Apparently Peter Humphrey Carlisle hadn't wasted any time. We hurried back.

"... the surgery appears to have been successful and she's stable. I can't let you folks in to see her yet but she should regain consciousness within an hour or so and I'll get you in there as soon as I can. I'm sorry to have kept you waiting."

"So what does this mean? Does this mean she'll be alright?" I asked.

"It means all the signs are good. I can't make you any promises. But that lady is as strong as an ox. I think you'll see her up and around pretty soon."

I was afraid that if I breathed I would upset the tenuous balance of the universe that was allowing everything to be alright in this moment. I didn't move.

George thanked the doctor and Mr. Wong muttered something that sounded like a prayer.

"I am going to go and breathe the air," he told us. He put his hand on my arm and whispered, "I think you will be alright here."

George and I stood alone in the corridor, frozen in place. Without meaning to I shuddered suddenly and a huge sob escaped me. George was holding me tight before I could blink.

"Shh," he whispered into my hair. "Did you hear that? She's going to be fine. She's gonna be kicking ass in no time. Probably yours, maybe mine."

I cried into his chest. George didn't let go of me.

"She's not going anywhere, Liza. Nobody in their right mind would leave you."

"Just feel lucky and don't let go."

CHAPTER 41

I CLUNG TO HIM and he stood there and held me until my sobs subsided, which I have to admit took several minutes. When I was finally able to stanch the flow of tears, I helped George to wring out his shirt and scrounged up some tissues from the ladies' room. He kept his arm around my waist as we walked the halls.

"That was really something, what you did back there," I said.

"That was nothing."

"It wasn't nothing." We had reached the exit into the courtyard and I pushed through the doors.

The night had cooled off substantially. The air felt so good. My body was exhausted, as if I'd been running for a long time.

He had stopped a few paces behind me. "I did it again, didn't I?"

"What?" I asked.

"The thing you hate. Threw my weight around." He was crestfallen.

"No," I told him. "No, you didn't do anything that I hate. There is nothing about you that I hate."

Neither of us knew quite what to say or do, for fear the other one was thinking something else altogether. The silence seemed to go on forever. I couldn't take it.

"You said you went to my place tonight?" I ventured.

"I did say that."

"Why did you do that?" I was almost afraid to ask.

"I was on the roof of this high-rise watching the fireworks. At Dominique's place. And the view was so incredible." He paused for a long moment. "I hated it. I didn't want to be there."

I waited.

"I'm sorry I ruined your reading."

"You didn't," I said.

"I'm sorry, Liza. I'm so sorry for everything."

"I know. Me too. So sorry."

We stood there with our hands in our pockets. George looked at his shoes.

"I went to your place tonight to tell you that."

Oh. Just that, huh? My heart sank.

"Oh."

"Damnit," he said, "I'm not saying anything that I wanted to say! I went to see you tonight because I haven't wanted to be anywhere since I've been without you. And because you were right. The way I've been ... I'm sorry I let you think it was all your fault."

With every word he said I felt myself lift an inch off the ground.

"And then Jeremy told me what happened and I didn't think, I just wanted to get here. I just wanted to help. I know I was probably the last person you needed to see tonight. I know I'm probably the last person you want to see ever, but, Liza—"

"Stop. Please stop. Please just stop," I said. I threw my arms around his neck and I kissed him. It was like coming home.

He held me tightly and I was anchored to the earth again. Suddenly everything was the way it was supposed to be.

"I love you," he said. "And after the other night I thought you were gone forever and I couldn't ... I didn't know what to do with myself."

"I couldn't be gone forever. I couldn't be gone at all. Believe me, I tried."

"You see?" he said. "I am kind of an asshole."

"Can we please forget that, please?"

"Forgotten." He laughed.

"You're wonderful," I told him, "which I know is the one thing I never said enough. So please just give me the chance to tell you that a few thousand times, okay?"

He smiled. "So does this mean I'm officially a 'friend of the family' again?" he asked.

"After what you did in there, I'd say Aunt Fran is going to kick me out and make you her niece."

"Nah, I don't have the legs for it."

"Should I be at all concerned that so many of our important moments happen in hospitals?" I asked.

"Concerned? No. If I start taking you to dinner in the cafeteria we might need to discuss it."

I doubt the hospital courtyard had seen so much necking in a long while, but who am I to say? I can only hope that there was nothing good on TV that night and that we gave some convalescing patients a cheap thrill.

Aunt Fran did regain consciousness early the next morning. Finally, they said we could see her, but only one at a time. I went in first.

Considering her last twenty-four hours, Aunt Fran didn't look so bad. Of course it wouldn't surprise me if she'd paid one of the nurses to do her makeup.

She sounded a little raspier than usual, but the first thing she said was "You look like hell, kiddo."

I could have kissed her. "I know," I said. "You'll have to forgive me. I was up all night."

"You kids and your parties."

"That's it," I agreed.

"So did it work?"

"Did what work?" I asked.

"My little scheme. Did he come back?"

I thought maybe she was still groggy. "Who, Aunt Fran?"

"George, your handsome suit! It worked, didn't it? I bet he's here. Bring him in here!"

I didn't dare argue with her, and we would never discuss it again, but somewhere in the back of my mind I will always question whether perhaps Aunt Fran had somehow engineered her own cardiac episode in order to bring me and George back together. I would have doubted anyone else in the world, but with Aunt Fran you really have to wonder.

"He's here, isn't he? I told you I'd think of something."

"He's here," I confirmed.

"You look like you've been attacked by fairies. I thought you didn't like trysting in hospitals."

"It's growing on me. Aunt Fran, you should have seen him last night."

"I'm gonna see him plenty. Smart men don't let extraordinary women slip away twice. Now, send Wong in," she said. "You have one heart attack in bed and men get spooked. I'm going to have to deprogram him as soon as possible."

I did as I was told.

George took me home a few hours later, but Mr. Wong stayed with Aunt Fran. I guess her deprogramming worked, because only a few months later Aunt Fran would be bound for Beijing to meet the rest of the Wong family.

George forced a doughnut on me on the way home, as I hadn't eaten in twenty or so hours, and he tucked me into bed and crawled in next to me. Only the evening before I had thought I'd lost two of the people who make my life recognizable. And now I had them both back. I felt sort of like a lunatic.

George lay with his chest against my back and I could feel his heart beating.

"You should be asleep by now," he whispered.

"Are you kidding? This is the first time I've been happy to be awake in weeks."

"Would it help if I promised that awake is going to be a lot more fun from now on? If I have anything to say about it."

"It would."

"Then I promise."

"Good." I giggled. "Jerk."

"Oh, you think that's funny?" He was laughing. "You think you're pretty funny, don'tcha? Oh, she's a funny girl. She's a funny girl!" He was tickling me and I was laughing so hard I thought I might die. And as it often does, tickling evolved into more fun things. Things I'd been missing for weeks. Really missing. Like every second. When you've been getting it good, really, really good, fabulously, in fact, so good you had no idea it could be so good, and then you lose it, you're really, really, unbelievably glad to get it back. Very, very glad. Vocally glad.

I will be hearing about this from Jeremy until the day I die. He and Natasha had been asleep.

Really. Until the day I die.

"I just hope you're taking notes. And I need a refill."

EPILOGUE

IN THE FINAL SCENE, the two stunning people, who are obviously meant for each other, fall into a passionate and much-anticipated clinch just before the curtain falls. You've waited two hours for them to get it together and the act lasts only long enough to assure you that they have. Nobody ever shows you the morning after, or the following afternoon or the next week. No one would be foolish enough to write such a thing. Because there is nothing in the world more terrifying than the end of the chase.

Only when you finally ensnare your object of affection do things truly become complicated, what with the sudden introduction of real life as a backdrop to your *amore*. Anyone who tells you different is lying and you should kick them in the shins and run away.

Aunt Fran, wise old crone that she is, has always instructed me that the world's greatest romances are characterized by a sense that the chase has never quite ended, that lasting fervor is the product of a shared knowledge that either party could walk at any moment, only they won't because neither one could really live without the other.

"What you shoot for, Niece, is your classic Hepburn-Tracy dynamic."

"Aunt Fran, Spencer Tracy was married to someone else for the entire duration of his relationship with Katharine Hepburn."

"Which, I have no doubt, kept things hot."

"He died in her house and she had to call his wife."

"I'm not saying it was perfect! Listen up, Liza! Have you ever seen a bear caught in a trap?"

"Yes, on several of my many hunting expeditions . . ."

"Save the sass for the bedroom, Niece. The point is, if you let that bear go right away, he's liable to dash off into the forest, but if you leave that trap on his ankle awhile . . . well then things might just get interesting . . ."

Sometimes my feelings about animal cruelty render me unable to fully appreciate Aunt Fran's advice.

Certainly I can identify with part of the analogy; several times over the past weeks I've watched George sleeping and experienced a terribly strong impulse to shackle his ankle to the bed to make sure that he'll never ever go away again, but thankfully I've been able to contain this urge, thus far. Considering he met my entire family at the height of a crisis and is still around, I should probably relax. George might actually be the first thing Aunt Fran and my mother agree on.

And as fearful as the prospect of actually trying to "be together" may sound, it somehow becomes less fearful when you've experienced the dreaded "not being together." For the foreseeable future, George and I seem to be enjoying an incredibly blissful, horny, re-beginning. And I'm doing this whole, crazy thinking-before-I-speak thing, so we'll see how that goes.

Protective Jeremy was a little edgy for a while, as he hadn't quite forgiven George for his brief hiatus. Their early exchanges in the apartment involved few words and much tension. They would run into each other in the morning and just kind of stare in this weird territorial boy way, sort of like two bulldogs standing over a porterhouse. Until George brought over the Playstation 2. Now I think they may be blood brothers.

Parrot called me last night to inform me that she'd made reservations for the four of us at Tenement. George and I have been struggling with this double-dating thing, as frankly, we both find it slightly disgusting. As first-timers in the world of happy coupledom, we're fairly resistant to anything that might seem cute or inspire people like Tabitha to make cooing noises. Parrot, as usual, is to be denied nothing.

"You're totally coming so don't even think about trying to get out of it or I will order takeout and track you down besides if you don't come I just have to sit there and stare at Kirk like I don't do that enough anyway and the food is supposed to be really good and I heard Billy Crudup goes there by the way I signed Kirk up for *Queer Eye* so I'll see you at seven?"

At least she has projects.

George and I have been invited to Tabitha's wedding, and I guess unless we can come up with an excuse we'll have to go. Dr. Tim has apparently been made a groomsman, but he e-mailed me to say I shouldn't feel awkward about attending. He's seeing a new girl and he's pretty certain she might be "the one": they've been dating for three weeks.

I'm waiting to hear whether anyone's going to do my play. I'm sure no one will. Things are going too well—it makes me jumpy. One of these days the phone will probably ring and someone will tell me that I have an ancestor who built a house on an ancient burial ground and everything will go to hell. I might actually find this comforting. At least I would know what to expect.

Besides, I'm always going to need more material.

ACKNOWLEDGMENTS

Many thanks for their endless patience, faith and extraordinary editorial guidance to Annelise Robey and Micahlyn Whitt. And to Shauna Summers for her confidence and generous support.

I am immensely grateful for a group of readers and invaluable friends who offered such insightful feedback: Jessica Arinella, PG Kain, Laura Marks, Kate McGovern, Sara Sellar and Meredith Zeitlin.

Thanks to Samantha Bornemann and Shinygun.com for giving me a place and a reason to become a writer in the first place.

I am so indebted to Kelly Harms, who combined astonishing foresight with the sort of conviction that can inspire one to change careers.

Thanks of course to my wonderful family for their ceaseless encouragement in all things.

And to Jon, who inspires me in ways that I will spend a lifetime trying to thank him for.

ABOUT THE AUTHOR

Ellen Shanman lives in New York City. *Right Before Your Eyes* is her first book.